The
She
Behind

BOOKS BY NICOLE TROPE

My Daughter's Secret
The Boy in the Photo
The Nowhere Girl

The Life She Left Behind

NICOLE TROPE

Bookouture

Published by Bookouture in 2020

An imprint of Storyfire Ltd.
Carmelite House
50 Victoria Embankment
London EC4Y 0DZ

www.bookouture.com

ISBN: 978-1-83888-228-0
eBook ISBN: 978-1-83888-227-3

PROLOGUE

The winter air is sharp with cold, the wind howling around them, drowning out the sound of their pounding footsteps.

She cannot remember the last time she was outside after midnight, when light and the morning seem impossibly far away. She cannot remember the last time she ran anywhere, and her panting breath alerts her to her lack of stamina.

The cold sneaks in under her layers, finding exposed skin to taunt. It's hard to imagine summer ever returning. But then it's impossible to imagine tomorrow right now, to see a life for herself after this. How will she go on if the worst has happened? She risks a glance to the side. How will they go on?

He continues to up his pace and she struggles to keep up with him, her head moving left and right, dark patches and shadows surrounding her. Fear catches in her throat and she coughs.

Her breath condenses in front of her and she has a sudden memory of herself as a child standing outside on a winter's morning, blowing out and watching, fascinated, as her breath emerged in a cloud of white in the frigid air. She is no longer a child but she feels like one, overwhelmed by confusion, by her lack of control.

How has this happened?
How could I not have known?
Is this what I deserve?

The street is eerily silent, the barren housing plots looming large in the darkness, threatening them with their emptiness.

There is a slight hum of cars coming from the highway in the distance, where nothing stops the endless streams of traffic – not the dark nor the cold nor the late hour.

She is dressed for the weather, with her coat on and a beanie hat, but she regrets it now that she's running. Her hands are freezing but she can feel a trickle of sweat make its way down her back. She pushes her body to move faster, pushes against the wind that seems determined to send her backwards. They need to get there quickly.

We're coming, baby. We're coming.

'Come alone,' he had instructed.

But she's not alone.

'Don't tell anyone,' he had commanded.

But she has told someone.

'I just want to talk,' he had stated.

But what could there be to say?

'I won't hurt her,' he had promised.

She knows that's a lie.

CHAPTER ONE

Rachel

It's not a sound that wakes her, more a feeling, a thickening of the air that indicates a presence in the house. She sits up on her bed, her heart already racing as she strains to hear something. *Your imagination*, she tries to convince herself. She swings her legs over the side of the bed, sinking her feet into the plush carpet, grounding herself. 'Your imagination,' she whispers. They've only lived here for two weeks and she's not yet used to the night-time sounds of the house. In their old apartment she could tell the time by the movement of other residents in the building. Mr Hong always returned from his work shift at ten o'clock. He lived next door and she always felt herself relax as his key clicked in the lock, knowing it would soon be time for sleep. Mrs Davos, on the floor above, slammed her front door and huffed downstairs at six every morning to hang her washing in the communal garden. Milly from the first floor sang on her way out of her flat when she left at eight. She made up songs about the kind of day it was and how she was feeling.

She had not thought she would miss those noises but right now she feels her isolation, her distance from everyone else in her large, quiet house. The furniture they brought from the flat was not enough to fill it. Generous spaces, like the dining room and the formal lounge, remain open and empty.

She listens again, hoping she will hear nothing or that she will identify a sound as something familiar. She hopes that she's just had a dream as she dozed over her book, but as she leans forward, she hears something. A sharp thump.

It is obviously the sound of a foot bumping into something, a misplaced step by someone unsure of the layout of the house, someone who is unaware that there are piles of unopened boxes everywhere. She takes in a deep, shocked breath. It's not possible. Is it possible? She grabs her mobile phone off the bedside table and holds her breath so she can hear better, undisturbed by even the sound of her own breathing. *Swish, swish, thump.* Another misplaced step. She leaps off her bed and stands at the top of the stairs, looking down into the house where the entrance hall and kitchen lights are on because Ben will be home soon. She strains to hear something, afraid that she won't be able to hear anything over the loud thudding of her own heart.

Another sound, another misplaced footstep. Someone is in the house. Someone is actually in the house.

She opens her mouth to call out because maybe it's Ben. It could be Ben. But then she closes her mouth again. Her husband enters the house with noises she's grown used to over the last couple of weeks. He shuts the door that leads from the double garage to the kitchen and then he checks the lock: *click, click.* He drops his briefcase in the kitchen – *thwack* – and then he always reaches for a glass for some water: *gush, swish.*

Then if she isn't in the kitchen, he calls for her: 'Home, babe.'

Please say, 'Home, babe,' she prays. *Please say, 'Home, babe.' Please be bumping into things because you've had a couple of drinks or you're tired.* But there is only silence.

She swipes her thumb across her phone, checking her location app for Ben's phone. The noise has not come from Ben. Her husband is still at work, still forty-five minutes away, even in the light late-night traffic. She is frozen where she stands, her mouth so dry she can't swallow and she has to suppress a cough. She takes a step forward and a shape jumps out at her, making her stomach drop. She gasps in fear but the shape doesn't move and she realises that it's a stack of boxes, nearly as tall as her, filled with extra linen and towels, waiting to be unpacked. She holds her breath again, listening.

Downstairs the footsteps move with more purpose now. She bites down on her lip, holding back a cry of fear. She needs to get to Beth, needs to keep her daughter safe. She tiptoes, silent footstep after silent footstep, across the landing to Beth's room. Once inside she closes the door, grateful for its silent glide over the thick carpet. She turns the lock slowly, hoping that the click sound it makes when it catches won't alert the intruder. Once it's locked, she breathes a sigh of relief but then panic ricochets around her body once more. She can see her little girl is deeply asleep, her night light twirling, the butterfly shapes fluttering their pink wings in the dim light. The room smells of the strawberry-scented shampoo she uses to wash Beth's hair. Such an ordinary night. 'Head back, Beth, don't squirm. Story time now. Time for sleep, darling, night night.' Such an ordinary night filled with all the ordinary tasks raising a young child brings.

But nothing is ordinary anymore. Because someone is in her house. Her home that still doesn't quite feel like it belongs to her, that is not yet familiar but is supposed to be her safe space. She clutches her phone hard as terrifying images of her and her daughter being attacked flash through her mind. She is not safe. They are not safe.

She breathes deeply. *Calm down*, she tells herself. She needs to be calm, to think. The butterflies twirl and the strawberry scent gets stronger. Beth's chest rises and falls slowly, sleep holding her tight.

Rachel's hand shakes. She doesn't know what to do. She needs to… She can't seem to think straight. Panic swirls through her brain, smothering all other thoughts. 'Ben,' she whispers as if she could summon him. *Ben*, she thinks. *Ben will know what to do. Ben always knows what to do.*

She calls her husband, pinpricks of fear dancing over her skin. 'Someone's in the house,' she whispers. She explains – the sound, her fear, and he tells her what to do.

'Call the police, I'm coming, call the police.'

His voice is panicked. If he is panicked, she's in trouble. 'Relax,' he always tells her. 'It will be fine,' he usually says. Ben believes things will always work themselves out. But he doesn't say that now. 'Call the police,' he says, urgency hiking his voice.

Why hadn't she thought to do that? Of course, she should have done that first.

Her trembling fingers dial 000. When a voice answers, she has to squeeze her hand into a fist, her nails digging into her palm.

Don't ever tell, don't tell anyone. Promise me you'll never tell. Especially not the police.

The words are ingrained in her psyche, part of who she is – but this is different. Now, she is not telling. She is not bringing up the past at all. She is asking for help, just asking for help.

She gives him the details in a stuttering whisper, her heart pounding in her ears, almost unable to catch her breath.

'They're on their way now,' a man with a liquid-calm voice assures her. 'Don't leave the room, sit tight, they're coming.' Rachel wishes the man on the line were right here with her, sitting next to her, reassuring her as he is doing on the phone. She imagines him as a tall man with broad shoulders. He is certain she will be fine. He must be right. He has to be right.

She slumps down next to her daughter's bed, trying to control her breathing, her arms wrapped around her knees, her phone clutched tightly in her hand, turned to silent. The room is warm, the slight hum of the heater the only noise in the silence.

All is quiet but then she hears someone coming up the stairs, the unmistakable sound of footsteps on the plush carpet that still retains its slightly chemical new smell. A *whoosh*, a *thump*. A shadow appears under the door and she freezes, trying to disappear into stillness.

Is it Ben? Is he home? Is he playing some sort of strange joke on her?

No, it can't be Ben, of course it can't be. He wouldn't do that. She just called him. He told her to call the police. She's not thinking straight.

The door handle twists, slowly, quietly.

She glances over at her daughter, hoping she is still asleep. *Stay asleep*, she prays, *please stay asleep*. She touches her own chest, trying to still her racing heart.

The door handle twists again, a more violent movement this time as though the person outside is trying to break the lock. She can't let them in. She can't let them near Beth.

'I've called… called… called the police.' Her voice trembles as she speaks. All the lessons on strangers, all the warnings about crime float through her head. Is she about to become a statistic, a story on the news? And Beth? What will happen to her child? She stifles a sob, bites down on her hand to stop her terror escaping.

The door handle twists again. She feels like she might throw up.

Crawling towards the door on her hands and knees, she says, 'I've called the police,' her voice a little stronger this time. She is locked inside and they cannot get in. Can they get in? Where are the police?

She feels like she's having a heart attack. Is thirty-five too young for a heart attack? Is this how she dies? Right here, right now? What about Beth? What will happen to Beth?

She feels tears on her cheeks. She bites down on her lip. *Stop it, stop it*, she cautions herself.

And then miraculously, wondrously, a siren fills the air. She holds her hand across her mouth because she wants to shout with joy. They're coming, they're coming.

She senses that the intruder has moved away from the door. Then she hears the sound of running footsteps as they go down the stairs.

The atmosphere changes. The air feels lighter. They're gone – whoever they are –they're gone. She should just sit here and wait, but how will the police get in? She doesn't want them to have to break down the front door, scare her baby girl.

Slowly, cautiously, she opens Beth's door, grateful that the heavy sleep of childhood has kept her daughter lost in her dreams. She peers around the door, her hand ready to slam it in case they're still here, but she can feel they are gone. She's sure of it.

As the police begin pounding on the front door, she sees it.

At first, she thinks it's a trick of the mind, her imagination working overtime. She cannot be seeing what she thinks she's seeing. It's not possible and yet there it is.

It shouldn't be possible. Yet there it is.

She leans down and picks it up, almost expecting her fingers to move through it as though it were a hologram. But her hand closes around it; its small plastic weight is solid. She shoves it in the pocket of her pyjama bottoms and then she flies down the stairs to open the door for the police.

CHAPTER TWO

Ben

His mobile phone startles him, ringing with the song that played at their wedding, a title he can't remember. She changed the ringtone for him. 'So you'll know it's me calling,' she smiled. He likes it, likes to remember her in the floor-length cream dress with the ruffle of roses along the bottom. He had heard about the dress for weeks. The dress, the veil, the flowers, the food – but all he had cared about was getting to call her his wife. He had, before her, agreed with all his friends that he didn't want marriage, didn't need to be tied down, but then he met Rachel and he knew that he needed to tether himself to her. He wanted to watch the way people looked at him when he introduced himself as her husband. 'Batting above your weight there, mate,' his father had laughed the first time he'd met her. He had to agree. Her honey-brown hair, sage-green eyes and delicate features lent her an ethereal appearance, as though it were possible that she wasn't quite real. But she was, of course. When she laughed really hard her face scrunched up and she made a hooting sound. She loved Monty Python and funny birthday cards. She craved Indian food and hummed advertising jingles while she did the washing. She was shy and quiet in front of strangers and had only a couple of good friends, but she would stop and pet every dog she walked past.

He likes to remember the way she looked at their wedding, just before their song started playing, when she tipped her glass of champagne and winked at him at the same time, a promise of the night ahead. She lost some of her reserve when she drank, became flirty and funny. They hadn't prepared for their wedding dance so they simply swayed together, staring at each other, marvelling at what they had just done.

'You look beautiful, Mrs Flinders,' he told her.

'Why, thank you, Mr Flinders,' she replied and then she giggled like a child playing a game. It felt like pretend for the first year or so, as though they were just playing at being grown-ups.

He glances at his watch. It's after ten. Everyone else left long ago. The office is silent except for the slight hum produced by the computers. He has been concentrating and only now realises how creepy the empty space feels with only the leftover smells from lunch for company.

He looks down at his phone, confirming it's her. He imagined she would be asleep already, has been keeping himself calm by holding onto the image of his wife curled up in their bed, the midnight-blue duvet tucked around her shoulders, her brown hair spilling over the pillow. For hours now he has been promising himself he will get up and go home but he has instead opened another spreadsheet, looked over another column of figures, worked through another pitch, chewed his nails through it all.

'Get a degree and the world will be your oyster,' his father, Bernard, always said, but everyone has a degree now. Every year a whole new generation of graduates becomes his competition. He is losing. He can feel he is losing. A degree isn't enough, not nearly enough. He should have kept taking courses, kept learning. The business software industry moves too fast, and now the amateurs are better than the professionals. Teenagers have thousands of followers on Instagram just from posting random pictures. His company is struggling to garner any kind of attention for their product. He feels like they are shouting into the wind. No one can hear them.

'I thought you'd be sleeping,' he says when he answers the phone.

'Ben, someone's in the house,' she whispers desperately.

'Oh my God, what?' he asks. His heart rate immediately ramps up, the blood pounds in his temples. 'Rachel, are you sure?' He stands up straight, feels his shoulders stiffen. He has to protect her but he is forty or fifty minutes away from home.

'I'm certain,' she says. 'I was in bed and I heard someone moving around downstairs. I'm scared. Please come home.'

He can hear the terror in her voice and he searches frantically on his desk for his keys. 'I'm coming, Rachel. Hang up and call the police. Call the police now.'

'Okay,' she replies and he can hear she's crying.

'Rachel, my love, just calm down and call the police. Where's Beth?' Why hadn't she already called them?

'I'm in her room with the door locked.'

'Good, good, I'm on my way. Call them now, call the police.'

'Okay, okay I will,' she sniffs. He hears her take a deep breath, feels a tinge of satisfaction that he is able to calm her down. He likes to think that only he can do that. That's why she chose him. Of all the men she could have had, she chose him.

He leaves the office at a run, gallops down four flights of stairs before realising his stupidity, instead taking the lift the last twelve flights down to the parking garage. His car is the only one there, and as he races towards it, he imagines someone jumping out from behind a pillar. Anything is possible. Someone is in the house. Someone is in their home. Their new home where the dining room stands empty because they cannot yet afford the large table that will be needed to fill it. It's supposed to be their forever home, but now it has been invaded. Everywhere feels like a threat.

He is grateful for the late hour and light traffic. He puts his foot down, risking a ticket but hoping for a police car behind him as well. He will lead them straight to his house. He won't stop. He imagines them behind him, feels the relief that seeing their flashing red and blue lights would give him now. Has she called the police? Are they okay? Should he call her again? What if her mobile ringing gives her away to whoever is there? Could an intruder get through the heavy, solid door of Beth's room?

'Idiot!' he yells at himself. 'You bloody idiot!'

He shouldn't have worked late again, shouldn't have left his wife and child in a new house where a security system has yet to be installed. But the huge mortgage keeps him behind his desk every night, looking for ways to ramp up sales so he is not one of the marketing executives sent on their way as the company struggles to maintain a foothold in the saturated market.

He races up to a red BMW, changes lanes and changes back again to get in front of it. In his rear-view mirror, he sees the driver shouting and, he is sure, swearing at him.

Ben wishes this… What would you call it – a blip? Maybe but it feels like more than just a blip. It feels like a steady slide in the wrong direction. Whatever it is, he wishes it would have happened before they started building the house – long before. He would have made many different choices. They would have made many different choices, and right now Rachel and Beth would be safely tucked up in their small apartment, where help was only a raised voice away.

Rachel was, up until a few weeks ago, working part-time at a primary school, but it was an hour away from their new home, and just as she started looking for something closer to where they now lived, she was given the devastating news about her mother. He is bearing the financial burden now, and on days like today, it feels very heavy.

'I don't need such a big house,' Rachel said but he wanted, needed, to give her everything. He loves seeing her happy, seeing her smile and laugh, loves those moments when the slight sadness in her eyes disappears briefly. He still can't let go of the feeling that she is too good for him, too beautiful. If he gives her everything, she will never want to leave.

And it was time for a house, for a proper home. He is thirty-five already. His father had two children and a house in the suburbs by the time he was twenty-five.

'It's a different time,' his mother, Audrey, kept telling him. 'It's not easy to save enough for a deposit these days.'

'Don't stop him from trying to have it all,' his father said. 'If you can push yourself a little financially now, it will all be worth it in the long run.'

Bernard has always been big on his children pushing themselves. All through their school careers, if they took up a sport or an instrument, they had to display an almost unnatural dedication to that hobby or his father stopped paying for lessons. Ben's sister Louise played netball and piano and violin. She practised all three as though her life depended on it. Ben bounced around from soccer to tennis to guitar to karate and finally settled on nothing, much to his father's disapproval.

Every day he got up and felt the need to prove that he could do this whole husband, father, provider thing as well as his own dad had done. But now everything feels like it's changed. The optimism he had a few months ago is dissipating into thin air. He's started chewing his nails again, a habit he thought he'd kicked long ago.

He changes lanes once more, sliding in front of one car and then switching back again. He wonders how the person got in. Is it a man? It must be a man. What if there's more than one? His stomach twists. How will she defend herself against more than one of them? Are they there to steal something or do they have a more sinister intent? Who would want Rachel's two-year-old computer and their five-year-old television anyway? Is it a drug addict looking for some quick cash? If so, he hopes they've found Rachel's purse and left already. But he sees hands all over his wife and daughter, a man's hands, and he wants to vomit. He pushes his foot down further. If he gets caught now, he will lose his licence. So be it.

'Come on, come on,' he mutters as he turns into a single-lane road and pulls up behind a slow-moving truck. He glances at the road ahead and, finding it empty, pulls out onto the wrong side, accelerating past the vehicle and pulling back into his lane. The truck behind him honks at his stupidity. It was a dangerous decision but he had no other choice. Are the police there yet? Do they even know how to find the address? It's a new housing estate and the blocks on either side of theirs have yet to be developed. The only indication that anyone will ever live next door to them is a giant pile of building materials on one of the plots of land. But so far, no one has even arrived to begin the project.

There are empty lots all over the estate, all sold but waiting for their owners to begin building. Their house is one of only a handful occupied.

'Maybe we should rent for a while longer, just until more people are done building. It's going to be really noisy during the day and kind of creepy at night,' Rachel said when their house was ready to move into.

'We can't really afford to keep paying rent and the mortgage, babe.'

And now look what's happened – someone has taken advantage of their deathly quiet street to break in.

He races up to an amber light that turns red as he gets there but he keeps going, keeps pushing his foot down on the accelerator.

A fifty-minute journey, heart hammering the whole way, takes him twenty-five minutes with no police in sight.

By the time he turns into his street, he is dripping with sweat, his mouth dry with fear. When he sees the lights of the police car, he feels again like he might throw up. He draws up to the house, screeches to a stop and leaves his car door hanging open as he sprints inside to his family.

CHAPTER THREE

Little Bird

I creep quietly on tippy-toes into the bedroom where she is curled up in her bed. 'Mummy,' I whisper but she doesn't answer. I go right up to her, right up to her ear, and whisper again. 'Mummy.' She opens her eyes. 'Morning, sweetheart,' she whispers back. She is lying all curled up underneath her blankets with her legs against her tummy in her lacy white pyjama dress. I like to sleep like that too. Her room is still dark because she hasn't gotten out of bed to pull back the heavy grey curtains and let the sunshine inside. That's what she says whenever she opens the curtains: 'Time to let the sunshine in.' Whenever she says it, I like to imagine Mr Sunshine with his friendly smile, knocking on the window: 'Hello, hello. Can I come in?' I like it when she lets the light in, when she lets the happiness in from outside, because sometimes there's not enough happy inside our house. I scrunch my toes on her carpet. It's thick and Mummy told me its colour is dove grey. I like this carpet. It's soft, like feathers.

'I'm hungry, Mummy,' I say because I can feel my tummy talking to me. I have to wait until the digital clock in my room says 7 a.m. Sometimes I get hungry when there is a 6 on the clock but I always wait. That's a rule. There are lots of rules in our house. Lots and lots.

'Daddy is going to get you some breakfast as soon as he's out of the shower, okay? Just go down to the kitchen and wait. He'll be there soon.'

She stretches her legs out and opens her arms and I lean forward and put my head on her chest. I can hear her heartbeat going *boom, boom* inside her and I can smell the sweet flower smell of her skin. I wish I could climb into bed and snuggle down next to her but I'm too big to do that now. I don't know why I'm too big but Daddy said so and that means it must be true.

'Hello, Little Bird,' says Daddy, dragging wispy steam into the bedroom. He has a blue towel wrapped around his waist and I can see the hair on his chest, all curly and wet. He is big, bigger than me and bigger than Mummy, with lots of reddish-brown hair and big brown eyes. Mummy has golden-brown hair like mine. Hers is straight and soft but mine is curly. Mummy has green eyes like me too.

'Remember, you're too big to get into bed with Mummy now,' he says. He says it softly but I can hear that he is cross with me because I have my head on her chest.

I'm too big for lots of things now. When I was smaller, Daddy used to lift me high up onto his shoulders and then I would be bigger than everyone, but he doesn't do that anymore. He used to let me lie next to Mummy in the big bed and sit on his lap, but now everything has to stop because 'it's time she grew up'. I heard him tell her that last night. Mummy said I was too young to walk to school alone but Daddy says it's time so it must be time. Mummy said, 'I don't think so, Len. I'm not comfortable with it.' And Daddy said… He didn't say anything but now Mummy also thinks I can walk to school on my own. Daddy likes her to think the same as him. He likes everyone to think the same as him – me and Mummy and Kevin. We all think the same because Daddy is clever and big and strong. He goes to work in a high-up-to-the-sky office where he sells stuff called insurance. He makes money for our family so we can eat and have toys and clothes. He knows something called statistics about everything. He knows about how many car crashes there are and how many fires there are and how old people are when they die. He knows everything so he must be right about me walking to school.

School is not so far away but I'm scared of the big growly dog at number fifteen who likes to show me his teeth and tries to jump over the gate to get me. I want to tell Daddy about the big growly dog but he doesn't like to hear about anyone being scared. 'Man up,' he says all the time. But I don't know how to do that. He used to just say it to Kevin but now he says it to me as well. Daddy said to Mummy last night that I had been 'indulged'. I don't know what that means but I think it's bad so I'll try not to be indulged anymore.

'Ready for your first day of walking to school, Little Bird?' he asks.

'Tweet, tweet,' I say and then Daddy smiles.

'Leave Mummy now. I'll be down soon.'

I want to stay with her, but I know Daddy likes me to listen so I stand up and then I touch Mummy's cheek with my eyelash. An Eskimo kiss, because an Eskimo kiss is gentle and soft and I know I need to be gentle with Mummy.

Even though the curtains are closed, I can still see the flower, all red and purple, on her cheek. It's not a nice flower. It's a hurting flower. I don't want to hurt her anymore. Last night when I went to bed, she didn't have a flower, but now she does. They come in the night a lot, especially if she says to Daddy, 'I don't think so, Len.'

'Off you go now, Little Bird,' he says and I run downstairs to wait.

I'm seven years old and I can get my own cereal but Daddy likes to do it for me. I think if I'm old enough to walk to school, then I'm old enough to get breakfast by myself, but Daddy makes the rules in this house. He says I'll make a mess and he doesn't like mess. He doesn't like mess or noise. He doesn't like shouting or crying. He likes me to smile and be his Little Bird.

'Tweet, tweet,' I sing as I wait for him and I try not to think of the big growly dog. 'Tweet, tweet.'

CHAPTER FOUR

I sit up straight in the chair, my legs wide and my hands on my knees, as she pulls out her notebook, taking out her pen and staring at me, all bright-eyed and bushy-tailed. She's going to fix me. I can see she thinks she's going to fix me. I roam my eyes up and down her body, starting with her short black hair and ending with her feet, stuffed into blue ballet flats that look a size too small. I prefer my women to be a little more delicate, a touch more graceful. The best way I can describe Dr Amanda Sharma is square. She has broad shoulders and big hips and a strong jaw. I wonder if she has a husband or wife at home who sometimes says, 'Maybe don't take a second piece of cake, Amanda.'

I wonder if, when her partner says that, she meekly removes her hand from the plate or if she tells him or her to get stuffed. I wonder if she plays some strange sport for a woman, like rugby. I see her huffing across a field, charging into her opponent. In just a minute I have invented a whole life for Dr Amanda Sharma and I can almost hear her saying to her partner, 'I had a really difficult patient today, scary-looking and not inclined to accept help.' I want to tell her that I used to be a lot scarier. Age has wearied me.

But I could still leap out of my chair and beat Dr Sharma to a pulp. The large nurse standing outside the slightly open office door would stop me, of course, but I could get in a few good blows.

She's quiet while I look at her, giving me all the time I need. I return my gaze to her face, expecting her to at least be a little flushed. Most women find this level of scrutiny alarming but Dr Sharma doesn't even look mildly concerned. She is staring at me, her nearly black eyes fixed on my face. I lean forward and enjoy the way she moves subtly in her chair, as though trying to increase the distance between us.

'So,' says Dr Sharma when she decides she has let my silence go on for long enough. I'm surprised at the high, girlish voice that comes out of her. 'Do you want to talk about why you're here?'

I laugh, and I instantly dismiss Dr Sharma as a joke. Her approach is an insult to my intelligence.

But I'm here for twenty-one days whether I like it or not. Even an overpriced lawyer could not get me released any earlier. This is an involuntary admittance to a public hospital. There is a smell here, of antiseptic and desperation and fear. There is also a beaten-down exhaustion about the staff, as though they have little hope or expectation that anyone in here will get better.

This is not, as the saying goes, my first merry-go-round. The goal I have right now is to serve out whatever sentence the courts hand me in this hospital, regardless of how hideous it is. Because they will be handing me a sentence. Too many people watched what I did. Too many people will tell the same story. And I've been to prison before. I show a 'pattern of behaviour'. But I'm not going back. I would rather be declared insane so I can spend however long they sentence me to in here, dabbling with paint and attending group therapy.

I need to prove to Dr Sharma that this is where I belong. Here is better than prison. In here, the system, the doctors and the nurses are all easier to manipulate than the bunch of sadists who run the prisons. I'm not going back. Been there, done that – got the blood-spattered T-shirt. The first day I went out into the yard for some sunshine and exercise I could literally feel every single other prisoner eyeing me up and simultaneously plotting to beat the crap out of me just in case I thought my size was going to keep me safe. After the first week I had four broken ribs. After the second I had a broken arm. After the third I put another prisoner, a man named Malik, in the hospital and then everyone left me alone. But I was a lot younger then.

This is the third time I have been involuntarily admitted to a psychiatric hospital in the last twenty years. The first time it happened, when I came out of my drug-induced haze, I actually thought it might help. I had never been on a public psychiatric ward before. I had already had two stays in a luxurious private hospital set amongst lush gardens where the fees exceeded $5,000 a week. Wind chimes clinked and water fountains bubbled wherever I walked. I was there to manage my anger issues. I don't have issues with my anger but society sees things differently. The expensive private hospitals didn't work and the heinous public hospitals didn't work either. I still have 'issues' and I may have just overstepped a little too far this time.

Dr Sharma taps her pen against her notebook, impatient to hear my sad story, my plethora of excuses, my flawed reasoning for why I did what I did.

I could sit here in silence, I know that. No one can force you to speak, but I have to admit to a small amount of interest in Dr Sharma's opinion of me, in how she will perceive the life I have lived so far.

'I lost control,' I say slowly to Dr Sharma.

'Yes,' she agrees, 'you got drunk and almost beat a man to death, and when you were arrested, you threatened to kill yourself.'

'Yes,' I agree with her, 'so shall we assume that you know why I'm here and I know why I'm here and go from there?'

A flash of irritation breaks the neutral mask of Dr Sharma's face but it's gone as quickly as it appeared.

'Would you say you often lose control, that you are often violent?'

'That's two separate questions,' I say, because it is.

'Okay, would you say that you are often violent? Are you a violent man?'

I think about the word 'violent', about what it's meant to convey about me and who I am. The word has always reminded me of the colour violet, and so when I hear it, I can't help seeing that shade of purple. It's quite beautiful really. I think about the things I've done and things that were done to me. I muse about what I have planned for those who I feel have betrayed me, about the justice I intend to get for myself, and then I give her the only answer that I can give her under the circumstances. I give her a lie.

'No,' I say. She hears the lie but makes no comment other than to lift one eyebrow slightly.

'All right, and are you suicidal?'

There is a quick, sharp pain in my chest and for a moment I think I may be having a heart attack, but it disappears, leaving something dark and gaping inside me. I'm aware that suicide would be an end to everything. I know that it would mean I'd never have to open my eyes to the morning sun with so much anger holding me down, it's hard to breathe. Death would mean peace but I have no intention of leaving this world until I have meted out my own particular brand of justice.

I allow myself a dry laugh and look up at the ceiling. 'Maybe.'

'Let's talk about that,' she says.

CHAPTER FIVE

Rachel

'Are you sure you're okay?' Ben asks for the tenth time.

She bites down on her lip, trying to conceal a sigh. 'I'm fine,' she says. 'Mostly I'm embarrassed that I thought I heard someone, got you to come rushing home and dragged the police over here. I'm sure they had better things to do.'

'That's their job, babe. I'd rather you call them if you're worried. They were happy to tell you they couldn't find any evidence of someone being here.'

'I know and they did a good job of looking around. Thank God they got here so fast. I was worried they wouldn't find our street.'

She pictures the faces of the two constables who had been standing on the doorstep when she flung open the front door. 'I heard…' she began and then she realised that she couldn't say anything else, that she shouldn't say anything else. 'Something…' she finished lamely, trying not to meet the bright blue eyes of the woman in the police uniform standing next to her partner with short spiky hair. They both had their hands hooked into their belts, their stances wide and shoulders back, ready for anything.

'Is anyone else in the house?' the constable with spiky hair asked, relaxing at the sight of Rachel, a small woman.

'Oh, Beth,' she said and she raced back up the stairs, followed by the police officers. Her daughter was as deeply asleep as she had been, much to Rachel's relief.

'Have you lived here long?' the constable with the blue eyes asked after following her back downstairs. She looked around the entrance hall where boxes were stacked on top of each other and a rug was still rolled up, standing against the wall.

'Two weeks,' Rachel answered, hoping that was enough to explain the 'just moved in' state of the house.

The constable nodded. 'Why don't you get yourself a cup of tea,' she said kindly.

Rachel obediently turned and walked to the kitchen to put the kettle on to boil, her heart thudding in her ears, as the constable and her partner walked quietly around the house. She listened to their footsteps, comforted by a sound that had, only minutes ago, terrified her.

'No signs of forced entry,' the constable with the blue eyes informed her.

'Oh,' she said because she had no idea what else to say. *How did he get in?*

Ben laughs now, dragging her away from the way the constable had smiled at her, believing that Rachel would be reassured that she was safe.

'I thought that our street wouldn't be on their maps yet,' he says.

'Thank goodness it was a false alarm,' she blurts out quickly to cover the slightly too-high pitch of her voice. *It's just one more lie*, she tells herself even as she is aware that this lie is more than just a lie. This is the card right at the bottom of the house of cards, the card that could topple everything. She hates lying to him, has always hated it.

I'll never tell, I promise.

She and Ben are speaking in the empty dining room, where one day they hope to put a large table and chairs. Beth knows nothing of what happened last night and they want to keep it that way. Their daughter is sitting happily at the kitchen table, chasing her Cheerios around her cereal bowl. Rachel can hear her singing to herself as she chews.

'Let it da, da, da, da,' she sings in between mouthfuls of cereal. Beth's world has not been touched by what happened last night and Rachel intends to keep it that way.

At seven years old, their daughter spends a lot of time immersed in her own imaginative world where monsters lurk under the bed and there are fairies in the brand-new park just a street away from their brand-new house. Rachel doesn't want her to know that the monsters are real. She doesn't ever need to know that.

This morning as she brushed her little girl's soft, glossy-brown curls, Beth wriggled away and came back again, making a game of it. Rachel wanted to cry at her daughter's innocence, at the impossibility of always being able to protect her. She dropped a kiss onto her child's strawberry-scented hair, inhaling the comforting fragrance. Beth wriggled away, impatient to be done.

'Now I will brush your hair,' Beth said after her mother had twisted the elastic, finishing off her ponytail.

Rachel sat down on the chair in front of her dressing table and stared into her own green eyes as Beth's little hands moved the brush through her hair. The child leaned forward and put her head on her mother's shoulder, staring at the reflection of the two of them. 'We look the same,' she said and Rachel turned her head and planted a kiss on her daughter's soft cheek. 'We look the same,' she agreed.

'But now your hair needs to be brushed,' Beth said and she resumed her slow, calm movement of the brush through Rachel's hair. She found herself wanting to sit there for the whole day, just the two of them, safe from the world outside.

'All done, my dear lady,' she said after a few minutes, making Rachel laugh at her imitation of her own hairdresser.

'I'm fine, I promise,' she says to Ben now, and she leans forward and kisses his cheek, feeling the slight stubble that's always there.

Someone was in the house, Ben, she thinks, *and you won't believe who it was because I can't believe who it was.*

I'll never tell, I promise.

She bites down on her lip to stop these words escaping and goes back into the kitchen to continue making her own breakfast. She won't think about this right now. She won't.

After popping a piece of bread into the toaster, she wipes up a spill of milk on the counter, admiring the brown and gold threaded through the beige-coloured marble. The benchtop had been the more expensive choice but it matched the cream-coloured cabinets so well, creating an air of calm harmony in the kitchen. She loves this kitchen with its soft-close drawers and swing-out shelves in the cabinets. It is everything she has ever imagined a kitchen should be. It was more than she had ever dreamed of really. It had never occurred to her that she would be able to look around a room like this and know that it was hers. She knows that her mother had a kitchen like this once. Her mother's kitchen had a white countertop and white cabinets, giving the whole space an air of sterility.

Rachel thinks about the succession of small, sticky, unworkable rental kitchens that she and her mother lived with over the years after they left the white kitchen behind. Her mother never seemed to mind drawers that stuck or stoves with burners that didn't work.

'It's fine,' she always said when Rachel complained, 'don't think about it – it's just a kitchen and nothing more.'

Was he in the kitchen last night? Did he walk through her harmonious space, tainting it with his presence? Did he touch the two boxes she needs to make time to unpack today? Did he run his hands over her counter, checking if it was clean?

Rachel jumps a little when the toaster pops. She grabs the bread and looks over at her daughter. 'Do you want a piece of toast as well?'

'Maybe,' says Beth, which Rachel knows means yes.

'And would you *maybe* like some peanut butter on it?'

'I might,' says Beth and then she giggles. She is imitating the way her grandmother speaks. Veronica never commits to anything, instead using 'maybe' and 'might' and 'perhaps'.

Rachel gives the piece of toast to her daughter and makes another one for herself.

Ben joins them in the kitchen and slumps onto a chair. He already looks tired. He begins his usual scrolling through his emails, checking what has come in overnight. He absent-mindedly sips a cup of coffee. He hates eating breakfast but he likes to sit with his wife and his daughter in the morning. He is often still at work for dinner so breakfast is the only meal they are all together for. Rachel would like to tell him that if he's on his phone, he might as well not be here at all, but she can see his eyes narrow and his brow furrow as he reads an email. Things are not good at work. He hasn't said anything to her but she can see that something is up. In the last few weeks he has developed a wariness when she asks about it. His usual reply of 'yeah good' when she asks him about his day has been replaced with 'fine' or simply a shrug of his shoulders.

She could push him to tell her what's going on, but right now she knows she doesn't have the energy to deal with anything else. Not after last night. *Someone was in the house, Ben, even though the police found no one. Someone was here.*

He looks up from his phone and catches her gaze, giving her what she knows is a hopeful smile. He wants her to be okay. Her husband is worried about her, even more worried after last night. He keeps stealing glances at her, as though he's waiting for her to do or say something. She is worried about him and he is worried about her and yet they are both sitting here in the kitchen, acting as though nothing is troubling either of them.

Beth continues to sing and Ben rumbles the next line as he reads an email. The song has become as familiar to her and Ben as anything they have ever listened to.

'That's not where I'm up to, Daddy,' laughs Beth.

Ben is one of the good guys. He's always been one of the good guys. The kind who escorts a drunk girl home from a party and makes sure she's safely tucked up in bed. The kind who brings you soup when you feel sick and listens, really listens, when you talk. He's one of the good guys but she has wondered every day since she met him if he is good enough to handle the truth about her, about her life. She's never had the courage to test him. And she made a promise – a promise to never tell.

When they met, he was studying marketing and IT and she was studying early childhood education. They wouldn't have met if his twin sister Louise hadn't been taking Rachel's course. She had found herself drawn to Louise, to the only other student with as serious an approach as she had. She was so grateful to be at university. She loved the idea of shaping young minds, of watching and helping as the fundamentals of reading and writing became clear. Louise loved children as well but she had a plan, an ambitious one for her life as a teacher. She wanted to change the way things were done. She wanted to run things. 'The whole education system needs a shake-up,' she liked to say.

They gravitated towards each other, both disliking the general culture of drinking and ditching classes that seemed to pervade the first year of university. They met in a tutorial on dealing with aggressive behaviour in young children. It was held early on a Monday morning and they were the only two who paid attention, who asked questions and got involved, and eventually they found themselves in conversation only with each other as the rest of the students stared at them, dazed and hungover. Rachel hadn't wanted it to end, was almost afraid she would never see the intense woman she was speaking to again.

'Want to compare notes from the lecture?' Louise asked Rachel as they left that first tutorial.

'Um, sure,' Rachel replied, wondering as she looked at the young woman with pixie-cut dark brown hair and chocolate-brown eyes if anyone ever said no to her. While Rachel had looked around the room as she spoke, concerned that she was irritating the other students, Louise had simply carried on, only stopping to try and force someone else to get involved.

Louise was dressed casually in leggings and what Rachel was almost sure was a pyjama top, as though it didn't matter to her at all what people thought. Rachel couldn't help comparing her own curated outfit of jeans and a light pink T-shirt, matched with small pink studs in her ears and strappy sandals that she had laid out on Sunday night. 'I like to see my girls looking pretty,' she had heard more than once when she was a child, striking fear into her about whether she was pretty enough. She couldn't imagine not caring how people viewed her, not watching others carefully to note how she was being looked at or listened to. It was so easy to say or do the wrong thing.

'I'm Louise,' she said with a grin. She had a lovely smile and perfect, even teeth. Rachel found herself thinking that she was the kind of girl that got described as handsome when she was older. She would always have an air of elegance about her, even in a pyjama top. She was taller than Rachel, more solid, as though she was more tethered to the earth than Rachel was. Rachel's fine brown hair, light green eyes and pale skin always made her feel slightly invisible. Sometimes she looked in a mirror and felt like she might be disappearing. She understood that feeling had little to do with her looks. She had always felt as though she wasn't as connected to the world as everyone else was, probably because she had never lived anywhere long enough to put down roots that would hold her to the earth.

She had been amazed when Louise introduced her to Ben after a couple of weeks. They were sitting in a coffee shop, moaning about how many assignments they had, when he walked in. Outside it was supposed to be autumn but it was still as hot as the middle of summer.

'Wouldn't it be amazing to just take off our shoes and go out there onto the cool grass under the fig tree?' Lou said.

Rachel looked out of the window of the café at the rolling green lawn. 'Yes,' she sighed, 'but Professor Hendricks needs a 2,000-word essay on contemporary perspectives of childhood development by Friday.'

'Don't you hate the way he keeps digging in his ear when he talks?'

'Yes.' Rachel laughed. 'It's so gross.'

Rachel glanced towards the door because she saw Lou's gaze stray there and then she immediately looked back at her friend. 'That guy looks—'

'Just like me?' Lou laughed. 'Over here, Benjamin,' she said, waving at him, and he came over to their table, his smile as wide as hers, his eyes the same shape and colour.

'This is Rachel. She's the one I told you about in my course.'

'Oh yeah.' He dropped into a spare chair at their table. 'Louise thinks you and I should go out.' He was wearing a tight blue T-shirt and jeans that hugged his hips. He smelled strongly of wood and spice.

'Benjamin!'

'No sense in beating around the bush, Lou. I agree. And call me Ben, everyone does except my sister. She thinks I sound more intelligent if she calls me Benjamin.'

'As if,' snorted Lou.

'Ben,' Rachel had repeated. Just the word, just his name and her stomach flipped. She wanted to lean closer to him, to inhale his scent.

'So, do you want to? Go out, I mean? We can have dinner or see a movie, whatever you want.'

'I'm… Yes, yes I would like that.'

'You can say no, Rachel,' said Lou. 'You can just tell him to go away.'

'Yeah, you can tell me to go away. I'm fairly easy like that. Lou tells me to go away all the time. I don't take it badly,' Ben said with a grin.

Rachel laughed. 'No… I don't want you to go away. I want to have dinner. I really do.'

'It's a date.' He smiled. 'And now the complex world of IT calls. Rachel, I have your number because Lou gave it to me already. I'll call you.'

Rachel was unable to stop her cheeks from flaming red.

'I knew you would be perfect for each other,' Lou said with a smile, 'and now I get the last bite of this chocolate cheesecake because I have made the perfect match.'

Rachel was only able to laugh.

Lou has never found her perfect match. 'I'm married to the job,' she likes to say but sometimes Rachel wonders if that's the truth or bravado. There is still time for Lou to find someone and have a family, she's only thirty-five, but at a joint birthday party with Ben last year, she confessed that while she loved teaching young children, she wasn't sure she ever wanted one of her own. 'I'm happy being the best aunt in the world. I feel like being child-free allows me time to look after all the kids under my care.'

Ben was Rachel's first serious boyfriend but she's never admitted that to him, not even after all these years. They never stayed anywhere long enough for her to make real friends or find a boyfriend, and with each move she grew quieter and more reserved in each new environment. By the time Rachel felt she had settled down enough to start relaxing, they had to move again. She never knew when they were going to leave. They would move into a new apartment and she would begin a new school and Veronica would find a job and everything would drift calmly along for a few months or even a year and then her mother would start looking worried. 'I think someone's been asking about us,' she would tell Rachel.

'Someone… you mean?'

'No… I don't know. A woman at work kept asking me questions, question after question about how long we've lived here and where my husband was and…'

When she was little, Rachel wouldn't even wait for her mother to finish telling her why she was concerned. She just started packing.

'You haven't told anyone, Rachel? Tell me you haven't said anything.'

'I haven't, I promise,' she would reassure her mother but then she would always worry. What if the truth had somehow slipped out without her knowing when she was talking to the girls she skipped rope with at lunch or the boy she sat next to in class?

She was scared all the time of being found because she knew she and her mother were being looked for. She knew it and only keeping the secret of their past would keep them safe.

When she was sixteen, she finally put her foot down. 'I'm not leaving, Mum.' She was nearly an adult by then and she imagined that she would – she had to – deal with whatever came. She was resentful to be running from the past, from him, after so many years. In her mind he was still a monster, still terrifying, but his outlines were not as clear, and the threat seemed more imagined now. It had been years and years and the memories were fading a little. He had never found them.

She can remember the look her mother gave her and then she said, 'Rachel you need to know something—'

'I don't want to know, Mum. I don't want to talk about it.'

She and her mother could talk about anything with each other. Rachel had never felt the need to become a secretive teenager, instead sharing all that she was thinking and feeling with her mother, knowing that Veronica would listen attentively and counsel her wisely. But they had managed to never talk about that night, to never talk about him. Even now, twenty-eight years later, they still do not discuss it.

And she knows that this is, mostly, her fault. There have been times over the years when she has caught her mother looking at old photographs, staring down at the smiling faces pictured there, tears in her eyes.

'Why do you do that to yourself?' she asked when she got old enough to pose the question.

'I just… I miss him, you know, and I wonder if maybe, maybe things would be better now.'

'They wouldn't,' she always says. 'They wouldn't and you know that's the truth. We can't tell because then he'll find us. We can't talk to him because he'll come and find us.' Her voice shakes and the fears that governed her childhood come rushing back. 'Please promise me, promise me you won't try to talk to him.'

'I won't, Rachel, I won't, I promise. Please calm down, I promise I won't.'

But at sixteen she was done with running. 'I want to finish school here. I'm not leaving.'

'And if he finds us, Rachel? What then?'

'He won't find us, Mum. He hasn't found us because we haven't told anyone and we haven't contacted him. He won't find us. He's probably forgotten us anyway.'

'You never forget those you loved, Rachel,' her mother said quietly.

'I don't want to leave,' she repeated, her tone strident, her fists clenched.

'Okay, we'll stay,' Veronica eventually said, and Rachel saw her mother's shoulders slump.

Rachel wasn't sure if it was relief or defeat. She smiled at her mother, thrilled that she would be able to stay in one place for as long as she wanted to.

After last night she understands how arrogant this was. She had no one to protect but herself then. Now she is a mother with a child of her own. Now she understands why her mother needed to keep running. He has never stopped looking for them.

Suddenly his image is right here and now her memories are flooding back, sharp and clear. Why has he returned to her life now? Why now after twenty-eight years, and what does he want?

She picks up her phone to call her mother because Veronica needs to know what has happened. And then she remembers, as she has done frequently over the last few weeks, that her mother will not be able to answer the phone and talk this through, helping her decide what to do. Her mother is at the top of her contacts list, and just seeing the word 'Mum' physically hurts her chest, as though she has been hit right in the centre of her body.

She turns to Beth to get her to finish her breakfast. 'Hurry up, sweetheart. I want to go and visit Nana this morning. I need to drop you off a little earlier but there will be a teacher on duty.'

'Nana's in the hospital,' says Beth. She nods as she speaks. She has her mother's tawny-brown hair and green eyes and her father's ready smile. Rachel feels like she brings sunshine into a room whenever she sees her. She is the happiest child she knows, and she should be. She is adored and protected, and both her father and mother can't believe the miracle of her existence.

She remembers being afraid of what would happen when she was pregnant, afraid of how having a child might change Ben, might change her. She had not been prepared for the difficulty of those first months, but then she wasn't just a mother struggling with a newborn. She was a daughter struggling with a mother's illness as well.

'She is sick,' Rachel agrees.

'She has some bad stuff in her stomach.'

'She does.'

'But the doctors are going to make her better.'

'They are going to try.' They have tried already. Tried and tried and tried.

Her mother is not going to get better but she keeps hoping. Veronica is like a climber dangling on the side of a mountain with only one finger left clinging onto a rock. She will fall any minute now, any minute.

Rachel puts another glass into the dishwasher and then stops and bites down hard on her lip. *Please, Mum, don't die today. Please be okay when I get there.* She doesn't know how she is able to have a thought like this and not simply collapse onto the floor. But then it is inconceivable that she is standing here in the kitchen, getting through breakfast like she did yesterday after what happened last night. She is an expert at compartmentalising, at not thinking about things she cannot bear to deal with.

But she will have to deal with her mother. She closes her eyes and wishes as hard as she has ever wished for anything for some miracle to have occurred overnight and for Veronica to be sitting up in her bed eating breakfast when she visits her. When Rachel opens her eyes, she realises the futility of this fantasy and her heart aches once more.

'Okay, I'm off,' says Ben, standing up and draining the last of his coffee. She takes a deep breath and blinks but Ben sees the tears. Placing a hand on her shoulder, he squeezes gently, and then when she turns to face him, he rests his forehead against hers. He doesn't need to ask why she's crying because he knows. What he doesn't know is that today her tears are laced with fear. Today she has another reason to cry.

'Call me if you need me for anything.'

'I will,' she says, watching him plant a kiss on his daughter's cheek.

'When is Jerome coming to live here?' Beth asks.

'Who's Jerome?'

'Oh, I forgot to tell you,' she says. 'We met him – not Jerome but his father.'

Ben looks confused. 'You told me – you said he was a big guy with dark hair, remember. His builders dumped that load of material on the site and left. He came to apologise for the mess, isn't his name Raymond or something?'

'Oh him, no, different guy,' says Rachel. She hadn't liked Raymond. Even though he'd told her he had an eight-year-old daughter, there was something creepy about him, about the way he smiled, but she imagined there was no reason for her feeling. Some people had a certain look that disturbed her.

'This is someone else, from the other side,' she says. 'Two days ago, when I was pulling out into the street to take Beth to school, I noticed a man standing in front of the house next door with one of those... um... tripods – you know, like surveyors use?'

'Yeah.'

'I stopped and he introduced himself. He's bought the land next door and he's going to build. He's a property surveyor by trade but isn't able to work here at the moment because he's Canadian. His name is Bradley Williams. His wife and son are finishing the packing in Canada and then they'll be here.'

'Cool,' says Ben. 'Does he seem nice?'

'He has a hairy face,' says Beth.

Ben laughs.

'Yes, he seems nice. He said their build will take about eight months.'

'Ages and ages and ages,' says Beth.

'It will go quickly. Love you both,' Ben says as he leaves his two girls.

'Get your shoes, Beth. Mrs Weiner is on morning duty today. Maybe she'll read you a story.'

'Okay, okay.'

As Beth goes to leave the kitchen, she stops and turns around. 'Did the monster go away, Mummy?'

Her heart pounds. 'Monster? When was there a monster?' She feels like Beth has seen straight into her soul.

'Last night. You came into my room and the monster tried to get in. You told it the police were coming. Did they come, Mum? Did the police make the monster go away?'

Beth sounds panicky. Rachel cannot believe what she's hearing.

'There was no monster, Beth. It was a dream,' she says, trying to stop her voice from shaking. 'It must have been a dream.'

'It turned the handle on my door, Mum. I saw it. It wanted to eat me all up,' she whispers. Her eyes fill with tears.

'Listen to me, sweetheart,' Rachel replies, swallowing her own fear and holding her daughter gently by the shoulders. 'It was just a dream. No one and nothing was here last night. You went to bed and Daddy came home late and nothing else happened.'

'Nothing else happened.' Beth sniffs and she nods and Rachel nods along with her, wishing she could believe her own words.

'Nothing, I promise.'

'Okay.' Beth smiles, her trust in her mother absolute.

'Get your shoes,' Rachel says faintly, and her daughter bounces up the stairs to her bedroom.

'So, nothing has been taken?' the police constable with the icy blue eyes asked Rachel last night as Ben held her hand.

'No, nothing,' they replied in unison. It had only taken them a few minutes to look through the house and determine that nothing was missing. Most of their stuff was still in boxes anyway. Rachel was wearing the most expensive piece of jewellery she owned, her engagement ring. The television and computer were still there, as was Rachel's car and Ben's digital camera.

'But you're sure there was someone here?'

Rachel started nodding her head but then she realised what she was doing, changing it to a shake. 'I don't know… I thought I heard…' She looked down at her feet, unsure of how much the constable would be able to discern by looking at her face. Weren't police trained to spot a liar?

She opened her mouth to tell, to explain, but an ingrained promise to keep the secret, to never ever tell, kept the truth deep inside her. 'It could have been a possum,' she said, because it could have been. Lou was tormented by the possums who ran across the roof of her small house at night. 'They sound like grown men stomping up there,' Lou said.

'It was probably a possum,' she said and she looked up, meeting the constable's blue-eyed gaze.

'Well, we've looked around and there really is no evidence of anyone breaking in, so let's just put it down to a noisy possum, but call us if you have any concerns at all.'

Now Rachel drops down onto a chair. She thought Beth was asleep. She thought her baby was asleep the whole time. And now she has lied to her daughter, the same way she has lied to her husband, the same way she has lied to everyone she has ever met since she was a child.

Someone was here.

Nothing was taken.

But something was left.

CHAPTER SIX

Ben

The long drive into work is exacerbated by a truck and car collision. He doesn't see it but he hears about it on the radio, listening to the announcer telling him he should try for an alternate route, as though he's not already stuck right in the middle of everything.

He lets his mind wander, still feeling panicked at the idea of someone being in the house. *There was no one there*, he reminds himself. *The police found nothing. Rachel made a mistake.* Yet he's not sure that he buys the possum idea. There are no big trees on the new estate, nowhere for a possum to be, really. There are only tarred roads and dirt and rock-filled empty spaces everywhere. The trees that once crowded the space have been razed to make way for the ever-growing city. But anything is possible. It may be that this was just a lost possum, searching for the tree that was once his home. He's been over at Lou's when they run across the roof. They do sound like grown men, heavy and big and loud.

He touches his screen to call his sister, knowing that she will be having a quiet coffee before her day begins.

'What's up?' she says as she answers the phone. She's not one for pleasantries.

He fills her in on his night.

'Scary,' says Lou. 'At least there was no one there. It must feel weird for her to be there on that huge empty estate.'

'Yeah, I'll get hold of the alarm people and ask them to move up our installation so that might be of some comfort but…'

'But what, Benjamin?'

'I don't know, she seems… I don't know.'

'Her mother is dying, Ben,' says Lou gently.

'I know but I feel like it's more than that – last night was weird.'

'You have to be patient with her. It's a really tough time and we just have to be with her until the end.'

'I know, I'm trying to do that, I am.'

'Are you okay? Is everything okay at work?'

Ben doesn't say anything for a moment. His sister can still read him so well but he doesn't want to get into this now. 'Fine,' he says.

'Good. Oh hell, I'm being beeped on the other line. Listen, hang in there, baby brother – it will all work out and thank heavens it was only a scare. I'll give her a call later, maybe arrange a time to help with some of the unpacking. Sorry, I really have to go.'

'No problem,' he says quickly. He smiles as he thinks about Lou calling him her baby brother. He is only the baby by about three minutes.

He lets his car roll forward in the traffic that is now barely moving at all. What worries him is that there *could* have been someone in the house. There could have been. The suburb is close enough to the highway and empty enough for someone looking for some easy money to consider it a good risk. Even he finds the estate a little creepy at night. Putting out the bins last week he had stood in the street and looked down at the only other house that had its light on. As he examined it, the lights in every room went out one by one. It was obviously the owner going to bed but he had found it unsettling to watch, as though those in the house knew he was looking.

He had longed for the peace and quiet of the suburbs after the noise and bustle of their block of apartments, but there is too much silence here. No owls hoot at night, no bats fly over, no passing pedestrians or loud neighbours. There is only the hum of traffic from the nearby highway.

It will be different soon, he comforts himself.

The alarm will be installed next week if he can't get them to do it earlier. It can't come soon enough. It's expensive but it's not something he would take a chance on. He wishes he could have found a way to stay in their apartment but the mortgage was huge and rent was not exactly cheap. 'Move in with us for a bit,' his mother had suggested but he didn't like that idea. He loves his parents but Audrey and Bernard have very definite ways of doing things. His mother serves dinner at six o'clock every night. His father likes to watch the news while he eats. They both allow themselves breakfast in bed on a Saturday after a long week at work. They take a walk at exactly the same time every morning and they hate even the smallest amount of mess in the house. His father is particularly fond of neatness and order.

His mother had been more relaxed when he and Lou were kids but once they both moved out to get on with their own lives, he could almost see her decide that it was finally time to have her home looking the way she wanted it to look. Renovations had been carried out and furniture replaced, and when Beth was little, he had found it stressful to take her over there, worrying about the white couches and the pale embossed wallpaper. But his parents had earned their peace and quiet after raising twins. He smiles now as he remembers himself and Lou at around four years old deciding to shampoo the couch, and at five years old smothering a wall with their artwork. Lou was always the instigator but he was always a willing accomplice. 'My adorable terrors,' Audrey used to call them.

When he and Rachel returned from their honeymoon and were waiting for their flat to be painted, they stayed with his parents for a couple of weeks. They had honeymooned in Venice, right in the middle of the European summer, enjoying all the cheesy things tourists did, like hiring a gondola for a ride down the canal and taking photographs in front of St Mark's Basilica. They had eaten pasta and pizza and ended every meal with a different flavour of gelato, eventually agreeing that the delicious pistachio flavour was the winner. Ben had seen a different side of Rachel, a carefree, less wary side. She laughed longer and talked more, even starting conversations with strangers. She embraced everything about travelling, loving being on an aeroplane with the joy of a kid. She was almost a different person because she was in a different country. Every morning she woke him with a kiss and a long list of things she wanted to do that day. She never ran out of energy and wonder at everything.

'I've never been overseas before,' she said with a grin. 'It's all so completely amazing.'

It had been a wonderful holiday but when they returned and moved in with his parents he had seen, had almost felt, Rachel shrinking back into herself. Her voice grew softer and he noticed a slight rounding to her shoulders. His parents were easy enough to get along with despite being set in their ways but Rachel was terrified of offending them, of getting something wrong – as though she were a child instead of an adult. 'I don't mind if you want to,' she had said to him when he suggested moving in with them for six months as they waited for more houses to be built around them, and he had known that it was not something she wanted to do. So, they had moved into the mostly empty suburb where at least roads were paved and the park was completed.

Rachel seemed fine this morning, but he could tell there was something. Maybe the fear of the night before had lingered, just like it had for him, despite the efficient constables checking the house thoroughly. He hates to think of his wife being scared or worried about being alone in the house that is meant to be their dream home. It took such a long time to save for the deposit, so many years in the small, cramped flat where he couldn't take a step without tripping over baby toys or full baskets of laundry waiting to be put away.

He prefers things to be tidy and orderly and he guesses he has grown up to be like his father, but Rachel seems cut from a different cloth. She never seems bothered by mess. When they first started living together, he had grown frustrated with the chaos in the kitchen one night and said, 'Why can't you just clean up as you go? Why does everything have to be in such a mess all the time?'

Her reaction shocked him. 'I'm sorry,' she said as she began putting things away. 'I'm sorry, I'm sorry, I'm sorry,' she repeated and he could see her visibly trembling.

'Hey, it's okay,' he found himself saying, 'it's fine, don't worry.' He knew there was a story there, something she was holding onto, but she never wanted to discuss it.

They moved into the house two weeks ago and it still looks like it did the day they arrived. He is finding it frustrating to never be able to find anything but he knows that she is doing the best she can. Her mother is nearing the end and he can see it is tearing her apart. He will do a whole lot of unpacking on the weekend, take some of the burden off her. He feels better after making this decision. There are a lot of things he can't control right now but the physical unpacking of their books and even some unopened wedding presents that have been waiting for a big enough house is something he can manage.

He can see, can feel – and has since the day he met her – that there is something fragile abut Rachel, something delicate. Lou set it up, of course, because Lou can never stop herself from interfering. 'She's just gorgeous,' his twin sister told him after she'd known Rachel for a couple of weeks. 'She's a little quiet and a bit shy but so pretty that all the boys in the class keep staring. I'm telling you, she's amazing. Stop by the coffee shop near the quadrangle at eleven tomorrow. When you see her, you'll want to date her – and she's clever and sweet. What more could you want?'

Lou had been right, she always was. He had stood at the door to the coffee shop, his hands in his pockets as people moved around him, just staring at the young woman sitting at the table with his sister. Her fine wavy brown hair hung down her back and her delicate hands flew through the air as she spoke. She smiled at something Lou said, and then she laughed and covered her mouth with her hand as though embarrassed. He moved forward to introduce himself, wanting to be the person making her smile and laugh.

Sitting next to her he had tried to be funny as he made sure he kept his hands well away from her, knowing that he wanted to reach out and touch the creamy skin of her arm, knowing that he didn't want to stop there.

After their first date he was smitten. There was something about her, something more than just her beauty, a kind of grace in the way she moved and spoke. And there was also the tinge of sadness in her startling green eyes, a shadow that never left. He wanted to know everything about her and it was only as he lay in bed that night, going over their evening, that it occurred to him that he knew virtually nothing about her beyond that she lived with her mother and her father had passed away from cancer when she was seven.

When he asked his sister about her, they realised that Lou also knew very little about Rachel. When he pressed Rachel on her childhood, wanting her to share her memories with him, wanting to unpeel her layers, she always glossed over it quickly and moved on.

'What was your dad like?' he asked her.

'Oh, you know. He was just my dad. He was nice to me; I mean of course he was but I don't remember much. He was tall. I used to think he was a giant when I was about four.' She stared into the distance. 'A giant,' she repeated and then she looked at him. 'But you know, I was a kid so… I had a big imagination.'

'Was it hard when he got sick?' he asked, squeezing her hand.

'Harder on my mum than me. She kind of protected me from all that. It was quite quick because it was pancreatic cancer and they didn't discover it until it was too late for treatment. Mum told me that he decided not to get chemotherapy. When it was near the end, she didn't let me see him anymore because he looked so bad. I wish I remembered more about him but I don't really.'

'It must have been hard for her to accept that he didn't want to get treatment.'

'She understood, at least that's what she's said to me – she understood his decision. It was too late and the drugs would only have made things worse.'

He has seen pictures of her father, a tall man with broad shoulders and a head of thick dark hair. His smile was nice but there was something about him… It was almost as if his smile didn't quite seem to touch his eyes. Rachel and her mother don't talk about him much but he supposes that's because he passed away a long time ago.

They have been married for nine years now and he still feels that he doesn't quite know Rachel, that she is holding something back from him. She never argues, refuses to argue. If there is something they disagree on, she will simply retreat, either agreeing with him or walking away. It drives him mad sometimes. He has grown up with his mother and Lou, assertive women who are forever standing up for themselves. If anyone had asked him who was the head of the family, he could only have answered that it was his mother. He can remember the rows his parents had when he was younger, not just about the domestic stuff in their lives but about politics and religion and movies. And Lou likes to make sure that everyone in a room knows her opinion on everything. She is headmistress of a primary school now and has no intention of getting married or having kids of her own – so very different to Rachel. Rachel loves teaching but was happy enough to scale back when her daughter arrived. 'All I really want is to be a mother and create a happy home,' she told him.

He was sure that by now he and Rachel would have had a second child but each year she has put off the idea. Things were difficult when Beth was born. Veronica was diagnosed with cancer for the first time and Beth was a baby who hated sleep and could cry for hours on end. Rachel struggled through it all. Because Veronica was wading through her first rounds of chemotherapy, she wasn't able to help with the baby very much. His own mother was working full time and he had only been granted a couple of weeks' leave before he had to return to work.

When Beth was four months old, he came home from work one day to find his daughter wet and screaming in her cot and Rachel curled up on their bed, staring at the wall.

He took his tearful daughter from her cot and bathed and changed her and then he took her to her inert mother. 'Rachel, Beth needs feeding,' he said and Rachel obediently took Beth from him. Finally, there was silence as Beth latched onto her mother, her little body shuddering as she drank.

'What happened?' Ben asked.

'She just wouldn't stop crying,' Rachel replied, her tone flat. 'She wouldn't stop crying and I was trying to talk to my mother but then she had to go and throw up and I knew that I should have been with her. My mum has no one with her, Ben, and I'm here with Beth and she just won't stop crying.'

'Okay,' he said, 'okay we're going to sort this out.'

Even though they couldn't afford it, Ben reasoned that using some of their savings to hire a babysitter a few days a week was well worth it. A lovely girl named Patricia was with them for six months so that Rachel could leave Beth and spend some time with her mother.

Their daughter was sleeping through the night by then and Veronica's prognosis was good, her cancer chased into remission, and suddenly life simply settled. From then on Rachel adored being with Beth, singing to her and talking to her and playing with her all day long.

But those first few difficult months left their mark and he knew that Rachel was scared of having another child. He had assumed she was finally ready when they had been choosing stuff for the house. She had deliberately picked neutral colours for the third bedroom, saying, 'I think it might be time for a brother or sister for Beth.' But then Veronica's cancer returned. He cannot forget Rachel's face after the phone call from her mother. Veronica had gone alone to her regular six-month check-up because Rachel had to work. They had all assumed that everything would be fine, just as it had been for five years, but it wasn't fine. Veronica phoned around dinner time and Ben is sure that she called when she knew he would be home, knowing just how devastated her daughter would be.

'Oh no, oh no, Mum… no… no… no,' Rachel had moaned and he had felt goosebumps along his arms. He knew it couldn't be good news. He took Beth into the living room and put on a favourite DVD for her, knowing that his wife would need him.

'I should have been there,' she kept repeating as she sobbed in his arms. 'She had to get the news all alone.'

Veronica had gone back to war with her cancer but this time it would not be vanquished. Now there is no more hope of her recovering, and any thoughts about a new baby have disappeared from Rachel's mind.

He is not sure how Rachel will cope with her mother's death. She doesn't seem to be coping now. Did she actually hear someone in the house or was it just a nightmare brought on by the stress she is under?

He shakes his head. Anyone could make the mistake of assuming that a noise they heard was someone breaking in. He's sure the police are called out all the time only to find nothing.

Turning into the parking lot of his building, he tears his thoughts away from Rachel to go over the list of things he has to do today. He pulls into his parking space, remembering the first time he did this four years ago, remembering the small spark of pride he felt seeing his name on the wall in front of the space, the bright yellow paint still wet to the touch. He had been excited about coming to work in the fancy large new building, designed to capture the attention of the whole city. The building, with its slight curve and floor-to-ceiling windows, had won the architect an award, and the space made Ben feel like he was walking on air when he stood right up against the glass. He thought he had finally made it. He thought he would see out his career working for Colin, becoming his right-hand man and eventually running the whole business. Everything feels very different now.

As he wearily gets out of the car, he leans down to get his briefcase on the floor of the passenger seat and his hand grazes something there. He twists his body and leans down to pick it up. It's a tiny doll, not one he's ever seen before. It's made of plastic and has pink hair that sticks straight up and an ugly little face. 'A troll doll,' he murmurs. He thinks there may have been a movie made about them a few years ago. Rachel must have taken Beth to see it. He's sure Lou used to collect these. The little doll is incongruously wearing a pink tutu and it's very grubby. He slips it into his briefcase. Beth is probably attached to the thing if she's been carrying it around.

He makes his way across the parking garage. The structure, designed to be light and airy in the summer, somehow turns into an underground wind tunnel in winter, and he shivers as the cold air whistles through the space.

He gets into the lift, relieved at the heating, and presses the button for the sixteenth floor when he sees a man hurrying towards him. He holds his hand against the door and waits. The man steps inside, slightly puffed from moving quickly, and nods his head at

Ben in thanks. He's a big man, taller than him by a whole head, and Ben instinctively moves ever so slightly away.

'Cold out there,' Ben says.

'Yep,' says the man, and then the lift doors open and he gets out on the third floor.

When the doors close, he is alone again. 'Well, good morning to you too,' he mutters to himself. He's never seen the guy before but that means nothing. Hundreds of people work in this building.

He wonders for how much longer he will be one of those people.

CHAPTER SEVEN

Little Bird

After school Andy's mum gives me a lift home even though I can walk. 'Your mum asked me to drop you off. She's not feeling well today,' she says.

'I know.'

'Do you know what's wrong with her?'

'Her head hurts,' I say because that's what I'm supposed to say. I'm glad I didn't have to walk home alone. The dog at number fifteen has sharp teeth and he was angry, angry that I walked past him, and he growled and barked and then I had to run because I knew he was going to jump over the fence and eat me all up. Mummy knows about the dog and that's why she asked Andy's mum to drop me home, but I know she will tell me it's 'our little secret'. Mummy and I have lots of 'our little secrets'.

So, when Daddy asks me if I walked home, I will say, 'Tweet, tweet.' And he will smile because he will think that means yes but sometimes I say 'tweet, tweet' so I don't have to tell a lie. I don't like lying to Daddy but I like that Mummy and I have our little secrets.

If Mummy's head is sore, she has an afternoon nap and that's our little secret.

If I don't get ten out of ten on my spelling test, Mummy just puts it in the bin and says, 'You'll do better next time.' That's our little secret.

If I have a bath and spill water on the floor, Mummy helps me clean it up before Daddy does his inspection, and even though she's not supposed to help me, that's our little secret.

Andy's mum nods when I tell her that Mummy has a sore head, like she understands about sore heads, but I don't know if she's ever really had one. She is always happy and her face is always just one colour and on hot days like today she wears shorts and I can see that her legs are all golden and smooth. She doesn't have any hurting flowers on her face or her body so I don't think she knows about sore heads at all.

Mummy never wears shorts, only long skirts because Daddy likes her to look pretty.

Andy talks and talks and talks, telling his mum about how he climbed to the top of the climbing frame and how he got full marks on the spelling test. I also got ten out of ten but I don't say anything. I'm worried about the big flower on Mummy's cheek. One time her head got so sore that she couldn't wake up from her afternoon nap so it couldn't be our little secret, and when Daddy came home, he said, 'Mummy's feeling a bit lazy so I'll have to cook tonight.'

I don't like the food he cooks but I have to eat it or he gets mad and says I'm not allowed to leave the table. He thinks food is about 'fuelling your body only'. But I'm not a car and I like things that are tasty. Daddy makes chicken with the skin off and broccoli that's still raw and crunchy and green-tasting and other stuff I don't like to eat. One night, after he made pink fish and Brussels sprouts, Daddy got cross that I wouldn't eat and told me to stay at the table until my plate was clean, clean, clean. I sat there so long that I fell asleep. In the morning Mummy found me there and she hid the food away in a packet to throw out in Mrs Jackson's garbage bin. Daddy smiled and smiled when he saw my empty plate and Mummy said, 'Looks like she got hungry after all… You were right, Len.'

'I told you – all that's needed is some consistent discipline.' Those are Daddy's favourite words, 'consistent' and 'discipline'. He says them nearly every day.

Mummy throwing away Daddy's yucky food is also our little secret. We don't just keep our little secrets from Daddy, we keep them from Kevin as well because he's meany-mean. Mummy says I shouldn't say that because he's not really mean. 'He's just trying to find his place in the world,' or she says, 'One day you'll be a teenager too,' or, 'Try to just stay out of his way,' or, 'He was such a good baby and such a sweet, kind little boy but…'

Sometimes Mummy lets me look through all the old photo albums and she has one with lots of pictures of her and Kevin from when he was a baby. In the photos he is always smiling and Mummy is too, and in lots of them they are hugging each other. Kevin doesn't like to hug Mummy anymore but she says that's because he's 'just a teenager'. I don't want to be 'just a teenager' because I always want to hug Mummy.

I don't remember when Kevin was sweet and kind. I only remember him when he was mostly mean and just a tiny bit kind.

I try to stay out of his way every day, but I get into his way anyway. If I'm watching television, he comes and sits right next to me and says, 'My turn now,' and then he takes the control from me and changes the channel. If I'm in the bathroom, he bangs on the door, making noise all over the house even though Daddy hates noise, and he shouts, 'My turn now.' It's always Kevin's turn now.

The only time it's not Kevin's turn now is when Daddy is home because then it is always Daddy's turn. Kevin doesn't take the control from him and he doesn't bang on the door when Daddy is home. But he's still mean to me. 'Get out of my way,' he whisper-snarls like the big growly dog. He doesn't like Daddy to hear him because then Daddy takes his big hand and slaps Kevin's ear, making it go all red. He doesn't tell Kevin to be nice to me – he just slaps him and walks away and then Kevin looks at me like he wants to bite me into pieces.

Kevin is afraid of Daddy and his slaps. Daddy doesn't slap me. I am his Little Bird and you can't slap a Little Bird. I think. I think you can't slap a Little Bird but I don't know.

'Just you wait,' Kevin says to me when I drop food on the floor or spill something or take too long in the bathroom. 'Just you wait until you're big enough and then you'll see.'

I close my eyes and wish for Andy's mum to drive faster and faster.

'Thank you for the lift,' I say when we get home. I get out of the car quickly. I need to see how Mummy is.

I ring the bell and wait for her to open the door. Andy's mum waits in her car watching, watching, watching. The door opens and Mummy doesn't come outside, just sticks her arm out and waves and Andy's mum drives away. Inside the curtains are all closed and the house is dark and so, so hot.

'I'll put the air conditioner on,' she says. 'How was your day?'

She cuts up an apple and puts a spoon of peanut butter on a plate for me. I tell her about Andy shouting in class and Mr Stanley making him sit on the 'have a rest' chair and about Maisie and me skipping ten times together before the rope got tangled and about my new reader with a little black-and-white dog on the cover.

Mummy nods and smiles and smiles but I can see the smile hurts her face where her flower is growing.

'Is your head feeling better?' I ask and she nods.

'Much better, love. Why don't you get your homework out now? We can do your spelling words together while I get dinner ready.'

I sit at the kitchen table and Mummy and I sing the spelling words together. She makes roast chicken with a golden, crispy skin and crunchy potatoes because that's Daddy's favourite. She makes broccoli as well but she covers it in cheese that goes all bubbly in the oven. Roast chicken is my favourite too. But I think Kevin doesn't have a favourite food. He eats everything. He even likes Daddy's yucky food. He just sits down and eats and eats until his plate is empty and then he says, 'May I be excused?' Daddy likes us to say, 'May I be excused?' Even Mummy has to say it if she wants to go away from the table before Daddy is finished eating.

Kevin comes home later when the sun is nearly going to bed.

'Did you have a good day at school?' Mummy asks him and he shrugs his shoulders. Then he looks at her. 'What happened to your face?' he asks and Mummy doesn't say anything because he knows about her sore heads but he still likes to ask her and then he shakes his head like he's cross with her and he goes to his room.

She makes sure the kitchen is clean and sparkling before Daddy gets home and she gives me another snack because Daddy says we must all wait for ages and eat dinner together because we are a family but I get hungry.

I have my bath before Daddy comes home so I am clean and sparkling just like the kitchen, and Daddy brings a big bunch of flowers because he is sorry that Mummy's head is sore. It's so big that Mummy has to put it in her biggest blue glass vase. The flowers are yellow and purple and they match the yellowy purple flower on her face. I open my mouth to tell her about the matching but then I don't say anything. Mummy doesn't like to talk about her hurting flowers.

We all sit down as a family and everyone gets to talk about their day.

'And what did you do with all your free time?' Daddy asks Mummy.

'I cleaned out the linen cupboard,' she says softly and Daddy nods because he likes things to be clean and sparkling.

After dinner Mummy reads me a chapter from a book about a pig named Wilbur and a spider named Charlotte, and I want to cry when the farmer wants to hurt Wilbur but then I am happy when Charlotte makes words in her web that say Wilbur is 'some pig'. When two chapters of the book are finished, Mummy cuddles up to me while I fall asleep. I close my eyes and pretend I am already dreaming when I hear her start to cry. I feel some of her tears splash onto my pillow near my face so I know she is crying a lot but I don't open my eyes because I know that she wants me to be asleep if she's crying. She doesn't like me to hear her crying.

I think her head is still really sore and I don't think Daddy's yellowy purple flowers made it feel any better. Not at all.

CHAPTER EIGHT

The food in hospital is revolting and I find myself longing for the nutritionally balanced meals of the private sector prepared by chefs. But I remind myself that this is better than prison. I look down at my plate of colourless food and think mildly about flinging the tray against the wall and then I force myself to remember where I am. I can eat bland food easily enough, but looking down at my dry piece of chicken and overcooked broccoli, I feel slightly sick.

I take a deep breath and remember that I can eat anything if I have to, and I need to maintain control so there will be no flinging of trays. I mostly manage to keep my anger in check. It may not seem like it to someone viewing my life from the outside, but mostly it is in check. It helps sometimes to visualise my anger, to see it as a simmering black sludge that pools at my feet. When it's out of control, when I cannot stop myself from doing the kinds of things that get me shoved into a hospital or thrown in prison, I imagine that it's because I have allowed the sludge to bubble up from my feet and take over my body. Sometimes I catch it just as the dark sludge starts to rise and I can imagine that I'm holding a giant bucketful of cold water. The water thins the sludge, settles it down. I can't remember which psychiatrist taught me that visualisation technique – probably the first one I went to see. Dr Gorman had a bushy grey beard and hairy nostrils. I spent a lot of time looking at his nostrils. I couldn't believe that anyone would allow themselves to walk around like that. He had a picture on his desk of a woman and two children so presumably he was married and his wife could have said something to him.

Dr Gorman's method only works to a point, obviously, so here I am again.

Dr Sharma wants me to write in a journal. Every psychiatrist I have ever met wants me to detail my thoughts and feelings and experiences in a journal as though that's the answer to everything. Feeling suicidal? Write in your journal. Want to kill someone? Write in your journal. Hideously damaged by the psychopath who raised you? Well, of course, write in your journal.

Each time I leave the hospital I leave with a collection of journals. I am a prolific writer. It's the most useless activity I know of and that includes the ridiculous arts and crafts I'm always expected to take part in. Basket weaving has an almost soporific effect on me. As soon as I get my hands on the thin strips of bamboo, I want to fall asleep.

Lunchtime in a psychiatric hospital is the worst time for food. You can't really screw up cereal and toast, and dinners, for some reason, tend to be okay, but lunch is always hideous. It's usually some strange mix of leftovers from dinner the night before.

I stare down at my plate and wonder whether I should write an entire journal detailing the reason that so many patients in hospitals are angry and aggressive is not their mental issues but rather the awful food. I chuckle to myself as I eat the lot, swallowing every bland, mushy mouthful. At least there is an apple on my tray as well. You can't mess up an apple although I wouldn't put it past the Lyndon Public Hospital to try.

I wouldn't be here if I hadn't decided that whisky was probably the best way to drown out the voices in my head.

'You're a real disappointment of a human being.'

'Your behaviour is the reason you're alone.'

'It is impossible for people to love you.'

'What is wrong with you?'

'You make me sick.'

'You're pathetic.'

'You have completely failed.'

'No wonder every woman eventually leaves you. How could anyone tolerate a life with you?'

You have to hand it to my father – he doesn't need to say something more than once for it to become embedded in my brain. He doesn't need to be here for the words to repeat themselves on a loop. I imagine he wouldn't even need to be alive – I would still hear his disappointment over and over again. I savour the idea of him being dead for a moment, swallow it with a mouthful of broccoli mush.

'Why do you keep going home?' my one and only friend asked me the last time I returned from yet another sojourn at a mental facility. 'You're too old to keep going back. You can live by yourself.'

I didn't know how to answer. I have tried to figure it out as the years go by, and the nearest I can come to explaining it is that I'm still tethered by the chain he has always held me by. I imagine the chain being linked to an ankle bracelet, and if I try to leave him, it cuts into my skin and I can't function because of the pain. He is all I have. I don't want to have no one. I don't admit this to anyone because it makes me feel pathetic.

He's right anyway. I am a complete failure. He is a success. He was and is a very productive member of society. He was the smartest person in his firm, the guy with the best-looking wife and the man with the biggest, neatest, most impressive house. My father did everything right. But when he closed the front door, locked it behind him and looked around at his perfect life, the rage he'd been concealing all day had to go somewhere. He doesn't need therapy, though. So I'm in here and he's in sustained denial.

He doesn't have an issue with my rage. He has an issue with my inability to hide it from the world at large.

I should have just taken that bottle of whisky back to my small, square motel room where free Wi-Fi was the biggest drawcard they felt they had. But I like people-watching. I shouldn't really have enough money to go to bars but my father is kind enough to supply me with supplemental income.

'You could have been anything. Your IQ is in the genius range. You could have been anything and yet you've chosen alcohol and failure.'

Poor Dad. Things have definitely not worked out the way he hoped. He had a plan for perfection. The perfect house, the perfect kids and the perfect wife. He had an idea of this Christmas card, picture-perfect family, all smiling widely in matching red sweaters.

The trouble is, we live in Australia. It's too hot around Christmastime to wear sweaters. You have to wear T-shirts and T-shirts don't hide bruises very well.

The trouble is, his wife and children hate him.

The trouble is, you can't beat perfection into someone.

Although he tried, he really tried.

Poor Dad. We were all just a whole lot of trouble for him. And yet he keeps giving me money. I suppose he has no one else to give it to. He does little else with his life now except tidy the house, over and over again, moving things one inch to the left and one inch to the right, making sure there is no dust anywhere. Obviously, he should be in here right along with me but he's old now, not really capable of hurting anyone, at least I don't think so. He spent years doing that. Now he just cleans.

I chew up the last bite of my apple and look around at the other patients. So many of them are staring at nothing. Everyone is doped up on something for their depression, anxiety, bipolar disorder, schizophrenia, general not fitting into society illness. I am also doped up – according to my drug regimen at least. I stare and look vacant when I can and I am amassing quite a collection of pills behind the toilet in my room. We have to clean our own bathrooms. It gives us purpose apparently. I think that's something Dr Sharma decided on.

It suits me. I know how to make things clean and sparkling as my father used to say.

I'm still hungry but I won't go up for more food. I can feel I'm gaining weight. It's all the white bread and processed crap they feed us. I don't want to be overweight and unfit because I have a plan to leave soon.

If I can just convince Dr Sharma I'm normal enough to be released but too sick to go to prison, I may have a small window while the courts wait to decide what to do with me. My theory is this: I am going to be charged for what I did. I am going to land up in prison or in this hospital for years. And if that's the case, then I'm going to make sure I've dealt with the reasons for my rage. It doesn't matter what I do now – I'm screwed – so I'm going to do what I've wanted to do for years.

It's my intention to get myself some justice. After that I would like to simply disappear but I understand that's probably an unlikely outcome. I'll get caught and that's fine, but before I do, I have a plan. It's not exactly a fully formulated plan but it's a plan of sorts. In truth, the idea has been brewing for years.

It started when I was only seven years old so I've been thinking about it for decades.

I look around the dining room, measuring myself against the nurses. There are no security guards here, even though this hospital does hold violent offenders, but rather just a collection of nurses and orderlies who look like they have been trained to kill you.

I'm big but not as big as nurse Bobby, who is at least six foot six and looks like he could lift me off the ground with one of his heavily tattooed hands. He seems to be here every day. If he wasn't, I believe I would refuse to deal with all the bullshit therapy sessions and art classes and journal writing crap I am dealing with. I would just waltz right out of here. But Bobby seems to be keeping a special eye on me. I look over at him. He catches my eye and folds his arms, pushing his shoulders back and planting his legs apart. I shake my head and smile.

'I'm not going to cause any trouble,' I would like to tell him but that's not really the truth. Not at all. Once I leave here, it is my intention to be nothing but trouble.

After lunch I am given fifteen minutes to make my one phone call. I don't have anyone to call. I don't have anyone I should call and yet I dial my home number anyway. I really can't help myself.

I listen while a robotic voice asks my father if he will accept the charges. He hesitates before he says yes. He knows I'm listening. When I stayed at the private hospital, I was allowed to phone him as often as I liked, within reason. I was stopped from making calls after he complained that, one day, I had called him and hung up twenty times. 'It was a joke,' I explained to the head psychiatrist, whose name I've forgotten. But my father didn't think it was funny. He never finds anything funny.

'I'll accept the call,' he says. 'How are you?'

'I'm fine, sir. How about you?'

'I am, once again, speaking to my son while he is locked away. I simply cannot believe we are doing this again, that you are doing this again.'

'I'm sorry,' I mumble, and the instant the words are out of my mouth, I regret them. Yet I can't help saying them. They were the words of my childhood. 'I'm sorry, I'm sorry, I'm sorry.' I said it so many times, despite all indications that apologising didn't work. I still said it again in the hope that somehow, some way, this time would be different. As the words leave my mouth for the millionth time now, I feel something tiny stirring inside me. I realise that some small part of me is still hoping that it will help.

'Don't be sorry. Develop some consistent discipline about your life. Grow up. You're forty-one years old. Who lives like this at forty-one? By the time I was your age I was head of the actuarial division at my company. I had this house and a family. What do you have? You have nothing.'

'I'm sorry, sir,' I say again and I gently hang up the phone. I can feel the sludge bubbling up from my feet. I make my way to my room, skirting around other patients, knowing that if even one of them touches me or looks at me wrong, I might kill them.

Sorry, sir. Sorry, sir. Sorry, sir.

He likes it when I apologise, when he's reduced me to a child again. It reminds him he's still in control of something and someone.

Every time I find myself in hospital or in prison, I promise myself that this time when I leave, I will take that control from him. I know that every time I return home, I simply hand it over again but this time… this time is going to be different. I know it. I can feel it. This time it's going to be very different.

CHAPTER NINE
Rachel

As she pulls into the parking lot she goes over the list in her head. There's still so much unpacking to do and she knows that she needs to stock up on fruit and vegetables. Her list is comforting. It's filled with practical things she can achieve, and as long as she's going over it again and again, she's not thinking about last night and about the sinister little gift that was left for her. She hasn't thought about him. She hasn't said his name but she has summoned the monster anyway.

She had tried to look for him once, when the whole world could be found on the internet. Curiosity and fear had driven her fingers and she had typed his name into the search bar and taken a deep breath, ready to push enter. But then her hand had begun to shake, her heart to pound. Would searching for him somehow summon him? Would she bring the monster back into her life if she acknowledged his existence? She had deleted everything and closed down her computer.

'I need apples,' she says aloud, pushing away everything else, 'and pears and oranges. I need to find my slow cooker so I can make some stews to have for dinner.' There are still so many boxes to open. She has no idea how they had so much stuff in their small flat.

It was not a good time to move, not now, but as Ben pointed out, how could they have known? The movers had been booked for a month and they'd given notice on their apartment. The landlord expected them out by a certain date and had already rented the place to another couple. They had no choice but to go ahead.

'It will be fine,' said Ben. 'Everything will just work, don't worry.' She would like to throw those words back at him now but she understands that would be unfair. How could he have known?

Her mother had been fine up until a few weeks ago. Well, not fine, the cancer was back. In the last two years nothing had worked completely and now it would not be stopped. It was, as Veronica's oncologist had said, terminal. Terminal. But her mother had been determined to live out the last months of her life with the same energy she had always brought to everything she did. 'I look at you and I look at Beth and I know that I've done something wonderful with my life, darling,' she told Rachel. 'It's enough for me and I'm so grateful that I got to experience being a grandmother. She's the great joy of my life.'

But Rachel did not want her mother to simply accept what was happening.

'I think I'm going to stop treatment,' she told Rachel six months ago when she was told that the new drug regimen was not working as expected. Rachel had winced as her mother said the words, the unimaginable, remembering how she had told Ben that her father had refused treatment for his cancer, simply stating the words without considering their true meaning. She had not imagined Veronica would ever make such a decision. But the treatment had, in fact, achieved very little beyond sapping Veronica's energy and stealing her appetite.

'Even the blandest food tastes too spicy and everything makes me so sick. I miss food. I miss eating.'

'Please don't, Mum, please – you have to keep fighting,' she had begged her.

'Oh, sweetheart,' her mother had said, stroking her face. 'Dr Lawrence said the only thing it will do is prolong things a little. I want to be able to spend the rest of my time with you and Beth, not hooked up to a drip and fighting nausea every moment of the day.'

'But you can't just give up, Mum. You have to try.' And her mother had tried again. Dr Lawrence had given her stronger drugs with more side effects. She had been handling the chemotherapy up until two months ago when her body seemed to simply lose its ability to fight anymore. Rachel had been with her at her last round of chemo, had held the bowl as she weakly vomited into it, her body shuddering with the effort of it. 'Please,' she had begged Rachel. 'I have to stop this. I don't think it's helping.' And Rachel had felt ashamed at her own cruelty. She wanted her mother around for years to come but the treatment was causing Veronica an abundance of suffering and she was only doing it for her daughter. She had looked at her mother's pale face, her lips dry and cracking, and she had been unable to stop the tears. Her mother leaned over and stroked her back. 'I'm sorry I can't fight for you anymore, my darling. I'm sorry I've failed you.'

'Oh, Mum,' she had cried, 'you haven't failed me, you've never failed me. I'm sorry I pushed. You can give up. You can stop now.' She had rested her head on her mother's lap and wished away her cancer, but they both knew that wishing was of no use. It was over. Veronica's fight was done.

Dr Lawrence had agreed that a break was needed and her mother had time to lie quietly in her bed and recover, but just three weeks ago she had begun to find even short walks to the bathroom difficult. She hadn't seemed to recognise Rachel at times and she had lost control of her bodily functions completely. Rachel had taken her for more scans even though she knew, absolutely knew, that the news could only be bad. The cancer was everywhere, just everywhere. Everywhere and growing fast, spreading its tentacles through Veronica's body and up into her brain. Dr Lawrence had called Rachel to prepare her so that she would be able to support Veronica as she heard the devastating news.

'I want to speak to you before you and your mother come in for the appointment tomorrow,' she had said, her warm voice tinged with sadness. Rachel had been standing in the middle of a sea of boxes at the time, the phone pressed against her ear as she anxiously tried to pack up her flat in readiness for the move and convince herself not to worry about the results of her mother's tests. She had sunk down onto the floor, knowing what the doctor was about to tell her.

'You need to look into palliative care,' Dr Lawrence told Rachel.

'No, not that? Surely it can't be time already.'

'I'm afraid it is, Rachel. The cancer is simply everywhere now.'

'Maybe I can convince her to have more chemotherapy, maybe she could get better. Maybe we shouldn't tell her it's spread.'

Rachel hated the way Dr Lawrence sighed, a soft, sad sigh, and she imagined how the woman's grey eyes would shine with sympathy.

'I have to tell her, Rachel, I'm her doctor – but I think she knows already, if I'm honest. We always know our own bodies better than anyone else.'

At the appointment Rachel bit down on her lip, drawing blood as she watched her mother receive the news. She had expected tears from Veronica, tears and disbelief, but her mother merely nodded. 'I thought so.' Rachel could see she was distressed but she could also see something else – relief, she thought. Veronica was so tired and so ready for things to end. 'Not fair, not fair, not fair,' Rachel wanted to shout and stamp.

She looked away from the doctor and her mother, carefully concealing her anger. She needed her mother to defy the odds, to fight the cancer. Yet she seemed happy to give up. 'But what about a trial? A new experimental drug? We'll find the money, just tell us where to go.'

'There's nothing left to do, we've done everything we can,' the doctor replied gently.

'I can't believe that.'

'You have to believe it, Rachel,' said her mother.

At the end of the appointment she helped her mother out of her chair and Veronica's scarf slipped a little, revealing her head covered only in tufts of grey hair. The terrible vulnerability in her mother's face as she lifted a small hand to straighten the scarf cracked Rachel's heart into two. Right then she transferred her anger onto herself. Her need, her ache, for her mother was preventing Rachel from seeing Veronica as a woman suffering in the last months of her life. She didn't want to be suffering anymore.

Since the appointment three weeks ago, her mother has grown weaker and weaker. Seven days ago, Rachel stopped fighting both her mother and Dr Lawrence, instead helping Veronica move into the Lady Grey Hospice.

'Maybe it's time to talk to him again,' her mother said to her as Rachel packed up her things to take with her to the hospice.

Rachel remained silent for a few moments, not knowing what to say.

'How can I? He will still be that person who liked to hurt.'

'Yes, maybe or… maybe not… but it may be time. I think it's time.'

'If that's what you want,' Rachel said and then she left the room to use the bathroom as her heart thrummed and her forehead beaded with sweat in the heated apartment. She just wanted the past to stay there and yet she couldn't deny Veronica this chance to say goodbye, even to someone they'd been running from for decades.

When she returned her mother was asleep, and when she woke, she seemed to have no memory of the conversation.

All Rachel felt was relief and then she felt guilty for not bringing it up with Veronica, for pretending that the conversation never happened. And now it is too late. She wonders if Veronica has somehow made contact, has somehow let him know that she is sick.

And in doing that, has she brought the monster back into Rachel's life?

Or has the monster actually been watching them all along? When they stopped running, did he find them and then just decide to watch and wait, like some kind of predator? Rachel shudders with horror at the thought.

The hospice is a long low building with a slate roof and a lovely manicured garden. Even on this chilly winter's day she can see people walking around, taking a break from sitting by the bedside of a loved one slowly disappearing. A young man is sitting on a wooden bench, in a giant puffer jacket and beanie hat, a thick blanket wrapped around his legs. He is reading in the fresh air as he does every day. Rachel squints as she gets a bit closer, seeing that he's reading *The Adventures of Tom Sawyer* today. He is rereading all his childhood books, capturing, Rachel thinks, a time when he had his whole life before him. His name is Luke and he refuses to be inside if he can be outside. 'I want to feel the cold on my cheeks,' he has told Rachel. 'I want to feel too hot or too cold so that I know I'm still alive.'

Each day the bones on his face grow more prominent, his flesh slowly disappearing. Next to him sits his mother, who comes every day, just like Rachel does. Rachel raises her hand in greeting and Elizabeth waves back. His mother sits with a piece of cake on her lap, a thick slice of chocolate cake covered in a cream cheese frosting. She occasionally puts a sweet morsel between her son's lips, a mother bird feeding her baby until the very end. 'I make one every Sunday night and bring a piece for him every day,' Elizabeth has told Rachel. Rachel knows that each afternoon, before she leaves, Elizabeth tips most of the slice of cake into the bin, admitting to herself time and time again that her son is simply no longer able to eat. But she still returns each day with another slice. Elizabeth is also still hoping for a miracle. Everyone is in this place.

She thinks about Beth, who will be in class now, shouting out answers to the ever-patient Mrs Weiner. She cannot imagine what it would feel like to lose a child, cannot fathom how Elizabeth will find the strength to go on. She is desperately struggling with losing her mother and that is the natural way of things. How terrible it is when the natural order of the world is reversed and a parent has to bury a child.

Inside she greets the nurses – the patient, quietly moving staff who exude empathy with each gesture – and she sits down by her mother's bed in her small, tidy room where machines hum and beep softly.

Veronica is mostly sleeping now as the pain becomes worse and worse. Rachel would love to be able to release her, to set her soul free from the pain she is experiencing, but she also wants her to remain with her, to never leave her alone. Even though they can no longer speak to each other, at least Veronica is still here, still with her.

Ben has told her she can spend every day and night here if she wants to. 'I'll pick Beth up from school. We'll make it work.' But she knows she needs some time away from this tiny room where her beautiful mother's body is shrinking and her life is ending.

She takes her mother's hand, stroking the soft, thin skin. There is some lotion that she keeps by the bed and she warms some up between her own hands before smoothing it over her mother's and gently massaging the dry, papery skin. 'I'm not ready, Mum,' she whispers, her voice thick with tears.

It's something she says every time she sits here, hoping her mother can hear her, waiting for the chance to see her open her eyes again. She wonders if her mother can feel her soothing her hands, can hear her whispering.

'I'm still struggling to get the house unpacked. I know it's driving Ben mad but he's trying not to say anything. He understands I have to be here.' She has a sudden memory of her and her mother packing up yet again to move and finding a box filled with things they had been looking for, for months. 'Do you remember when we were getting ready to leave that awful flat on Julie Street and we found the box with the kettle and the toaster in it and realised that I had been using it as a side table the whole time?' She cannot help laughing into the quiet of her mother's room as she remembers that both she and her mother had been unable to stop giggling and had eventually found themselves lying on the ugly green carpet in the living room, laughing at nothing.

She takes a deep breath and the memory fades, and with it her laughter.

'Beth loves her new room,' she continues, moving aside her mother's blankets so she can massage some cream into her feet. 'She can't believe she has so much space. Last night she crawled into the cupboard and told me she wasn't coming out until she found Narnia. I bought some unicorn decorations to put up on her walls. You know how much she loves unicorns.'

Rachel stops speaking as the lump in her throat begins to feel as though it will stop her breathing. She drops her head onto her mother's bed and allows her tears to fall. 'I'm so sorry you never got to have a better life, Mum. I'm so sorry you had to struggle so. I love you. I hope you know how much I love you.'

Her mother doesn't wake for the next hour.

Rachel wants to tell her about last night, about what happened, how scared she was, but somehow the words won't come. She doesn't need to burden her mother with them anyway. If she could hear her, she knows her mother would worry. She doesn't need to worry anymore. She has raised Rachel and kept her safe all these years, and now it is Rachel's turn to keep her mother safe. It's the least she can do.

But the words need to come out. She whispers, almost too quietly to hear the words herself, 'He's found me, Mum. I thought he had stopped looking but he's found me.' She looks at her mother, who hasn't moved, and then she tips her head back against the chair and closes her eyes.

'Hello, Rachel,' says Sam, an older nurse with kind blue eyes. 'I'm just popping in to check on the drip.'

Rachel opens her eyes and gives Sam a small smile.

'Maybe take an hour or two off? You look like you need a break,' he says.

'I'm so worried that I won't be here if she, when she… and I'll have to leave at three to get Beth anyway. I'm fine.'

'There are signs when it's getting closer, love. We'll call you. I promise we will call you immediately but I think we've a few days to go.'

Rachel trusts Sam. He's been working in hospice care for over forty years. Sometimes she wonders if he ever gets to laugh. She hopes so. 'Maybe I'll just get a coffee,' she says quietly.

There is a room set up with coffee and tea and biscuits for visitors. Rachel sits silently in a chair overlooking the garden as she takes small bites of a chocolate biscuit, letting it melt in her mouth. She is not hungry but knows it's better to eat a little. Her mother loves dark chocolate covered roasted almonds. In her bedside drawer she has two unopened packets that Rachel brought her, hoping that against all odds Veronica would open her eyes and ask for a last taste of her favourite treat.

Rachel studies the white stone paths that lead people from one side of the hospice to the other, keeping them off the grass and out of the colourful flower beds. She watches a couple with a teenager walk slowly towards the front door. They stop before they pull open the heavy glass doors and Rachel knows they are composing themselves, mentally preparing themselves to see the person they have come to visit. Patients change overnight, shrinking and growing frailer with each passing day, every passing moment. It's why Rachel has made the decision to keep Beth away. She wants her to remember her grandmother smiling, helping her with a puzzle, rolling out dough for cookies, laughing at the jokes Beth likes to make up, vibrant and alive. She does not want Beth to remember the emaciated woman in the bed who seems to be barely breathing.

She is aware of other people coming in and out of the visitors' room but this is a place where conversations have to be invited. Everyone here is grieving for someone. A mother, a father, a son, a daughter, a brother, a sister. This is a place that levels everyone. Rachel can spot the more well-to-do families by how they dress and the cars they drive, but grief looks the same on their faces as it does on hers. They all wear the same misery, the same disbelief. It seems that here, right at the end, who you are means very little. Everyone here feels for others going through the same tragic loss, and the compassion that the world most needs is readily on display.

On her way back to her mother's room she finds herself feeling jumpy and looking around as though it were possible that he could turn up here today as well. When she was little, she knew he was all-powerful and that nothing could stop him. She knew that the only way to get away from him was to run and keep running. Right now, she feels she is a child again, a frightened child, losing her mother and afraid of the monster.

At three she kisses her mother goodbye. She has barely moved in the hours she has been by her bedside. 'I'll pop back later tonight, Mum,' Rachel says, hoping that Ben will be home early enough for her to do so, and that she won't fall asleep on the couch as she has done so often in the last few days.

As she pulls out of the parking lot, letting her tears fall freely, she tries to distract herself with her list of things to do. The first and most important thing is to check all the doors that lead into the house again. She needs to know how he got in so she can prevent him from ever getting in again.

She could have told the police the truth, could have shown them the small token left by a man she thought had disappeared from her life completely, by a man she has told everyone she knows is dead, but she hadn't been able to find the words. How could she have explained it all, and how could she have explained it in front of Ben, who has an entirely different version of her past?

I'll never tell, I promise.

She had been a child with secrets, a child who knew how to hide things. Even now, as an adult, it feels impossible to suddenly start telling the truth. She feels safer when things are not discussed, when she can pretend that what happened never happened. It is how she has managed to survive.

It had to be him. Only he would have left the small plastic doll for her. Only he knew how much the doll meant to her. It was definitely one of hers. She had known every single one of them, had loved every single one.

For a moment, when she found it last night, she thought that it could have belonged to Beth, that it was simply dropped in the hallway between their rooms. But she knew it wasn't. Beth didn't have a toy like it, and it had not been in the passage when she had darted into Beth's room and locked the door. It wasn't lying in the hallway either. It was standing up straight on the carpet, balanced carefully there by someone who was sending her a message.

It's been so many years. She assumed he had stopped looking, had stopped caring about where they were. She has even, if she has ever thought about it, imagined him moving on and creating a whole new family to torture. So why is he here now and what does he want?

She stops at a traffic light and takes a deep breath. She's exhausted. Last night, once the police had gone and Ben was breathing steadily in sleep, she crept into the bathroom and rummaged around in the bottom of the hamper where she had pushed the doll under the dirty laundry. She pulled it out and looked at it carefully, making sure she recognised it as one of hers. She was unable to prevent a small smile as she stared down at its big eyes and funny nose, the rainbow hair that stuck straight up. But her smile disappeared quickly as fear made her tremble. She held the doll tightly, the little plastic hands digging into her palm. She had named this one Riley Rainbow for its hair. She can remember combing it with a tiny brush her mother bought for her. 'Riley Rainbow,' she whispered and then she stuffed it back down to the bottom of the hamper so she could throw it out in the morning.

This morning she'd looked at the suitcases of clothes that still needed to be unpacked and fought the urge to grab them and just run because she knew how to run. She was very good at running.

She pulls up to the school where Beth will be rushing out to greet her in a moment. A typical day, a typical task and something she has long taken for granted. She wonders how much longer she will be able to do this. He obviously means to do her harm, means to harm her family even if he is older and weaker. His strength lies in his ability to manipulate and control. Age doesn't take that away and he would still be a big man, despite how many years have rolled by. She knows that on nights when the terror of him finding them kept her awake as a child she would fantasise about him being in prison, would imagine that he had taken his violence outside to the world and found himself punished for it.

The urge to run overwhelms her. Only running kept them safe. She will need money for that. Just in case.

She thinks about telling Ben, about explaining. Because he has found her. She is no longer safe and there is no reason to keep the secret anymore.

I'll never tell, I promise.

What will Ben think of her, of all the lies she has told? What will he think of her mother? And how could she explain it to him so that he would understand? Only she knows why the little doll is a threat. She can almost imagine Ben and the police laughing at her.

She simply needs to know that she can run if she has to. The thought of leaving Ben, of leaving everything, forces more tears from her eyes. Even as she already mourns her mother, she knows that she is lucky, that she is loved and safe with Ben. How on earth could she leave him, leave her life? How could she go back to the terrible rental apartments, always looking over her shoulder, and how could she do that to their baby girl? Maybe she could tell Ben and they could all leave together? But he would never agree to that. He would want to stay and sort things out. He would not know how afraid he should be. He wouldn't understand.

She was seven.

Beth is seven.

She needs to get ready, like her mother was always ready. Always ready to run, always ready to leave, always afraid of being found.

Climbing out of the car and walking to the school gate, she hears the final bell ring for the end of the school day. She forces a smile onto her face so that Beth will only see a happy mother, so that everyone at the school gate will see that Beth has a happy mother. The movement makes her cheeks hurt, as though she hasn't smiled in a long time, but she holds it as she looks for Beth and nods at other mothers waiting for their children. Even though it's only three thirty, the sun is already low in the sky and the air is growing cooler. It will be dark by five and once more she will be alone in the house with Beth. Will he be back tonight?

She spots her daughter and waves. 'Mummy!' shouts her daughter, her face lighting up as she sees her mother. An ordinary winter's day but Rachel knows that nothing is ordinary anymore.

CHAPTER TEN

Ben

Before he switches off his computer, Ben takes a quick look at their bank account to reassure himself that the rental bond has been returned and that there is enough money to cover the mortgage, which is coming out in the morning. He hears some laughter from the corridor. One of his colleagues, Angela, pops her head in. 'We're going for a drink, want to come?'

'Thanks, but I want to get back in time to put Beth to bed and read her a story.' Outside, the night has descended and the cold wind has picked up. It's only six o'clock but it feels much later. He can't wait for summer to return so that he can get home when it's still light. It feels like he's living then, not just commuting into the office as the sun rises and returning long after it sets. In the office the temperature and the light are always the same but outside the lone tree on the pavement sixteen floors down bends as it is assaulted by the winter wind.

Two days after her desperate phone call to him, Rachel is still on edge. The alarm system was fitted yesterday after Ben explained his fear for his family to the woman at the company responsible for the installation. 'You poor dear,' she had said sympathetically. 'I'll move some things around and get Mark to come over at the end of today.'

Last night he had arrived home to find Mark still finishing up the installation.

'Thanks so much for doing this, mate,' he said.

'No worries, I understand how much you need it. It's really quiet out here at the moment. I have a friend who's going to start building next month and he told me no one was living here yet.'

'Yeah, well, our builders were really quick.'

Mark nodded as he placed the last sensor above the kitchen door. 'The latch that closes the sliding door that leads to the garden was a little loose but I tightened it up for you.'

'That's good of you, thanks.'

So now they have an alarm and Rachel has a remote with a panic button she can press if she needs to. He assumed it would make her feel secure but she's still jittery. It's not just because of what's going on with her mother – it's something more, he's sure. Last night, after Mark had left, he had stood behind her in the kitchen after he had come down from his shower. She was talking to herself, whispering what he assumed was a list of things to do, and he had listened, trying to figure out what she was saying. Then she turned around and saw him, dropping the bowl of salad she was carrying. 'Why did you sneak up on me?' she yelled. He was too shocked to respond. Rachel never yells.

He got down on his hands and knees to help her pick up the spilled vegetables. 'I'm sorry,' he said.

'It's okay, it's not your fault, it's me, I'm just… well, you know.' She waved a hand in the air to indicate everything and anything. He didn't know and he wanted to know, would have liked her to talk about how she was feeling about her mother and the break-in, which wasn't really a break-in, but she didn't seem to want to discuss anything other than Beth and school and work – the safe subjects. She is only home for a snatched hour or two at the moment, spending most of her time with her mother.

Every now and again Ben finds himself having a terrible thought about Veronica, a sort of wish that it would end quickly now, that her life wouldn't keep lingering on, torturing both her and her family. The hospice is a shocking place to visit. A beautiful building filled with the dying. He should go more often than he does but he can't seem to force himself over there. He doesn't even want to contemplate what it will be like for him when it's one of his own parents slowly wasting away. He sighs and rubs his eyes, chasing away the morbid thoughts that make him feel like an awful person.

He realises Angela is still in his office doorway, waiting for his attention. 'You're such a good dad.' She smiles and he feels like she's making fun of him. Her frosted pink lipstick has been freshly applied, shimmering in the office lights. Ben flushes. Angela seems to enjoy flirting with him, despite his lack of response. He knows that she's slept with more than one person in the office and he also knows that should he ever give in to her invitation, he would regret it for the rest of his life.

'See you tomorrow,' she says when he doesn't say anything else.

'Yeah, have a good night.'

Once she's left the room, he looks over the bank account, noting that the electricity bill has been paid today and that Rachel has withdrawn $300. She must have bought something new for the house. They have been discussing the need for some prints for all the empty wall space. Why else would she need so much cash? He knows it wasn't for groceries because she used her card for those yesterday. He sighs. He doesn't want to question her on the money, especially not now when she is so stressed, so on edge about the move and so heartbroken about her mother.

Veronica and Rachel have always been so incredibly close, just the two of them against the world. She introduced them after they'd only had a few dates. Ben hadn't ever met the family of a girlfriend so early into a relationship but he knew things were different with Rachel. He felt like they had just clicked and as though they had been together for much longer. He was nervous about meeting Veronica but could see how much Rachel wanted him to.

They had gone to a burger restaurant for their first date. It was
a favourite restaurant of his and he knew that between the music
and the atmosphere, if they didn't have much to say to each other
they could still muddle through. As it turned out they had barely
stopped talking long enough to eat and had eventually asked their
waiter to pack up the cold burgers and fries to take home. He had
driven them to the beach and they had walked along the water's
edge with their shoes off and jeans rolled up, enjoying the last
dash of summer in the air. The inky black sky had been cloud-
less and studded with stars, and the sea spray had covered them
lightly, cooling them down. They had talked and talked. About
everything from their favourite colours to countries they wanted
to travel to and what their dreams for their future lives were. They
had reminisced about television shows and books they had both
loved as kids. She had made him laugh as she poked gentle fun
at Lou's intolerance of other students in their course who didn't
do the readings before class. It's been a long time since she made
him laugh, since they made each other laugh really. Things have
become so complicated and so difficult, it's like the people they
were on the beach that night have completely disappeared.

He had felt, after that first night, as though he knew everything
about her and only later had he realised that real details, the deeper
details, about her life had not really been shared. He assumed they
would get there.

When he met Veronica for the first time, Rachel buzzed him
into her building and he found himself standing in an entrance
hall that showed its age. It was a small, red-brick building on the
outskirts of the city with six apartments, a concrete surround and
only a few spindly trees in some planter boxes. Inside, Ben had
looked around as he searched for the staircase that would lead
him up to Rachel's apartment, noticing the cracks running down
the walls and the strange musty smell of an old carpet. He had
thought about his own family home where he and Lou had their

own bathrooms and living areas, almost like two small flats inside the grand house surrounded by an emerald-green lawn and large evergreen trees. 'So you'll stay home a bit longer,' his mother had told them, not wanting to let them go.

'I want you to meet my mum,' Rachel said excitedly when she opened the door, giving him a quick kiss on the cheek.

'Sure, yeah, of course,' he said as he tucked his shirt in, a schoolboy about to be marched into the principal's office.

He could see the flat was in need of a coat of paint, and it was comfortably messy with books piled on every surface and an overstuffed sofa covered in colourful blankets.

Inside, her mother was seated on the sofa but stood up as soon as she saw him, and Ben found himself looking at Rachel twenty or thirty years from now. The same fine brown hair, although hers was streaked with blonde highlights, and the same grey-green eyes, with only a few lines around them, and a thin scar on her cheek to distinguish the two.

'Hello, Ben,' she said, her voice soft and deep like Rachel's. 'Rachel has told me so much about you, and of course I know all about Lou as well. It's wonderful that she's met such lovely people to spend time with.'

'Hi, um, thanks, yeah, Lou is great... She introduced me to Rachel, so... yeah.' He was surprised to find himself a little lost for words. Veronica's stare was intense, and he felt that she could see how nervous he was. He had a moment of panic at the idea that Veronica wouldn't like him, which he knew would be a deal-breaker for her daughter. After just three dates he already knew how close they were, and he was desperate to make a good impression. He felt like an awkward boy as he held out his hand to her. 'I'm Ben,' he said, forgetting that Rachel had already told her mother his name.

'I'm Veronica,' she said shaking his hand. Then she laughed and her daughter laughed along with her and Ben could feel their bond, hanging thick in the air as though it was something that could be touched because it was so strong. Lou and his mother were close but there didn't seem to be the same intensity there was with these two. He assumed that it was because they had been alone for so long, Rachel's father having succumbed to cancer when she was just a child.

Now he knows that their love for each other sustained them through that ordeal. Before Veronica got sick, they would speak at least twice a day and have lunch together whenever they got the chance. After she was diagnosed, Rachel had, for a time, seemed to be trying to squeeze in a lifetime with her mother. Even up until recently they shopped together and read the same books at the same time so they could compare notes, and sometimes they seemed to communicate without actually saying anything. 'I was thinking…' Veronica would say, and Rachel would reply, 'Yes, I think so too.'

'What?' Ben would ask, confused. 'What are you two talking about?' eliciting gentle laughter from both of them. He hopes that when Beth grows up, she and Rachel will be as close.

Ben turns off the computer. How cruel it is that Rachel lost her father to cancer and is now losing her mother to the same awful disease. He thinks again about how much of the unpacking he will get done this weekend so she doesn't have to worry about it. He decides he will also take Beth to the park, so she can have some fun. He knows he cannot understand the depth of Rachel's grief right now but the least he can do is take care of the things that he can manage.

He lets his mind drift as he makes his way through the rush hour traffic, thinking about how small and thin Veronica is now, how fragile she looks, as though a single touch might break her. It is soul-destroying to watch. He's glad that Rachel has stopped taking Beth to see her grandmother. It would be too much for the little girl to see her so altered.

He is relieved to get home, to find his wife and his daughter in the kitchen laughing over some silly joke.

'Good day?' asks Rachel.

'More of the same. We're not selling enough units – how can we sell more units? If we don't sell more units, jobs will have to go.'

Rachel concentrates on turning the lamb chops she is frying. 'Are you worried?' she asks and he wants to tell her that he's more than worried, that he thinks they've bitten off more than they can chew with the house and that he spends more time fretting over losing his job than actually doing it.

'Nah,' he smiles at her, 'not worried at all,' he says, and he is cheered by the smile she returns. Her trust in him, her faith in him, makes him feel ten feet tall most days. But sometimes, like now, he wishes he could hand some of the burden over to her, that he could tell her what's really going on at work instead of keeping things from her because she is already dealing with so much. He squashes the thought down and turns to his daughter, who is a little carbon copy of her mother.

'Now how was your day – did you make important year-one decisions?' he asks Beth as he sits down.

'I decided to go across the monkey bars three times at lunch even though my hands got freezing,' she says. 'Charlotte brought her Barbie doll to school and Mrs. Weiner said that "the classroom is not a place for toys".'

Ben laughs at her imitation of her teacher's voice.

'Oh,' he suddenly remembers, and he gets up again to grab his briefcase, 'look what I found in my car the other day. You must have dropped it.' He digs inside the case and finds the troll doll.

Beth takes it from him. 'It's not mine,' she says. 'Can I have it?'

'Can you have what?' asks Rachel as she places their plates in front of them.

'This, look, it's cute and kind of ugly beautiful, it's a troll doll, you remember we saw the movie, Mum? Charlotte has some troll dolls. We played with them when I went to her house that one time.'

Rachel's face loses its colour. She falls into a chair with her hand on her heart.

'Rach? What's wrong, you okay?'

'Oh yes, yes… I just need to eat,' she says. 'Where did you find that thing?' He watches her hands move as she cuts up Beth's lamb for her. She has lost too much weight in the last few weeks, as though she is wasting away with her mother.

'It was on the floor of my car. It must be yours, Beth, unless there is another little girl who calls me Daddy.'

'Silly Daddy, I'm the only little girl who calls you Daddy,' she says and she giggles. 'I love my dolly and I'm going to name her… Pinky, because of her pink hair. See, Mum, see Pinky?'

Rachel nods her head but she doesn't look at the doll, instead looking down at her plate, where she is cutting her lamb into smaller and smaller pieces.

'That's a great name,' says Ben, conscious of Beth's smile disappearing. 'Mum's just really hungry now and so am I. Come on, eat up, and then you can play with Pinky.'

'Put it down and eat, Beth,' Rachel says, sounding as though she is speaking through tears.

Beth looks down at her plate. 'I love you, Pinky,' she whispers to the little doll, who is standing on the table gazing at her with giant bulbous eyes.

'I said eat, Beth,' Rachel snaps, 'and put that stupid thing away.'

'But Mum,' says Beth, her eyes filling with tears that quickly spill down her cheeks.

'I tell you what, Beth,' says Ben, standing up, 'I think that just for tonight and just because you have your new friend Pinky, you can watch television while you eat dinner. That will be fun, won't it? Maybe I can find the *Trolls* movie on Netflix.'

'Maybe Pinky is in the movie!' shouts Beth, her tears drying instantly.

Ben looks over at his wife, worried that she might protest, but she is staring down at her plate again. He picks up Beth's plate and takes her to her playroom, where she has a television. He sets her up with a small tray table and finds something for her to watch when he can't find *Trolls*, convincing her that it will be on some other time.

Returning to the table, he slides silently into his seat, watching his wife, unsure of what to say, unsure if there is anything he can say that will make things better for her.

Rachel eats little and is mostly silent.

'You okay?' he finally asks quietly.

'Fine.' Rachel sighs and then she wipes her cheek and blows her nose, giving up all pretence of eating. 'Mum didn't really wake up today.'

'That's not... I'm so sorry, sweetheart,' he says and he leans across to touch her hand but Rachel stands up quickly.

'I feel like she's gone already... like... I don't know,' she says picking up her plate, her tears returning.

Ben takes his own plate over to the garbage and scrapes off the remains of his dinner. 'Why don't you sit down and let me do this?' he says.

'No... no, I'm... I'm okay to clean up but could you... could you just get Beth to bed? I'm not really...'

'Of course,' he replies eagerly, pleased to have some concrete way to help, 'of course, don't worry about it.'

Beth sits Pinky on the side of the bath to watch while she builds a soap tower out of frothed coconut-scented bubble bath. Ben sits next to the bath, listening to her talk to the little doll.

'And I'm gonna build you a house and you can have a bed and a swimming pool like Charlotte has...'

He tries to prevent himself from looking at his phone as it buzzes in his pocket with incoming emails. His daughter lies on her stomach and kicks her legs in the tub.

Once she's in bed, Beth holds the doll up to him. 'Mum doesn't like Pinky,' she says.

'Of course she does, Beth. She's just a little sad tonight. Everyone gets sad sometimes.'

'Is Mum sad because Nana is sick?'

'She is because she loves Nana. We all love Nana and we don't like it that she's sick.'

'I love Nana a million billion,' says Beth.

'I know you do, darling, now lie down and I'll snuggle you.'

'You lie down with me,' she says as he tucks her pink duvet tightly around her the way she likes.

He angles his body next to hers, revelling in the strawberry and coconut smell of her. She turns off her light and together they watch as their eyes adjust and the moon and stars appear on her ceiling. He will lie next to her until he can hear she is asleep, her tiny chest rising and falling, just the way his father did for him and Lou when they were little.

'Mum cried today,' Beth says softly.

'I know, baby. Mum's very sad about Nana.'

'Yes, but I don't think she was crying because of Nana. I think she was crying because of the monster.'

'The monster?'

Beth turns on her side so she can look at him. She puts her little hands on his face and whispers, 'There was a monster here in the night. He tried to get into my room to eat me all up but Mum called the police. Then she cried and cried and I think she cried today because she's scared of the monster even though she said there wasn't a monster. I know there was.' She lets go of his face and turns away from him. 'I know there was,' she whispers again before she puts her thumb in her mouth.

'What monster? When was this?' Ben asks quickly. But Beth doesn't reply and her even breathing tells him she's asleep. He gets off her bed feeling queasy. Rachel told him Beth was asleep when she called the police. The police said there was no evidence of anyone in the house. What was Beth talking about?

Downstairs Rachel is flicking through channels on the television. 'I'm going to go back and spend some time with Mum in a few minutes,' she says when he joins her.

'Um, yeah... Rach... Beth just told me the strangest thing.'

'What's that?' says Rachel, her eyes on the television.

'She told me you cried today because of the monster who was in the house. She said he tried to get into her room.'

'What?'

'She said that a monster made you cry today. A monster who was here in the night. I think she means a couple of nights ago, obviously, but I thought... I thought she wasn't awake for that?'

Rachel shakes her head. 'She wasn't. I made certain. You know she wasn't or she would have been awake when you got home. Anyway, as the police pointed out, there was no one here. What a strange thing for her to say to say – she's obviously seen something on television or something, don't you think? She wasn't... she wasn't awake. I know she wasn't.' Rachel speaks quickly, almost babbling, listing all the reasons Beth may have been mistaken.

Ben lays a hand on her arm and she stops speaking, finally taking a deep breath. 'I'm afraid I did shed a few tears in the car when I picked her up from school. I'd just been to see Mum and I thought about how sad it was that Beth will never see her again.'

Ben nods. 'That's okay. It's just that she might have been awake and then maybe we should talk to her about it? Maybe just let her know that we thought someone was here but that the police came and everything is safe.'

He strokes her arm as he speaks, conscious of her darting eyes and the stiffness in her body.

'Maybe, but I don't want to worry her. I want her to know her home is safe. She should feel safe.'

'I'm sure she feels safe, Rach. She's always safe with us.'

'Yes, she is,' says Rachel, nodding her head. 'I think we should just leave it now, just let it be over.'

'Okay,' says Ben slowly. He would like to ask his wife why she doesn't want to discuss what happened or the fact that Beth may have heard more than she thinks, but she seems so fragile right now. He's afraid to push her. And she's probably right. Beth has a child's imagination. She sat in the bath earlier and talked to Pinky as though the little doll was engaged in the conversation. She told him that the fairies in the park leave little flowers as presents for her. She could have simply imagined the monster. Telling her about the police coming might frighten her.

He slouches down onto the sofa as Rachel stands up so she can leave to go and see her mother. He's making more of this than he should, he's sure of it.

'Give her my love – I mean if she wakes up, tell her we're all thinking of her and we love her.'

Rachel nods, walking towards the kitchen to get her bag.

'Are you sure she was asleep, Rach?' He cannot help asking once more because for some reason he doesn't believe his wife.

'Absolutely sure,' says Rachel, her tone clipped.

Ben doesn't say anything else. He listens as she leaves the house, the garage door sliding up, her car reversing, and only when he hears her roar off down the street does he relax, wondering why he doesn't believe what she's saying.

Why doesn't he believe her?

CHAPTER ELEVEN

Little Bird

On Saturday night Mummy and I watch a movie on television. It's about a nanny who comes to take care of two little children. Mummy says that she loved the movie when she was a little girl just like me, and so now I love it too. 'No story time tonight,' says Mummy at the end and I know that means I can read my new book but only for a few minutes. Mummy is tired today because she cleaned and cleaned and cleaned.

She only stopped cleaning to change the bandage on her cheek when a bit of blood came. 'I was so silly,' she told me this morning, 'I opened the bathroom cabinet to get my toothpaste and I hit myself,' and then she laughed and I laughed as well even though my laugh wasn't a real laugh. I don't think a cut on your cheek is funny.

'You need sleep to grow so you can only read for a bit,' Mummy says. I think Kevin must have slept a lot when he was seven years old because he's nearly as tall as Daddy now. He has the same colour hair as Daddy too and brown eyes. Black-brown eyes that look mean. I think Kevin has mean eyes.

I go quietly up the stairs because Daddy is working in his office and he doesn't like noise. That's why me and Mummy had to make the television soft, soft but we could still hear most of the talking. When I get to my room, I see that Daddy is not in his office. He is in my room looking at my dollies lined up on the windowsill.

They are all in a straight line, neat and tidy, just the way they are supposed to be. I feel my tummy fill up with scared and I look around my room quickly. My bed is made, the covers smooth, the pillow lying on top with the folded blanket. My heart jumps anyway because Daddy is sitting on the floor and then he turns and looks at me. My room is clean and sparkling but Daddy looks upset. I wonder if some mess is hiding somewhere. Daddy is good at spotting things that are hiding.

'Hello, Daddy,' I say slowly. I don't like it when he comes into my room without me. My room is my favourite place because I'm allowed to close the door but not lock it. It has a light pink carpet and dark pink curtains because I told Mummy that pink was my favourite colour, and for my last birthday, she took all the Little Bird stickers off the wall that she put up when I was a baby and painted it white with a little bit of pink. Daddy didn't help her but she didn't mind. Then she painted butterflies all over one wall. Big ones and small ones. Some are sitting on flowers and some are flying in the air. They have patterns on their wings and so many colours I can't count them all. Sometimes, one of our little secrets is that Mummy will call me a pretty butterfly. She only calls me that when it's just the two of us because she knows that Daddy likes me to be his Little Bird. I like to think of myself with wings covered in colours.

'Amazing how far a degree in fine art can take you,' Daddy said when he saw my room and then he laughed but it wasn't a happy laugh and Mummy didn't laugh with him. She just looked at her shoes. I don't think Daddy likes the wall of butterflies but I love it and I told Mummy it was the best birthday present ever. I don't think Daddy should come into my room if he doesn't like the wall of butterflies.

I am not allowed in his and Mummy's room unless Mummy is there. I am not allowed in Kevin's room ever, ever. But Daddy is allowed to go into any room he likes. I stand quietly and wait for him to tell me where the mess is hiding. I don't think he's here to read me a story. Daddy doesn't read stories to children.

'I thought you loved these dollies,' he says.

'I do,' I say, nodding my head. 'I love them all.' They are my special dollies with ugly faces but big smiles and beautiful coloured hair. I have twenty-nine of them. Daddy buys them for me all the time and Mummy does too because they are small. Every night Mummy and I count them together and that's why I am the best counter in my class and I always get ten out of ten on my maths test.

'Then why,' he says, 'don't you treat them nicely? Look at how messy they are, and see here, these two, just lying on the floor?'

I look at them lined up neatly on the big windowsill and I can't see that they are messy, but if Daddy says they are messy, then they are. Then I look where he is pointing, behind my side table, where two dollies had gone on a little holiday. I forgot they were on holiday when I tidied everything up. I open my mouth to explain but then I close it again. Daddy won't understand about a dolly holiday.

Daddy stares and stares and waits for me to say something. 'Maybe they fell off. They were next to the others,' I whisper. My face gets hot and I know it's turning red. It always turns red when I tell a lie. Daddy will know I'm lying and he doesn't like liars.

'I don't think they fell off, Little Bird. I think you left them on the floor after you were done playing with them even though you know that things need to be kept neat and tidy. Even though you know that if you love something, you must take care of it.'

'I'll tidy them up, Daddy, I promise,' I say quickly. My cheeks feel burning and I want to cry. Daddy smiles at me and then he picks up one of my dollies and shows it to me. It's the mermaid one with the silvery pink tail and blue hair and it's one of my favourites. She wanted to go on holiday so she could swim in the sea. 'I don't think you love this one enough. She was just lying there on the floor like you didn't care about her at all.'

'But I do care, Daddy. I'm sorry. I'll never forget her on the floor again.'

'I think you're lying about that, Little Bird, and I hate liars.' He wraps his big hand around the mermaid's head. He twists and pulls until it snaps right off.

'No, Daddy, no!' I shout. But the doll is broken. Daddy throws it on the floor and then he grabs me by my shoulders, his fingers digging into my skin. 'Don't raise your voice at me, don't you ever raise your voice at me,' he hisses.

'Sorry,' I say and my tears splash onto my shoes and my nose starts to run. I can feel my heart inside me, trying to burst out because I am so sad for my dolly and so scared of Daddy.

'What's going on, Len?' says Mummy, and I turn and see her standing in the doorway.

'What's going on is that you still haven't managed to teach your daughter how to keep things neat and tidy, and I have been so patient, so patient with both of you.'

'I'm sorry, Len. I'll make sure it doesn't happen again.'

'I believe you,' says Daddy and he stands up and pats me on the head. 'Don't cry, Little Bird, I'm sure you won't leave your dollies in a mess again.'

I nod my head.

'Let's have a drink,' he says to Mummy, and she looks at me and her eyes are sad and I know she wants to stay with me. But then she turns and goes downstairs with him.

I sit down on the floor and look at my broken dolly, who is still smiling at me. I hear a sound from downstairs, a *thump*, a *crack*, and I know Mummy will have a sore head again. Maybe she forgot to make everything clean and sparkling as well. Mummy has a sore head a lot on the weekend. Daddy stays home from work and he makes sure that everything is just right. That's how he likes things to be, he says – just right.

I make sure all my dollies are in a straight, straight line on the windowsill and then I brush my teeth and change into pyjamas and I climb into bed, holding my broken little mermaid. 'I'm sorry,' I whisper to her, and she smiles and smiles and I know she forgives me. I close my eyes and I hope that Mummy's head won't be too sore tomorrow. I hate the weekend when Daddy is home all the time, just looking, looking for hiding mess. Kevin doesn't hate the weekend because he doesn't come home. He goes to his friend's house for a sleepover and he only comes home on Sunday night. Kevin's room is always clean and sparkling because he's never here for a long time.

He rides his bike to his friend's house, and when he comes back, he always makes sure that the bike is put away in its special place in the garage. It's not a very nice bike. Kevin found it on the side of the road and he cleaned it very carefully and painted it and put some special oil on the chain, but it's still not a very nice bike. He used to have a nice bike. It was shiny and red and he got it for his eleventh birthday but one day he came home and put it in the garage but he didn't stand it up straight enough. Daddy showed him how to make sure the bike is standing straight so he won't scratch his car when he puts it in the garage. He didn't scratch his car but he still didn't like that the bike wasn't standing up straight enough so he pulled the bicycle out of the garage. Then he called Kevin and he made him watch while he drove his big car over Kevin's bike.

Kevin got tears in his eyes. I remember even though I was only five because I had never seen Kevin get tears in his eyes before. He didn't shout and he didn't say anything. After he rode over the bike, Daddy got out of the car and said, 'You left me no choice, Kevin.'

'Yes, sir,' said Kevin. Daddy likes Kevin to call him sir. 'It's what I called my father. It's a mark of respect,' he told Mummy. I am allowed to call him Daddy but maybe when I am big like Kevin, I will have to call him sir too.

I felt some sorry inside myself for Kevin. He really loved his shiny red bike. After Daddy went back in the house, Kevin sat on the ground next to his bike and patted the smooshed white seat. Mummy tried to give him a hug but he didn't want her to hug him.

'Just leave me alone,' he said. I didn't understand why he didn't want a hug from Mummy because she gives the best hugs. I always want Mummy to hug me.

When I am nearly asleep, I hear Mummy come into my room. She puts a soft kiss on my forehead and whispers, 'I'm sorry, Little Bird. I am so sorry.'

CHAPTER TWELVE

'Can you tell me about the house you lived in when you were a child?' Dr Sharma says.

Dr Sharma is really starting to disappoint me. I thought she would try something different but I've had this question from at least three different doctors. I don't think I would have seen any doctors if the school hadn't told my father it was necessary. I started seeing the school psychologist at fourteen and then she ran out of options, calling my father in and telling him I needed professional help.

Her name was Ingrid and we were allowed to call her Ingrid, instead of Miss Andrews. Her office was covered in hundreds of inspirational signs. *The only way is up. It's not the destination, it's the journey. Find your passion. If you believe, you can achieve anything. Life is tough but so are you. He believed he could so he did. Mistakes are proof you're trying. Live, Laugh, Love.* They covered the walls all the way to the ceiling, and when my father was sitting next to me, opposite Ingrid as she explained slowly that my anger issues would affect the rest of my life if I didn't learn to control myself, I watched my father's eyes roam up and down the walls. He didn't even let her finish talking.

'I'll get him some professional help,' he said, standing up. 'You're obviously incapable of dealing with anything beyond this silliness.' He gestured around the room. Ingrid had blonde hair and freckles and I couldn't help laughing when her face turned beetroot-red. My father put his hand on my shoulder. 'Nothing to laugh at here, son.' When I took off my shirt later, I had his fingerprints on my back.

I think about the house question because I can't stop an image of it from appearing in my mind. It's meant to be an easy leading question that takes you back to childhood in a non- confrontational way. The idea is that I describe the physical characteristics of the home I had when I was a child and that leads me into a discussion about what my childhood was like and who hurt me, etc. It's boring but I don't want to be regarded as a recalcitrant patient. They tend to start upping your meds then or they make sure to watch you swallow them because surely if you were taking all your meds you would be behaving. Surely.

'I lived in a very nice suburb,' I say.

She doesn't say anything, just leans forward and furrows her brows. I've never really noticed a woman's eyebrows before but hers are thick and dark and look like they could use some attention. Even in here I make sure to maintain my appearance. I like to keep things neat and I make sure I do my 200 press-ups and sit-ups every day. I like watching my muscles bunch and move. I like that other patients look at me and back away. Size is power. I know that. I am big enough to not have to worry about anyone threatening me. I'm the threat. I'm who people should be scared of.

'My father was an actuary,' I say and she writes that down, even though she has all that information already. My file follows me from hospital to hospital, doctor to doctor. It's pages and pages and pages on a computer. A nurse showed it to me once. She liked me, really liked me. We used to have sex in my room after lights out and I convinced her to show me my file on the staff computer. I read through it quickly enough, catching terms like 'psychopathic tendencies', 'dissociative disorder', 'attention deficit disorder', 'bipolar disorder'. My psychiatrists have never agreed on exactly what's wrong with me. I didn't quite understand her interest in me – I mean, she had obviously read my file – but then I realised she was just like all the other women I have ever slept with. She thought she was going to rescue me. It's strange that when my father suggests no woman will ever want to be with me, he forgets to account for all the women who think they can rehabilitate a damaged man. I have never had to look too hard for a willing body.

In my file I read that everyone had a different opinion and a different drug they thought I should try. But I don't need drugs. I'm pissed off. That all. I'm really pissed off. I ended it with the nurse after she showed me the file. She had nothing left to offer me.

'Your father was an actuary,' Dr Sharma says. She doesn't enjoy long pauses.

'He worked in insurance,' I continue, 'and he made a reasonable amount of money so we had a nice house in a nice suburb. We didn't have a pool because my mother really wanted a pool…' I stop talking, irritated that I have said more than I should have.

'Did your father not like the idea of a pool?' she asks, quick as a wink.

I ignore the question as the large bright green expanse of our garden appears in my mind.

My mother asked for a pool. I loved to swim and so did she – it was one of the few things we shared so naturally my father refused us a pool. He made the money, after all. Physical power and abuse are one thing, but I have no doubt that my father enjoyed the mind games even more. Every year for at least three years, as spring rolled around, my father would start bringing home brochures from pool builders. He would leave them lying around, and if neither me nor my mother said anything, he would begin reading them all the time. He would start asking our opinions about designs and what kinds of tiles would be good to use. He would spend time in the garden staring at the space, holding a brochure as though he was trying to visualise the pool. And every time he did this my mother and I would eventually suspend disbelief and start joining in the conversations. When our excitement reached fever pitch it would all stop, just stop. The brochures would disappear, and if either of us asked about it… I have a rib that never quite healed right – I call it my 'pool rib' for obvious reasons. I actually think he smiled as he hit me. I was stupid enough to utter the words, 'But you promised.'

'Everyone breaks their promises,' he said as his fist swung towards me. 'Remember that.' I learned that lesson but I didn't learn it from him, surprisingly. I learned it from my mother. When I was twelve, I broke my ankle at school during a game of basketball at lunch. I attempted a jump shot and landed strangely, rolling my ankle and cracking the bone. I was in the school office with my foot up on a chair and a cold pack on my ankle when my mother rushed in. I knew they had called her but I thought she would send my father, and I didn't expect the strained look of worry on her face. 'Oh, darling,' she said, smiling when she saw me, relieved, I suppose, that I was sitting up and basically okay except for the ankle.

'You came,' I said because by then my father was the one mostly dealing with the school over the problematic behaviour I had begun to display.

'Of course I came. I promise I'll always come for you if you need me.'

A year later, she broke that promise, and that's how I really learned that everyone – absolutely everyone – breaks their promises.

I don't tell Dr Sharma any of this, continuing my description of the house instead. 'It was a two-storey house with timber window frames that had to be sanded and cleaned regularly or they swelled in the wet weather. We had someone come in every six months or so. Both my parents loved timber and so there was a lot of timber in the house. We had timber floors – wide boards that were stained a kind of honey-brown – and timber doors in all the rooms, stained to match.'

'And what about your room? What did that look like?'

'A conventional room for a boy, I suppose. When I was younger it was decorated in blue and white with pictures of boats and trains. When I got older my mother took those down and my father bought me these giant framed pictures of cars. I liked cars.'

'What kind of cars?'

'I had a picture of a Lamborghini Veneno in red and a Bugatti Chiron in black and a Ferrari in yellow. I had models of them as well, small die-cast models. They were really expensive.'

I stop speaking and stare at the wall behind Dr Sharma's head. I am sitting in a leather armchair and she is sitting opposite me in the same kind of chair, and all that's between us is a rectangular wooden coffee table with slightly rounded corners because you never know what can be achieved by a lunatic with the broken corner of a wooden coffee table. The room is painted beige, that's the only way I can describe it – it's a plain beige square. It's a neutral room. There is nothing here that can trigger a person or upset anyone.

I should have loved my room at home. The few times I brought over a friend – one friend in particular, James – he was amazed at the double bed and the beautiful posters gracing the walls. He was also amazed at how neat it was.

My socks were lined up in colour-coded rows in my drawers, and my shirts were hung by colour in my closet. There were no plates on my floor or mugs under my bed. There was no underwear stuck behind my desk like a typical teenager's room. Everything was pristine.

'Do not show my mother this room. She will never get off my back,' he laughed.

I spent a lot of time over at James's house. He was one of four brothers and their house was always complete chaos. When I was twelve, I was allowed to start sleeping over at friends' houses and I took the opportunity to be out of our home whenever I could. I loved sleeping at James's. His family would sit down to dinner any time between five and eight in the evening when someone decided to cook. James was the youngest so he was never expected to do much, but his parents both worked so his brothers helped around the house. More often than not they would order takeaway for dinner, and then when it arrived the whole family would tuck in as they sat around the kitchen table, and there would be talking and laughing, and the food tasted amazing, and all of them would give each other shit about something or other. In my house the food tasted good when my mother cooked but it was always hard to swallow in the oppressive silence my father's presence led to. Only the clink and clank of cutlery made any noise at our dinner table unless my father asked a question that required an answer from one of us.

I remember one night when dinner was over, James's mother stood up from the table and said, 'Well, I'm exhausted and I'm going to have a bath. Clean this up, will you?' and then she just walked out of the kitchen. I couldn't believe that James's father allowed her to do that but he did. He smiled and said, 'Enjoy it,' and then he stood up, cleaned up a little and then went, 'I'll do the rest tomorrow.' Then he left as well.

I started tidying up and James said, 'Just leave it.' I loved being over at James's.

I realise that Dr Sharma is staring at me and that she can see I've drifted backwards in time. I really don't want her to ask me about that so I say, 'We had a big garden and the whole lawn was this amazing deep green. My mother took care of it with some help from a guy who came every week.'

'So, your mother enjoyed gardening?'

I shrug my shoulders. I have no idea what my mother did and did not enjoy except for swimming but that's not much to go on. When I think about her, she's a cardboard cut-out of a person.

She always looked good with her smooth brown hair neatly done and her make-up perfect and her clothes without a stitch out of place. She was very pretty – unless she had a bruise. That made her unattractive and far too real. I hated looking at her when she had a bruise.

I spent a lot of time not looking at her.

'Our house was always neat, always clean. There was never anything out of place.'

'That must have been hard for your mother,' she says. 'Children make a mess. I know because I have two of my own.'

'Oh, how old are they?' I ask and I smile and I watch Dr Sharma sit up straight and remind herself that she should not be giving away personal information.

'My mother liked to clean,' I say. She must have liked to clean. It was pretty much all she did. 'And my father liked things clean.'

And wrapped up inside those two statements is a whole, terrible, traumatic life.

I lived by myself for a couple of years when I was in my thirties. I had a job delivering those giant water bottles that they have in offices.

'Beneath your intellect,' my father said when I told him, and I thought about quitting right then but for some reason I got up and went in the next day. The work was easy, especially for someone my size, and it was difficult to have an issue with anyone since all I had to do was walk into the office, swap the empty water bottle for a full one, collect a signature and go.

I rented a small one-bedroom apartment an hour away from Sydney in a building built right on the highway. I was as far away from who I had been as a child as I could be. The noise at night was horrendous as giant trucks rumbled up and down the highway, shifting gears, but I quickly got used to it and I did well at my job. I bought cheap furniture and everything else that I needed, and it was my intention to allow the apartment to just be. I wasn't going to do my washing too regularly or tidy up or worry about dirt or about making everything 'sparkling clean'. I was going to let the space resemble James's house, with its chaos and its mess and the feeling of freedom that blew through the space like air. But I couldn't do it.

I would come home at night and no matter how tired I was I couldn't rest until everything was clean and the washing basket was empty. If I tried to leave it, my hands would itch and I would have to drink myself to sleep so I could cope.

I hated him for that, for turning me into him in every way possible. Maybe if I'd gotten some help and stayed away from him, I would have been okay. But instead the pressure built up and one day I stopped for lunch at a pub, got drunk and smashed the truck owned by the company. Just like that, I was back home in my childhood bedroom.

'Okay,' says Dr Sharma, 'what about you? Do you like things clean? And your sister? Did she like things clean?'

'My sister and I liked what my father liked. That was the rule,' I say. And then I decide on silence for the rest of our session. Sometimes I am worn out by these memories and these truths. Sometimes silence is easier.

Dr Sharma scribbles down some thoughts as I stare at the wall behind her. I think about the word 'sister'. She is thirty-five years old now. I imagine she looks just like my mother because even as a child she did. I see her as slight and pretty. But I have no idea who she would be. What she's like.

Maybe she's angry like I am or timid like my mother was. I like to think I don't care. But for some reason I do. I think my father cares as well. I know for a fact that he knows where she lives, where they both live, although he refuses to tell me. He's always had access to private investigators because he worked in the insurance game, and if an insurance company doesn't want to pay out, they need to catch you out. From the time they left, every few months some guy would turn up at our house clutching a buff-coloured folder that he handed over to my dad. He always came at night, kept his head down and his baseball cap pulled low over his face as though he was the one being watched. In winter he even wore a ridiculous trench coat, like he was Inspector Gadget.

My father hid the envelopes in his study, making sure I never got to see them and even taking them with him when he had to travel for work. When I was around eighteen, I realised that he had never travelled for work before they left, only after. He was finding them, watching them. I believe that's what he was doing. And as far as I know, he's still doing it, although, presumably, Inspector Gadget now sends emails.

I don't know if he speaks to them or just watches them but I assume that if he did make contact, they would run. If I was them, I would run. They know how to run at least. I don't know how to do that, am incapable of that. But maybe when justice has been done I will finally, finally be able to leave.

When I'm home I often find my father in my sister's room. It still looks exactly the same as it did when she was a child even though the pink curtains have faded with the sun. Her clothes still hang in the closet and her bed is perfectly made, a book with a bookmark next to her bed. He has this thing about lining up her small dolls on the windowsill. He rearranges them by colour or theme or something and then rearranges them again. 'Maybe I should send them to her?' he said to me the week before I landed myself in here.

'Maybe you should visit her,' I said.

'I might just do that.'

He has never gotten over them leaving. He may not be able to believe how I have messed up my life but he definitely still cannot believe what happened twenty-eight years ago. He still can't believe it and I think he needs – now that he's getting older and looking death in the face – to make them pay for messing up his picture-perfect Christmas card family. To really make them pay.

I want justice for myself, but my father… my father just wants good old-fashioned revenge.

CHAPTER THIRTEEN

Rachel

Rachel takes the money she has withdrawn out of the joint bank account from a pocket in the side of her bag. She wants to hide it before she leaves to see her mother later.

She counts the money again as though it could have magically grown since she withdrew it but it is still only $300. If she has to run, she will need more, a lot more.

The second doll was a warning, a threat. He wasn't just watching her – he was watching Ben as well. She has no idea how he knew that Ben would bring it into the house instead of simply throwing it away. Maybe he didn't care if she saw this particular doll or not. Maybe there are many more on the way. Twenty-nine. There were twenty-nine dolls. Twenty-eight. It has been twenty-eight years since she and her mother left, ran, fled. She took two of the dolls with her, two of her favourites. She left twenty-seven dolls behind. Will he send her all twenty-seven and then turn up to hurt her?

He wanted to let her know he was watching. She wants to scream in frustration. Beth has named the second doll Pinky, and when she was in her room this morning, Rachel looked at it properly to make sure she had actually recognised it, that it wasn't just some dreadful coincidence, but she remembers it well. She had named this one Petal because her hair was the colour of the lush pink petals on a rose bush that grew in the beautiful garden of the house where she lived, where the grass was a vivid green and everything was always neat and tidy.

How did he get into Ben's car? She feels invaded, insecure, out of control. Is he watching her right now? Where is he hiding? He is a much older man now. Is he cowed? Stooped? Frail? Or is he still the same psychopath she lived with? She thinks about his big hands and what they did, what they could do, and she shudders.

If she tells Ben, what would he be able to do? How could Ben stop him? No one could ever stop him, not until she did, until she stopped him and then they ran.

Beth is waiting for her downstairs. 'Pinky needs a house,' she declared when they came home from school. 'She needs somewhere to live and a bed to sleep in, and Charlotte says that she can bring her dolls over to play with Pinky. Charlotte has eleven troll dolls, Mum. I wish I had eleven troll dolls. They could all live together in the house we make.'

'Oh, Beth, I don't know… I have so much to do and I have to go back and visit Nana.'

Her daughter is completely taken with the doll and Rachel can see that soon Beth will drop subtle hints for more of the dolls and begin a campaign of nagging for them. Ben will give in because he always gives in, and soon their house will be littered with them. The thought makes Rachel feel queasy. Even if they aren't the same as the ones she had, they will bring with them a time in her life when she used to love and play with them. They will bring everything back, everything she has tried to forget. But it's all coming back now anyway. First Riley Rainbow and now Petal and it's all coming back because he's found her.

'You're always visiting Nana. You never play with me anymore. Please, Mum, please… Pinky needs a house,' whined Beth.

'Okay, just give me a minute.' She gave Beth her snack and raced upstairs to hide the money.

Now she sits down on her bed, staring at the drawer where she has stuffed the cash. Her bedroom is beautiful. It is a dream room in the dream house she and Ben had eagerly chosen finishes for, giggling like children with delight at how stunning everything was. In their bedroom they have chosen a rich blue carpet, pairing it with pale blue curtains. Their old wooden double bed looks a little incongruous in the middle of the large space but she hopes for new bedroom furniture once they feel like things are under control, perhaps when she finds another job.

She still has the suitcases filled with summer clothes to unpack. She knew she wouldn't need them right away. Her father must have hated the chaos in the house. He must have hated that the boxes are everywhere and that Beth's school bag was tossed in a corner by the front door. Sometimes, in the flat, she would find herself straightening the pantry, lining up canned goods and spices so that everything was straight, and then she would quickly mess it all up again, horrified that even after decades away from him, he was still haunting her. She doesn't like the mess in the house right now but at the same time she doesn't mind it. It means that it's her house, that it can never be a house he would be comfortable in. And yet he has been here. She can only imagine his fury.

It all feels tainted now. The two-storey brick house with black metal window frames was meant to be her forever home after so much of her childhood was spent moving around, hiding from the world. But now he's found her, he's found her and she feels the urge to pack her things and leave, to take Beth and simply run. Could she do that to her daughter? Could she give her the same kind of traumatic childhood that she experienced, even though it was a childhood filled with love?

She would like to ask Veronica what to do about him. At the same time, she doesn't want to say a thing. If, by some miracle, her mother wakes up, she doesn't want to discuss him, she refuses to. Her mother's breathing grows shallower by the day, and Sam said yesterday, 'You'll keep your phone right next to you, won't you?' She cannot ask her mother anything at all.

He couldn't have picked a worse time to come back into her life. Anytime would have been bad but it feels as though he knows how vulnerable she is right now, as though he's sensed it across the miles and years that separate them.

They became complacent, she and her mother. They stopped running when Rachel was sixteen, but after that she knew she still always had to be watchful and wary. She can't remember when that stopped because it must have happened gradually, but she clearly remembers walking through a parking garage one night at around eighteen years old and seeing a man. She remembers feeling the frightening vulnerability of being a woman alone and then understanding that she had been afraid because she had feared a stranger, not because she had feared that he had finally found her. She had managed to stop thinking and worrying about him, and the relief of that realisation had made her laugh out loud in the nearly empty parking garage, startling the man, who had hurried to his car.

'Muuum,' Beth calls, tearing her away from her fear. 'I've finished my snack even though I don't like pears. Please come and help me.'

Rachel laughs. 'Coming, and I thought you loved pears yesterday.'

She sits with Beth at the kitchen table, watching her daughter poke her tongue out as she colours the carpet on the floor of an old shoebox while Rachel cuts the lid and angles it to create a roof. 'Pinky will be so happy, Mum,' says Beth.

'Nana made me a doll's house when I was little.'

'Did she? Do you still have it? Can I have it? Maybe Pinky can live there.'

'It broke – we were moving and it fell on the floor and broke.'

'That's sad,' says Beth.

Rachel clearly remembers the elaborate house Veronica made for her. She had bought wood and cut and sanded and shaped a house with two storeys and then she had painted tiles on the roof and sewn material for curtains. The project had taken her months, a surprise for Rachel's ninth birthday. She had known what her mother was doing. There was no way to hide something like that in the small apartment they were living in but she had kept quiet and had forced herself not to peek under the cover her mother placed on it each night. Rachel had loved the beautiful doll's house and Veronica had slowly made her little people out of felt to live in the four rooms, knowing that Rachel still missed the dolls she had to leave behind.

'I can buy you some new ones,' her mother told her a few weeks after they left, knowing that Rachel had only taken two of her precious dolls with her; but even as a child she felt that this would somehow be a betrayal of the dolls she had loved and left. And then it would simply be one more betrayal. She was only seven but she understood on a fundamental level that she had encouraged her mother to do what they had done. She understood that it was her fault. Thinking about it now she feels a familiar sharp ache of guilt for who was left behind and for what his life would have been like without them.

The doll's house had been dropped and smashed on one of their moves. Rachel can't remember which one but she thinks it might have been when she was twelve. She mourned its loss but she was too old for a doll's house by then and hadn't thought about it for more than a few weeks. She thinks Veronica might have been more upset about it. 'It was so perfect,' she remembers her mother saying. It had been perfect with a perfect little family of four. A mother and smiling father and a boy and a girl who always liked to play together. She had recognised, in the faces, the family they had been. The father doll with his brown eyes and the mother and daughter dolls with their light green thread eyes. And, of course, there was the brother. His eyes were dark brown, almost black, and she had seen Veronica pick up the doll once or twice and stare down at it, sadness pulling at her face.

The house was perfect and the felt residents were always happy, and now that Rachel has a family of her own, she thinks that her mother loved the house for what it represented – a happy family. Something Veronica never got to experience. Her parents, Rachel's grandparents, had died within a year of each other when Veronica was only twenty. Was his large family part of the attraction for Veronica when she met Rachel's father? She thinks so. 'We had one hundred and fifty people at our wedding,' she remembers Veronica telling her. 'All of them were from your father's side and just about every one of them thought he'd made a mistake with me. I was too quiet, too shy, and they were quite loud and bubbly. I think it was their Irish ancestry. They liked to argue about everything. I never had the courage to join in their discussions.'

A picture of her parents' wedding had stood on the white mantel above the unused fireplace in their home. Her father hated the idea of the smoke and the mess it would create. In the photograph her mother is stunning in a close-fitted, white lace dress with short sleeves that she'd paired with long white silk gloves and a short veil on a pillbox hat. 'I tried lots of dresses,' her mother told her, 'but I was just lost in the full-skirted ones.' Her father stands like a soldier, his black tuxedo fitted close to his large frame, his arm looped through hers. Neither of them is smiling but Rachel remembers her mother smiling when she looked at the picture. She assumes they were happy once. They must have been.

The strange thing is that Rachel remembers seeing very little of her father's family when she was small. Her parents rarely went out and they certainly never had anyone over. She wishes she could talk to Veronica about all of this, ask her to explain what happened and why she found herself married to such a man, but it's too late now, and all these years she and her mother have had an unspoken agreement to not talk about their lives before her father's supposed death, before what they have always agreed was his death. Fear makes people do such strange things.

Even as she thinks this, Rachel realises that she is allowing fear to control her in a way she promised herself it never would, not since she told her mother she would no longer keep moving to avoid being found. But she cannot seem to help herself.

She has stuffed the money in the bottom drawer of her cupboard. This is how she remembers Veronica doing things. There was always an envelope of cash hidden in the bottom of a drawer so she and Rachel could make a quick getaway if they needed to. How much will she need if she has to run?

It makes her feel dirty doing this, guilty, lying to her husband, taking money they can ill afford. But what choice does she have? It feels like a compulsion, like she has to have the money ready and waiting or she won't be able to breathe.

She picks up her mobile phone and looks at it. It wouldn't take much to press Ben's number, to simply explain. She has no idea how she would start, but once she did, it would be fine. Ben would help her figure it out. He would calm her down and tell her that it would all be fine.

I'll never tell, I promise.

She puts the phone back in her pocket.

She cannot know for sure how Ben will react. If he cannot understand and forgive her, she may lose him. If he does understand and wants to try and protect her, what will happen to him? What might the monster do to him? It seems that whatever happens – if the truth comes out – she risks losing her husband.

She has never imagined she would ever contemplate leaving him. He is nothing like her father, and leaving him would devastate her – but what if she has no choice? To save her child she may have to run, she may have to accept the heartbreak of losing Ben and just run.

She briefly contemplates calling Lou but knows she will be at work and very busy. They try to catch up with a phone call once a week but they don't manage to see each other much now that Lou's the principal of her school. Her weekends are taken up with sporting events and rehearsals for musicals and endless paperwork.

She knows that Lou would tell her to confess everything and get the police involved. But Lou has grown up in a different world to Rachel, a world where Mum and Dad and home are safe people and safe places. She has never had to run from anything, to really fear anything. She has always been able to turn to her parents or her brother for help and support. Veronica and Rachel have only had each other, and everything else, everyone else, has been a threat. And soon Veronica will be gone and Rachel will be on her own. She will have Ben; she knows she will have Ben, but the only person who knows every single truth about her will be lost.

'Can we put some sparkles on the roof? I want purple sparkles,' commands Beth.

Rachel draws herself back to where she is. She should be enjoying this time with her daughter. She will be leaving to return to the hospice as soon as Ben walks through the door.

'I'll sort out dinner and bath time,' he told her on the phone this afternoon.

'I'll get sparkles,' she says, knowing they are in a box marked 'craft'. In the room designated as a playroom for Beth, she stands and stares at a tower of boxes. Exhaustion at the idea of having to unpack them all makes her sigh. She feels like the process of moving in will never be finished, that this will never feel like home. She starts moving boxes one by one until she finds the right one and manages to extract some purple sequins.

'Here you go,' she says, returning to Beth.

The front doorbell startles them both because they've never heard it ring before. The short, sharp burst of high-pitched sound is unexpected.

'It's a delivery,' says Beth. 'Maybe it's more troll dolls.'

'I really don't think so, Beth.'

Rachel leaves her daughter in the kitchen and, heart thumping, she pulls aside the curtain of a window in the living room from where she can get a clear look at the front door. When she sees a man, her throat constricts and the panic she felt only a few nights ago returns, but then he turns and she sees it's Bradley from next door.

'I'm going mad,' she whispers as she goes to open the door. She has no desire for a conversation but her car is in the driveway, ready for her to return to the hospice. He knows she's home.

'Hello,' she says, pulling open the door. Outside the air is chilly and fresh and she glances up, noting the gathering of dark clouds. It will rain soon.

'Oh hey, how are ya? I just stopped for a look at the site because I'm thinking about a pool and… it's a big expense but Jerome wants one.'

Rachel smiles and nods.

'Anyway,' he says when she doesn't say anything else, 'I found something outside the house this morning.'

'Oh,' says Rachel, unsure as to where the conversation is going.

'It's, um…' He puts his hand into his pocket, digging around. 'There you go, it's so small. Here, I found this little doll thing in the street. I thought it must belong to your little girl since she's the only child living around here right now.' He opens his hand and shows her what he's found.

Rachel catches her breath. Her fear makes her want to slam the door in his face but she cannot move.

'I was afraid I'd lost it. It's small enough. Is it hers?' he says when she doesn't reach to take the doll.

'I don't…' replies Rachel as she looks at the tiny baby troll doll with white hair and a painted-on nappy. She knows who this one is. This is Baby Doll, tiny and sweet and given to her by him when he came home from work one day. 'Look what I found hiding in my desk for Daddy's favourite little girl,' he said and then she had to prise open his fist, pulling fingers one by one to reveal the little doll.

'I know kids get attached to stuff like this. Jerome has these tiny transformers all over the house. I stepped on one once and he cried for an hour.'

'It's not… not hers,' says Rachel. Her voice is faint. She feels sick.

'Oh, okay then… I'll just chuck it.' He smiles uncertainly.

She nods and moves to close the door.

'Are you okay?' he asks. 'You seem a little… pale.'

'I'm fine, just fine,' she snaps and then she shakes her head. 'I'm sorry, that was rude, things have been a little difficult. My mother is… not well.'

Bradley closes his hand and shoves it in his pocket. 'Oh God, I'm sorry, I didn't mean to intrude.'

'No, no, it's fine. I'm sorry, you didn't do anything…' She trails off. She doesn't want to start off on the wrong foot with him. He has a child Beth's age and she doesn't want him to think she's strange. She struggles for something to say, for a way to lighten the conversation. 'Um… when will your wife be here?'

He smiles, takes out his phone and opens an app. 'Eleven days, four hours and thirty minutes,' he says. 'I have this countdown app.' He turns the phone around to show her and she nods weakly. She doesn't know how much longer she can be polite for.

'But I should get going,' he says. 'I'm sorry about your mom, I hope she gets better soon.'

'I don't think she will,' says Rachel and she is embarrassed to hear a sob catch in her throat. She has no idea why she is telling him but she realises, as she says it, that it's the first time she has acknowledged this out loud. Her mother will not get better. Her body heats up, even as the cold wind comes in from outside. Her mother will not get better.

'Oh God, look, I'm really sorry, I know… I lost my mom a while ago. It's… look I'll leave you. We'll talk in a bit.' He takes two steps backwards and then turns around and walks quickly down the driveway.

Rachel shuts the door and leans against it. She remembers that Baby Doll liked to sleep next to his mother. She had a tiny cradle for him. Petal was his mother. Petal, who Beth has called Pinky. She clasps her hands together and squeezes. She had wanted to reach out and take the doll, to reunite the pair, but she couldn't touch it.

Her father was everywhere. He was inside her house and in Ben's car and in front of the neighbour's house. He was everywhere and nowhere that she could see.

Where are you? she wants to scream. *Where are you?*

But Beth, her baby, is in the kitchen and so there will be no screaming. She hears the garage door go up – Ben is home. She will return to her mother at the hospice because there is nothing else she can do. She knows she will look behind her as she backs out of the driveway and as she gets out of her car and walks along the path to the front door of the hospice. She will look behind her when she gets inside as well.

She will look behind her because she had become complacent. Now he's back to make sure she will look behind her every day from now on.

CHAPTER FOURTEEN
Ben

He shakes his head as he looks through the bank statement. Rachel has taken $400 out this time. They have a small cushion of savings as an emergency fund but it won't survive such large amounts regularly going out of the account. What could she be taking it out for? What could she need that costs so much?

He gets up from behind his desk and looks out into the open area. It's quieter today than it's ever been. Two of the administration staff have been let go and the mood is sombre. Everyone is concentrating on their computers, appearing or seeming to appear incredibly busy. He knows that Angela has already begun looking for another job. His boss, Colin, has been locked in his office all day and no one has any idea what he's thinking. Ben has spent a little time this morning getting his CV into shape. He can feel his time is running out.

Marni's figures this month are a lot better than his. She's been out on a lot more presentations than he has, and even though she's been knocked back a lot, she's managed to bring in two new companies who've been willing to give the software a trial. He's been distracted. Too worried about losing his job to actually do his job. He's also been on the phone far too much talking to the builder and the bank about the new house.

He takes his phone off his desk and leaves his office. 'Just getting a coffee,' he says to Marni when he passes her in the hall. She nods at him and strides on. She is only twenty-five and single. If she lost her job right now, she would be fine, he thinks. It's not the same for him. It's not the same at all.

Outside he looks around him, noting some smokers huddled in a corner out of the wind. He isn't wearing his jacket and realises that he's cold. He looks up at the grey sky and then feels a drop of rain land on his head. He squeezes himself into a small covered corner near the front of the building, wrapping one arm around his chest.

He bounces on the balls of his feet to keep warm as he calls Rachel.

'Hey,' she answers him, almost whispering.

'How's your mum today?'

'She hasn't actually woken up at all. She did moan a little and I thought she must be in pain so I called Sam and he's upped her morphine. I hope it's helping. I hope she's not in pain.'

Ben swallows as he listens to her fight back tears. He feels like he shouldn't say anything about the money to her, not now. It doesn't matter. Nothing really matters except what she's going through, and the fact that it's something he's even paying attention to makes him feel like an awful person. It's just money. He hesitates for a moment and then he says, 'Um, Rach... look, it's no big deal but... I just wanted to ask you... I mean, you seem to be taking quite a bit of money out of the account and it's fine, I mean, if you need it – it's fine. I just... just wondered what it was for?'

There is silence on the phone and for a moment he thinks she's hung up.

'I'm sorry, I needed... some things for Beth... She's grown out of all her winter clothes and...'

'Okay but last week you took three hundred dollars and yesterday you took four hundred dollars. That's a lot of money for clothes for a seven-year-old. And things are kind of tight with the new mortgage. I know you're only doing what's best for her but it is quite a lot…'

'Some of it was for me,' she says. He can hear she's getting angry. 'I needed some stuff.'

He sighs. 'Rachel, I'm sorry to even say anything. I know you've got so much going on but could I ask you to cut back a bit? We need to be conservative right now… You never know what can happen and I just need to see that I can handle the bills and the new mortgage. Just until you get another job, you know.'

'Why, what's going to happen? Is something going on at work?'

'No, nothing… nothing… It's just…' He doesn't want to say the words, doesn't want to admit that he's a failure. He should be able to manage this while his wife looks after their child and her dying mother.

'You said it was fine, Ben. You said we could afford the house,' she says softly. 'I didn't know that we were in trouble. I would never have…'

'Would never have what?'

'I wouldn't have bought anything. Are we okay, Ben? Is something going on that you're not telling me?'

Ben sighs at the irony of her question. He was going to ask her the same thing. How has this distance grown between them where they are both watching their words and concerned about what secrets the other is keeping?

'Nothing,' he says, hoping that by saying it out loud he will make it true. 'Nothing's going on. Everything is fine.'

'Yes,' she agrees, 'fine, it's fine. I have to go now, Ben, sorry. Mum seems to be waking up.'

She ends the call and Ben stands in the street, staring down at his phone. What is he missing? She doesn't have time to shop, much less spend so much money, and she's never done anything like this before. Is she helping to pay some of Veronica's medical bills? Why not just say so? He would never refuse to help.

'Let's always tell each other everything,' he remembers saying to her on their wedding night.

'Everything?' she said. 'You already know everything about me. What more do you want to know?' She giggled as she struggled with the zip on the back of her dress.

'You're drunk.' He laughed.

'Drunk on you, Ben Flinders,' she said and then she tripped over and landed on the bed. She turned over and stared up at the ceiling. 'It was so nice of your mother and father to pay for the wedding. My mum was really grateful. I know she told them but I hope they know – I mean really know.'

'They know,' he said with a smile. 'Now let's get you out of this dress.'

'Don't tear it, I'll keep it for our daughter.'

'Our daughter,' he said, 'I like the sound of that.'

He is still waiting to learn everything about his wife, still trying to figure her out, and that seems to be getting harder and harder to do. What isn't she telling him? He wishes he could simply call her back and ask, 'What are you hiding, Rachel?' Maybe he is blowing everything out of proportion. It was just a few hundred dollars, really. He's reading more into it than he should because he's so worried about his job right now.

He thinks about a conversation he had with Richard from accounts at the Christmas party last year after they'd both had too much to drink.

'How long have you been married?' Richard slurred as he stood next to Ben, who was waiting for his double shot of whisky from the young barman, despite knowing that it was definitely time to stop drinking and go home.

'Eight years,' he replied, standing slightly apart from Richard, who was swaying back and forth, his nose red and his large face pale and clammy. 'How about you?' he asked politely. The barman handed him his drink.

'More for me,' mumbled Richard to the barman after he handed
Ben his drink. 'Was… was twenty years. Twenty… twenty… years.
Can you imagine?'

Ben had nodded politely, his attention drifting, as Richard kept
talking about his wife and children. And then Richard had stepped
forward, using a finger to poke Ben in the chest. 'You can't trust
a… a… a woman. They make you think everything is fine… fine
and then,' he waved his hands, 'boom. "What's wrong?" I asked her
when she got kind of… secretive and quiet… not like… like before.
And you know what she said? You know what she said?' Richard
belched and Ben felt his hot breath and smelled the sausage rolls
that were being handed out. His stomach turned over in disgust.

'No,' he replied, looking down into his drink, wondering how
quickly he could extricate himself.

'"Nothing." That's all she said: "Nothing." I knew she was lying;
I just knew it but what can you… say to that? She said nothing
was wrong so I believed her.'

He didn't know what to say. He stepped back from Richard,
muttered something about needing to call his wife and escaped.

'Get caught by Richard, did you?' Angela asked, coming up to
him as he stood behind a tall potted plant.

'Yeah,' he laughed, awkwardly.

'He's such a pig. If I were his wife, I would have left him as well.'

'Yeah, well,' Ben said, looking hard at Angela, who he had
always known enjoyed gossiping. 'Marriage is hard.'

'Well, not for Mrs Richard, not anymore. He came home one
day to find she'd taken everything. She'd cleaned out the bank
account and moved all the furniture out of the house. She'd been
having an affair with her builder.'

Ben remembers being overwhelmed then by a desperate need
to get home, away from Angela and her enjoyment of the scandal
of Richard's marriage.

He sighs now and puts his phone back in his pocket. He isn't achieving anything thinking like this.

He hears a burst of laughter from the group of smokers and bites down on his resentment at their snatched moment of happiness. He cannot imagine ever simply laughing with his wife again. How is this his life now?

He makes his way back to his office and sits down at his computer. He needs to concentrate on work. He slides his keyboard forward because it has somehow moved back on his desk and notices a piece of paper underneath.

When he lifts the keyboard, he sees it's a photograph, torn in half.

He picks it up and looks at it and for a moment he doesn't know what he's looking at, but then he realises that it's Rachel and her mother. If it wasn't obvious that the photo was so old because of the faded colours and slightly sepia tone, he would have thought it was Beth and Rachel.

In the picture, Rachel and her mother are not smiling. At Veronica's side there is half a head where the picture has been torn away, belonging – he thinks from the short hair and square jaw – to a man that he assumes must be Rachel's father. He has never seen this photo before and has no idea how it came to be in his office or why it has been torn in two. He hopes Beth didn't do it, imagining it was something she could play with. Maybe she dropped it into his briefcase as she has done once or twice before, sometimes leaving him a drawing to find when he gets to work. He knows Rachel and her mother don't have many photos of the three of them so he's sure she would be upset at the destruction of this photograph.

'We had a flood in our flat when we lived in Melbourne and a lot of our photo albums from when he was alive were destroyed,' he remembers Rachel telling him.

As he goes to put it in his briefcase, he looks at it again and notices a hand resting on Rachel's shoulder. It's not a man's hand so it couldn't have belonged to her father, and it looks too small anyway. It could be her mother's but he can see that Veronica, who is sitting down, appears to have both her hands around Rachel's waist, although one is slightly hidden by the ruffled red dress Rachel is wearing. For a moment he tries to adjust his body to see who the hand could belong to but he can't work it out. He will have to ask Rachel.

Looking back at his computer, he tries to concentrate on writing up a marketing pitch for a group of bakeries, but he keeps thinking about Richard, who has now left the company, and his wife and how he had no idea what she was doing.

He didn't want secrets in his marriage. He wanted a marriage like his parents', who to this day are best friends, but he can feel a shift in his own relationship and he doesn't even know why. He's keeping the trouble at work from his wife but she could be keeping something from him. Their daughter said there was a man who made her cry. She called him a monster but it might be a man. Is Rachel having an affair? Has Beth seen Rachel fight with her lover? Ben feels his body heat up with anger. And then he chides himself to calm down. Rachel said Beth had imagined it, and she wouldn't lie about something like that, would she? He's certain she wouldn't. And it's not as if she would have called him to come home, her voice shaking because of how terrified she was, if she knew the man in the house. He is jumping to conclusions.

He sits up straight. He needs to get back to work.

'Ben, a word,' says Colin. He has opened Ben's office door without knocking, startling Ben, who is grateful that at least his marketing proposal is open on his computer screen.

He saves what he's been working on and follows Colin back into his office.

CHAPTER FIFTEEN
Little Bird

Mummy is humming in the kitchen and I am humming with her. She is humming a song from the movie about the nanny. She is smiling today. Smiling and baking. I love it when she bakes. It means she's happy. The sugary smell of chocolate chip cookies getting all soft and gooey in the oven makes me hungry, hungry.

When the cookies are done, she slides the tray out of the oven and puts them on the rack. 'No touching now, they're hot,' she says. 'I'm just going to the bathroom, and when I get back, you can have one.'

I sit on my knees on the chair so my nose is high up in the air and I can smell the chocolate. I know how good the sweet darkness of the chocolate chunks will taste and I swallow and count to a hundred while I wait for Mummy.

But before she comes back from the bathroom, Kevin comes in. He's been at school where he had a detention because he was fighting. Kevin says that the boy said something mean to him and then he had to hit him because he had no choice and he gave him a black eye. The principal phoned and he wanted to speak to Mummy but Daddy said to Mummy, 'I don't think this is the sort of thing you're capable of dealing with.'

'It's not appropriate behaviour,' Mummy told him. Kevin's eye was all black and his nose had yucky dried blood at the bottom.

'Sometimes a person needs a good smack,' Daddy said and then he smiled at Kevin and they laughed together. I hope no one ever thinks I need a good smack. I think it hurts a lot.

Kevin smiles at me now and I get a funny feeling inside like I always do because I don't know if I should be happy or scared of him. Sometimes he's nice to me, like one time, when Daddy was angry about everything in the house not being sparkling clean, he helped me get the paint off my hands from school before Daddy saw. But sometimes he's not so nice, like when he goes into my room and pulls all the covers off the bed just before Daddy does his inspection.

I wait to see what he will do and I feel like the butterflies on my wall are all flying around inside my stomach. He looks down at the cookies that are getting cold on the rack and he sniffs. He also likes it when Mummy bakes.

'Mummy says not to touch,' I tell him. 'They're too hot. We can have one when she gets back from the bathroom.'

He comes over to me and grabs my hair, pulling it hard and messing up my neat ponytail that Mummy did for me this morning.

'Ow,' I say, and my neck goes backwards. I feel hot in my face and some tears come in my eyes.

'Do you think I care what she says?' he spits at me. He sounds like Daddy when he talks. Daddy also doesn't care what Mummy says. He lets go of my hair and I rub my head where it hurts. He goes over to the cookies and puts one in his mouth and chews it up. It must still be hot because he opens his mouth and lets in some cold air but he doesn't spit it out. I sit quietly and watch him. I don't like it when he hurts me and I don't want him to think I need a good smack.

When he has finished it, he picks up the other cookies one by one and crushes them in his hands. Steam from the hot cookies rises in the air but he doesn't stop. I feel my tears in my nose and my throat but I don't want to cry in front of him.

When Mummy comes back into the kitchen, she looks at all the broken cookies and then she shakes her head and says, 'Oh, oh, why would you do that?'

He doesn't answer. He just smiles at her and steps towards her. He is much bigger than she is now even though he's not a grown-up yet. He looks down at her and Mummy steps away from him and looks down at her feet. I can see that sometimes when she talks to Kevin, she also has butterflies in her tummy. I remember when I was smaller than seven or six or five and Mummy used to call Kevin 'my little man' and he would hug her all the time. But now he doesn't hug her anymore, and even though she says, 'Boys are difficult when they're teenagers,' I know it makes her sad.

Kevin doesn't say anything to Mummy. He just laughs and walks out again.

Mummy looks at all the crushed cookies and a few tears come out of her eyes because she is sad about her beautiful cookies being all crushed up.

'Don't cry, Mummy,' I tell her. 'They'll still taste good.'

She nods and sniffs. 'I'm sure they will. We'll put them on ice cream. That will be nice, won't it?'

I nod my head and she smiles at me with teary eyes and goes to get the ice cream. The cookies still taste nice and I eat and eat, keeping the sweetness in my mouth so I don't think about how sometimes I hate Kevin and I'm not supposed to hate him because he's my brother and you have to love your brother even if he's not nice to you.

'Are you going to tell Daddy what Kevin did?' I ask Mummy after my whole bowl of ice cream and cookies is gone.

'No,' Mummy says. 'No, and you mustn't either, Little Bird. It's our little secret, okay?'

'Okay,' I say but I feel hot and angry at Kevin. Only Mummy and I have our little secrets. But now he has one too and I don't like that. I don't like that at all.

CHAPTER SIXTEEN

'So, I would like to talk about your father today,' says Dr Sharma.

'Straight for the jugular, eh?' I laugh.

'Look, you've been here for a week now, and I understand that you've been through this before but I'm sure you're aware that you have serious assault charges against you. You are a highly intelligent man and I know that you know that the only two choices you have before you are prison or a stay with us for a long period of time until we deem you are no longer a threat to yourself or to society.'

'I am highly intelligent,' I agree, 'and I'm well aware of the charges. I didn't kill him.'

They measured my IQ at school once. They wouldn't tell me the number but they did tell me I was in the genius range. I knew that already. School found me difficult to deal with because I was at the top of every class but I never paid any attention. Instead I liked to make jokes, disrupt things, see how far I could push a teacher before they went running for the principal.

My mother was always whining at me to try and behave. At first my father thought it was funny, and the funnier he thought it was, the worse my behaviour became. But then out of the blue he would decide that it was enough, and a detention one week that merited only a set of raised eyebrows meant a fist to the ear the next week. His mercurial nature kept us all on our toes. We were his dancing monkeys.

I have, in some of my many therapy sessions, speculated – along with whatever psychiatrist is treating me – on what my father's childhood was like. Abusers aren't born, they're made. It takes a lot to turn a baby into a monster. I think I was a relatively sweet little kid. I have memories of my mother and I playing hide and seek, building block towers, cuddled up in bed reading books. Good memories from before I turned seven and everything went to shit. She used to call me 'sweet boy' and 'my little man'. I know that I liked being near her all the time. I felt safe with her, sure that I was someone worthy of being loved. At some point I stopped being worthy of being loved. I know that.

I understand, after many years of therapy, why I am like I am. I just don't seem to be able to control it. Or maybe I don't want to. So, I wonder what happened to my father. Who hurt him? Who turned him into the man he is?

The nearest I can get to an explanation is the one memory of having lunch with his parents, my grandparents. We saw them very rarely and then not at all but I do remember a Christmas lunch at our house when I was nine and my sister was three.

The day before had been reasonably frantic as my mother cleaned and cleaned and my father pointed out all the things she had failed to clean to his standards. On Christmas day we were given our presents and then we were locked in our rooms until our grandparents arrived. My father was one of three boys in his family but his two brothers were living overseas by then. Once my grandparents turned up, we were allowed to come down and greet them. I think they gave us money but we had no real idea of what to do with that. I remember my mother being nervous and smiling a lot. She kept moving this arrangement of flowers on the table a little to the left and then a little to the right, as though getting it absolutely dead centre was the most important thing she had to accomplish that day. She was wearing a sundress made of fabric printed with red roses. The dress had diagonal pockets on the side and when she wasn't moving the flowers, she kept her hands in her pockets so no one could see they were shaking. But I saw. I had to suppress an urge to grab one of her hands and hold it tight. I was too old to hold my mother's hand, according to my father.

I remember my grandmother didn't say much at all. She was a small woman with rounded shoulders as though she was carrying some great weight no one could see. I remember she touched my head when I said hello. No kiss, no hug, just patted my head and I remember how sad she looked, as though she were disappointed in my existence. I understood why she would look at me that way. I had been disappointing my father for years by then.

If my mother had stayed with my father, if they had grown old together, I imagine that this is how my mother would look today, bowed and deeply sad.

My grandfather was big, as big as my father, and loud. He talked and talked about all their relatives and how well everyone was doing. My father nodded and nodded, barely saying a word.

When we sat down at the dining room table, my mother brought out the turkey she'd been slaving over all morning along with roast potatoes, carrots and all the other stuff she usually made for Christmas. The air conditioner in the dining room was humming away because outside it was baking hot. I was dressed in long, stiff pants and a long-sleeved, starched shirt and I was itchy and sweaty and all I wanted was to be outside but I knew better than to say anything. I could feel something in the air. I didn't understand what it was but my stomach was churning, and even though the food looked really good, I didn't want to eat. I had been salivating at the smells coming out of the kitchen all morning as my mother chopped and stirred and fried enough food for twenty people instead of just six, but even as I looked at the honey-glazed carrots and the crispy brown potatoes, I knew it would be difficult to swallow. I didn't know how to explain it then but now I know that I was bursting with anxiety, too full of worry and fear and foreboding to eat a bite. But I knew I would force the food down. Not eating was an unacceptable option in my father's mind.

When my father stood up to carve the turkey, I held my breath. My grandfather watched him pick up the knife and the big carving fork and he said, 'No doubt this is going to be something to watch. How badly do you think you can screw this up, Leonard? Carving a turkey is a man's job.' And then he laughed, like he'd told the best joke. But no one else laughed. It was a long time ago but I remember exactly what he said because of the effect it had on my father. His hands started shaking and his shoulders hunched and I watched a bead of sweat make its way down the side of his face. My mother looked down at her lap and I could see that she was twisting her linen napkin around and around in her hands. We sat like that for about five minutes until my father finally spoke. 'Maybe you should do it, Dad.' He said it softly, deferentially, and his father stood up and said, 'That's right, boy, maybe I should.'

I was only nine but I could see from the way my dad sank into his chair like a whipped dog that he was scared of his father, of not carving a turkey right in front of him. It was the first and only small glimpse I had into where my father had come from.

When we all had our food in front of us, it was absolutely silent. I looked down at my full plate, nausea rising in my throat.

'You'd better eat every mouthful,' my father said, his voice tight with the promise of punishment.

I looked over at my sister and I could see she was struggling to eat as well, and I know that I reached for her hand under the table and squeezed it just a little. I don't know why I did that but I know that it made her smile and then she seemed to find swallowing easier. I did too.

I think I tried once, about five years ago, to discuss my father's family with him but he shut me down. 'Don't drag me into the sad little psychological exploration of your life,' was what he said. 'I turned out just fine.'

'You nearly killed him, the man you beat up,' says Dr Sharma, dragging me back into the therapy session I have no interest in participating in. Prison might just be easier. At least there I won't have to talk about my feelings. 'He will have many more months in hospital, and rehabilitation. Do you think you can explain your reasoning behind the assault? What led you to hurt him?'

I try to think about what my reasoning might have been. I really try. But nothing comes to mind. Nothing ever comes to mind when I think about the things I do.

'Do you know what it means when people say that they saw red?'

'I do,' she says. She's wearing a pantsuit today. It's too tight. I think Dr Sharma has been eating the cafeteria food here. It's all about starch. My father would never have tolerated my mother gaining weight. I remember her being small and delicate but I also remember her once reaching for a second helping of apple tart and my father simply laying his hand over hers and shaking his head. He liked her small and delicate.

'Is that what happened to you?' she asks. 'Did you just see red?'

I nod my head. It's the truth, in a way. I don't feel like I have the energy to explain about the black sludge – 'seeing red' is a close enough analogy.

'He pushed in front of me at the bar. I told him I was there first and he laughed at me.' He was not a big man. I didn't understand how he could push in front of me and then laugh at me when I called him on it. I didn't understand how he didn't lift his little rat face up to look at me and just say, 'Sorry.' Did he not see how big I was? Was he completely confident of getting away with his behaviour? That's what irritated me more than anything else. His lack of fear. He thought I would just smile and wave away what he'd done. You should be scared of someone bigger and stronger than you are. He was an idiot, and as my father always said, 'Sometimes someone just needs a good smack.'

'Do you remember that it took three men, three big men, to pull you off of him?'

I shrug my shoulders again. 'The first thing I remember is being in the back of the police van.'

I remember the other men pulling me off him. I remember the sounds of people, mostly women in the bar, screaming and shouting. I remember the smell of alcohol from the drinks that spilled as glasses hit the floor and shattered after I pushed him into tables. I remember someone shouting, 'Call the police.' I remember the police storming in as the men who had pulled me off him held me and I kicked and screamed. I remember everything but an insanity defence starts with no memory of what you did, and I know how to do that.

'Okay, so you understand it's my job to help you remember what you did and accept responsibility for it. I think we can get to the bottom of your behaviour if we look back into your past, but I'm not telling you anything new here. I think you *actually* want to talk to me. I know from reading your file that your father is a brutal man, and I know that you're aware that this is where a lot of your rage comes from.'

'Well, there you go, Dr Sharma. You've solved the case. My dad is mean and I'm angry. Stick me in a cell and be done with me.' The words come out with more feeling than I would like. I hate becoming emotional; I try to keep everything in check. Except my rage, of course. That serves a purpose. After they threw me in a cell I screamed and kicked for a while but then I went straight to sleep. I felt released, calm, peaceful. I always feel like that afterwards, and even though I have never asked my father if he feels the same way, I know it's the truth. I watched him once, after he had yanked my mother's head back and punched her in the stomach because the dishwasher was incorrectly stacked. I saw how he relaxed. He left her and went into the living room to watch television and I watched him slouch into the couch, peaceful and happy. My rage comes from my father and his rage came from his father, I assume. And on it goes. It's a good thing I haven't had a son who would inflict his own rage on the world.

I once dated a girl whose father was abusive, but only when he drank. Otherwise he was a nice, average guy. 'It changes who he is,' she told me. 'When he's sober, he's the best husband and father, but after four beers he becomes a different person.'

I was jealous of that, of her. I thought she was lucky to be able to have a concrete reason for why her father did what he did. Her father was only a monster sometimes, only some of the time.

My father drank in moderation. He never talked about an abusive childhood. My mother was practically a Stepford wife and yet he needed to hurt us, like an addict craves a drug. My whole childhood I assumed that I was an awful person. I was awful and my mother was worse and I knew that my sister was getting to the age when all her terrible faults would mean she stepped into my father's firing line. I understood he was the one hurting me. But I blamed myself. I hated myself and I was angry at myself for years until I turned that around. Then I hated everyone else.

'He shouldn't have pushed in front of me,' I say to Dr Sharma and I register the frustration that flits across her face. I don't care. She needs to work for her own insights. I am not providing her with them.

'Please, I'm trying to help you,' she says and I see something in her dark eyes, something more than just a doctor with a patient. I groan. She wants to save me. She must be somewhere in her forties, which means she's been doing this for a long time. I have no idea how she still has the enthusiasm she seems to have for her job. She is looking at me like my mother used to look at me on the very few occasions we found ourselves simply talking to each other after our relationship became this strange, strained ball of energy sitting between us. It's a look that says, 'I'm here for you and I'm listening.' It's a look that I used to trust until it was so thoroughly betrayed by my mother. It's a look I find difficult to resist and so I decide to give Dr Sharma the highlights.

'The first time he hit me, I was seven years old.'

CHAPTER SEVENTEEN
Rachel

She can feel herself beginning to sweat in the heated room. How had she imagined that Ben wouldn't notice the money being taken from the account? She should have prepared her lie better, should have at least stopped at a shopping centre on her way home from school with Beth and picked her up some new things. 'Stupid, stupid,' she mutters to herself. But it feels like she has no choice. Having the money allows her to breathe, to function. It's illogical but she needs it to be there.

She is clutching her mother's hand, holding it tight, probably too tight. She lets go and wipes her clammy hand on her jeans.

'I wish you'd wake up, Mum,' she whispers, conscious of Sam and the other nurses just outside the door. 'I wish you'd wake up so I could talk to you about this. I don't know what to do. I don't even know why I've got the money stashed away. It's not enough for anything.'

She knows that taking the money, hiding it, was an impulse, just an impulse because it was what Veronica did every time they found somewhere new to live.

'Our sprinting money,' was what Veronica called it because if he found them, they wouldn't just have to run, they would have to sprint away. They would have to move faster than they had ever moved.

But he never found them. If he got close, if someone seemed to be asking more questions than usual, they just moved.

'But how would he find us?' she knows she asked her mother when she was around thirteen.

'Private investigators. He worked with a lot of them. He used to tell me all the time that he could find anyone anywhere in the world.'

'So, we're not safe,' said Rachel.

'We're safe unless we tell,' her mother said, 'but if someone starts asking questions, I know it means that they are being asked the questions and it's time to go.'

And so, they had gone. They had run from one place to another to another until Rachel got to sixteen and refused to run anymore.

But now she knows she should have kept running.

She takes the brush off the bedside table, runs it through her mother's hair. Veronica has only a thin covering of hair after all her rounds of chemo but she uses the soft brush to neaten the strands. She feels peaceful and calm when she does this, just like she feels when she combs Beth's hair. 'If I tell Ben, I don't know what will happen. He doesn't know any of it, Mum, you know that. He thinks my father died from cancer when I was seven. I wish we had talked about what to do if he came to find us, to find me. I wish we'd talked about a lot of things, Mum. What am I going to do when you're not here to talk to? I think I need to tell. I know I promised not to but I need to tell the truth and I don't know what will happen when I do.'

She puts the brush down, lays her head on the bed and places her hand on her mother's chest, feeling the shallow rise and fall of her breathing. Her mother will be gone soon and, along with her, the secrets she has been keeping. What would he look like now? She was born when both her parents were thirty years old. That would make him sixty-five now, the same age her mother is. Would he still be fearsomely big? She stopped having nightmares about him years ago, but when she did, he was always the size of a giant, stalking her through a shiny, sparkling landscape of white stones and white trees and white mountains. In her nightmares she ran away from him, ran and ran, her feet pounding beneath her, her chest heaving, but she could never get far enough away from him, not until she panicked herself awake.

She stands up and looks out at the garden, where the grey clouds dull the colours of the winter plants. She shivers despite the heated room.

It would be comforting to think that age had mellowed her father but the dolls indicate that's not the case.

The dolls are a way for him to torment her. They are a threat, a way to unbalance her, a power play. The dolls mean he is still the same man. He knows how much they meant to her. He must know how broken-hearted she was to leave them behind. He wants her to know that he still has them, still has a part of who she was and therefore still has some control over her. It was always about control. It was the only thing he really seemed to take pleasure in. What might a man like that do to her, to Beth, to Ben?

If she tells, she will put her husband and child in danger. His anger at her and her mother for leaving would be extreme now. It's had twenty-eight years to fester. And he can only direct that anger at her now. It would have been directed at someone else all these years. The guilt, the remorse that is a stone inside her, makes itself felt.

She closes her eyes. She is so incredibly tired all the time. 'It's grief and worry,' Sam has told her. An hour ago, he came into the room to check on Veronica, and Rachel had jerked awake as he moved near her chair. 'Oh, I don't know what happened,' she said, embarrassed to be sleeping in the middle of the afternoon.

'Don't apologise. I can see how tired you are. Sleep is a natural defence for the body.'

'I shouldn't be asleep – what if she needs me?'

'I'm here, Rachel, and I can tell you that your exhaustion is natural. You know what's coming so you're already mourning her but you're also afraid of what's coming. It's normal, trust me. Try to take more breaks, to give yourself a little time off every now and again. Go outside and take a walk. It's cold but it's refreshing. It will help, I promise.'

She should take a walk outside but she can't seem to bring herself to leave.

Rachel looks around her mother's room with its pale blue walls and linoleum floor and thinks back to how excited she and her mother had been when they had signed the lease to rent their flat for two whole years when she was sixteen. It wasn't a nice building or in a particularly nice part of town but it was what they could afford.

It was the first time they had ever actively decorated their home. In all the years they had been moving around, Veronica chose to rent furnished flats, and so they lived with someone else's bed and sofa and, in one case, even their cutlery and crockery. Rachel had hated it. It felt like they were living in someone else's home, using someone else's stuff, and she couldn't help worrying that, at any moment, the owner of the apartment would return and tell them to leave.

When they finally moved into the flat in Sydney, Veronica began bringing home things from second-hand stores. Lamps with quirky-coloured shades and prints filled with colours. She bought an old timber dining table and reupholstered six chairs in a deep maroon velvet. The chairs were all different styles and shapes, nothing matched. The flat was forever messy because Veronica and Rachel always had two or three novels on the go, and piles of books littered the space.

'Who decorated the house we used to live in?' she knows she asked her mother one afternoon, after they had painted a purple wall in her bedroom. She had been admiring the way the sun changed the colour of the wall as it moved, transforming it into multiple shades, rather than just the one deep colour. It had been the middle of summer and all the windows were open as she and her mother hoped for the slightest of breezes to blow through the hot little flat. They were both sweating from their work but it had been so exciting to change just one thing in the room, to use a colour to make the space feel like hers and only hers. As she stared at the paint and waited for her mother to answer, she imagined the purple pillows in different shades that she would buy to scatter on the bed.

'He did. I had nothing to do with it. I hated the white walls and countertops and cupboards. There was too much white.' Veronica had stopped speaking and Rachel had known she was lost somewhere in the past.

'Why did you marry him?' she had whispered, hoping that asking the question quietly would mean she'd get an answer. They didn't look at each other, instead focusing on the wall so that speaking the truth was easier.

'I loved him,' her mother said in a quiet voice. 'He was tall and so good-looking and completely charming. I felt safe and protected when he was around.'

'And why did you stay? After things got really bad. Why did you stay?'

Her mother put the paintbrush down, picking up a rag to wipe her hands. 'I had children,' she said simply. 'I had no family who could take me in, no idea of how I would work and take care of you two. I was terrified of the whole world because I had always been protected by my parents, and then soon after they died, I met him and it seemed to me that he would take over where they left off. I should have waited. I should have lived on my own so I would know how to take care of myself, how to be on my own, but I was still grieving for them and bewildered by the world. He was kind at first. Kind and gentle – even afterwards. I pray you never have to learn what I learned, Rachel, and that is the intoxicating nature of abuse. The hands that hit were also the hands that touched gently, that touched me as I'd never been touched before. He would cause pain and then he would drug me with his tender touch and his words of love, with his attention and affection, and I would succumb and stay. Don't do what I did, Rachel. Don't get married without knowing who you are and what you want. Have a career and a plan for what you will do if things fall apart.'

Rachel nodded. 'But why—'

'No more now,' her mother said quietly, looking at her feet. 'No more.'

When she signed the lease on the flat, Veronica had obviously accepted that he wasn't trying to find them anymore. It had been nine years since they'd left. Nine years of leaving wherever they were every few months, of never having enough money, of never fully unpacking, of never making friends. It makes sense that Veronica thought they had outrun him, that she believed he would have moved on with his life and forgotten them. But he hadn't. He didn't.

She looks over at her mother, who is asleep but fitfully so, her breathing ragged and her eyelids twitching.

'I need you to wake up, Mum. I need you to wake up and talk to me,' she says firmly, hoping that a change of tone will penetrate the drugs numbing her mother, forcing her to open her eyes.

But Veronica sleeps on, in full possession of her secrets, and eventually Rachel knows she has to leave to collect her little girl from school.

She buttons her coat before she braves the cold outside the hospice, inhaling deeply as she walks out into the parking lot, taking the chilly air into her lungs and breathing out the smell and the stale heat of her mother's room. She listens to her feet crunch over the white stones that cover the parking lot as she tries to shake off her despair.

She tries, as she leaves, to centre herself so that she can be with Beth for the afternoon and really give her the attention she needs.

After breathing deeply again she stops in front of her car and stares down at something on the ground. She looks around at the rest of the car park but they are only in front of her car. If there was more wind, she assumes they would have blown away or that they could have simply been blown in front of her car. But though the air is heavy with cold and the threat of rain, the leaves on the large fig trees in the hospice garden are still.

She feels her stomach churn and her body heat up inside her coat. She leans down to gather the pamphlets up. There must be six or seven of them. She would assume that they had been dropped by someone walking through the neighbourhood, stuffing them in letter boxes, but they are all different, for different companies.

They are brochures for swimming pools. She flicks through them, her hands trembling. There is a brochure for an above-ground pool encased by steel and made out of plastic; three people sip drinks as they lounge with their arms over the side. There is one for an expensive in-ground pool, the water a sparkling blue, the surround a beautiful mosaic. There is one for a small child's inflatable pool and one that looks like it's for a sport's centre. Her heart beats in her ears, and she quickly opens the door to her car. Once, she would have loved a pool. 'I will love it and I'll swim and swim and swim,' she knows she said to her mother when she was only six years old and had just begun her swimming lessons.

'It's not up to me,' her mother said, her face tight and angry. Something she hadn't been able to understand.

She should have known not to ask her father, not to speak to him about it. The memories flood back; guilt engulfs her.

She rests her head on the steering wheel for a moment. She needs to get Beth, and if she doesn't leave now, she will be late. But she needs to calm down first.

A tap on her window startles her so much she yelps. When she sees it's Sam, she yanks open the door, fearful of what he has to say.

'Sorry, love, it's all right. Your mum's the same. I didn't mean to scare you. Didn't you hear me calling you?'

'I… no,' she says, looking into his kind grey eyes, wishing that she could tell him about the train wreck her life is becoming. She wonders how old he is. He could be her father's age. He has told her he should have retired last year but he loves his work.

'I saw this fall out of your bag as you were leaving. I didn't want you to leave without it.'

She looks down, and in his hand is another doll. First the pamphlets, now this. He is everywhere. He will not stop.

She stares at the doll and the doll stares back at her.

She doesn't want to touch it, doesn't want to have it anywhere near her despite remembering how much she loved this one.

It is dressed as a wizard with a pointy blue hat covered in decorative stars and a moon. She remembers believing that this was a magical doll, that if she whispered her wishes to it every night, it would make them come true. She had asked it for a happy family, for her father to be kind, for a life like the ones she could see her friends had. She tried that every night when she was six and then seven years old until the last night, until the night everything changed.

That was the night that she had seen this doll for the last time. That was the night she had looked at it and known that it wasn't magic at all, that none of her wishes would ever be granted. And so, she had left it behind.

'Oh… yes,' she stutters. 'It's Beth's… thanks, Sam… thanks.' She takes the doll from him, holding her hand stiffly so he can't see it shaking. She looks at him, noting that he is gazing at her curiously.

'You take care now,' he says and he gives her shoulder a squeeze.

She can do little more than nod. Her mouth is too dry to speak. He smiles again and then he steps back, allowing her to close the door. She starts the car immediately. She needs to get out of here, away from here. Sam lifts his hand and waves as she pulls out of the parking lot, still holding the doll and steering with one hand. She squeezes the doll tightly, feels it press into her palm. She wishes she were strong enough to crush it, to annihilate it. She wishes she were strong enough to deal with him, but all she can feel is an overwhelming fear.

'I'm sorry, Daddy,' she whispers, the words coming out automatically, repulsing her with the memories they bring.

She suddenly flings the doll on the floor of the car. There is no magic in this doll.

Her phone vibrates in her pocket. It's her alarm telling her to leave to pick up Beth from school. She can feel tears on her cheeks and she knows that she will fetch her daughter from school with red eyes and a puffy face. Beth must believe that she is incapable of smiling anymore. Rachel doesn't want her to think she is only ever unhappy.

She will have to throw the doll away without Beth seeing it, and she cannot help experiencing a pang of sadness about that.

'Look, Mummy, look at him, isn't he beautiful?' she hears, remembering how delighted she had been to spot the little doll on the counter at a newsagent. She and her mother had been out buying Christmas presents.

'He is, but I'm sure you'll get lots of dolls for Christmas. Come on now, home time.'

'But Mummy, look at his hat. He's a wizard and he's magical, I know he's magical. He can grant wishes and I can wish for so many things.'

'All right, sweetheart,' her mother had said, laughing, 'you've convinced me.'

As she pulls up at the school, she realises that Beth was right. There was a monster in the house.

'I wish he was dead,' she whispers as she picks up the doll and shoves it into her bag next to the brochures.

She removes her hand from the bag and shakes her head.

There is no magic. The wizard doll can't grant wishes.

He never could.

CHAPTER EIGHTEEN

Ben

He pulls into the garage and turns off the engine, sits in the car. He is unable to dredge up the strength to tell Rachel he's lost his job. 'I've lost my job,' he whispers aloud, trying out the phrase on himself. It doesn't seem real. It doesn't feel real. He feels his eyes prick, a few hot angry tears escaping, and he wipes his face roughly with his hand. He needs to get it together.

'I've had to make some hard decisions and I'm afraid that you're just not bringing in the revenue we need right now,' his boss told him.

'But things will get better, Colin, I promise you I'm giving it everything I've got. I'm working on a new proposal for Gumnut Bakeries and I've already had a chat to their head of accounts and she's really interested.'

'I can't rely on "interested" anymore, Ben. I need people who can bring in the business, and to be honest you seem more than a little distracted.'

'But I've just bought a house, you have to give me a little more time, please. I promise you I'll bring in the business. Things have been difficult at home; my wife's mother is dying and...' He stopped speaking when he saw the way Colin looked at him, his face a mask of pity.

'I just can't justify keeping you on. You're a good bloke, you really are, but I'm in some trouble here. I'll give you a great reference. If you could just transfer everything you're working on to Marni, I'm happy for you to leave today.'

'You don't even want me to finish up the week? I'm sure I can bring in the bakery… I have a good feeling…'

Colin rubbed his hand over his bald head and Ben noticed how tired he looked. There were heavy bags under his bloodshot eyes. He wanted to keep pushing but realised that it wouldn't help at all. His boss had made up his mind, had probably made up his mind weeks ago. Instead Ben stood up, admitting defeat. 'There will be a redundancy package – two months' salary, which should tide you over. I'm sorry, Ben, I really am.'

Ben nodded, understanding, feeling the fight go out of him. If he hadn't just bought a house, he would be glad to leave. He retreated quickly to his office but had caught glances from other staff. Everyone knew what a visit to Colin's office meant right now. He felt himself colour. He was ashamed at losing his job, ashamed at having to end the day with everyone knowing the truth. He waited until all his colleagues had left to quietly pack up his desk and leave. No one even came in to say goodbye or commiserate with him. They sent emails instead. He was sure that those who remained with the company didn't want to be seen with him, not wanting Colin to associate them with someone he'd just fired, to be infected by his failure. Angela had walked past his office at lunchtime and he had seen her deliberately look down at her phone as though she was dealing with something important. It was almost funny. He wanted to get angry but he knew he was the one who had lost his job. He'd been distracted and he'd failed to achieve his targets. It was as simple as that. The reference from Colin arrived in his inbox at the end of the day. It was filled with glowing statements about his enthusiasm and commitment and ability to be part of a team. Colin was a good man. He would be equally complimentary to any potential employers who called to discuss Ben. But Ben had to get an interview with a new company first. The thought of starting again made him want to sleep for a year but he didn't have that luxury. He had a family to support and a mortgage to pay. He couldn't afford to take even an hour off from searching for a new job.

He thinks about his friend Max, who is divorced. Max works in a bar and gets by on the minimum amount of money. Every winter he leaves the country for Europe, where he travels around by motorbike, picking up casual bar work and sleeping with twenty-year-old girls. He sends Ben emails filled with pictures of the beaches in Europe and photos of himself with his arms slung around beautiful women. He always has a drink in his hand, always has a smile on his face. 'Living my best life,' is always in the subject line. Ben is sure that this is not what he wanted for his life. He wanted Rachel and he wanted Beth but he had never imagined how heavy all this responsibility would be. He had watched his father perform the role of 'man of the house' with ease and he had assumed it would be the same for him. But it's not, it's not at all, and the urge to run suddenly feels overwhelming. He allows himself a small, dry laugh. Maybe Rachel feels exactly the same way. Maybe that's why she's taking money out of their account. He feels sorry for their little girl. She needs stability and security, not this. Not two parents who are slowly and steadily spiralling.

He had called his father as he left the office. 'I've lost my job, Dad.' But his father didn't understand, not really – how could he? He has worked at the same university for his whole life, at the same university he had studied at and received his doctorate from. He didn't have much advice beyond saying that everything would be okay and offering help if Ben needed it. 'Thanks, Dad,' he said before he hung up, not believing that everything would be okay at all.

In the car he takes a deep breath. Maybe he will get a new job quickly. He's already called Zach, an old friend from university, who now works in recruitment. Zach had promised to start looking for something for Ben but had mentioned that IT was a young man's game these days and that social media skills were important. Ben had never thought thirty-five was old but internet trends changed quickly and younger people seemed born to understand everything immediately.

Ben grabs his briefcase and hauls himself out of the car. He has toyed with the idea of not telling his wife but realises how ridiculous this would be. He doesn't want to have to pretend with her but he will make it seem like this is just a small detour, that soon he'll be back on track. That's not a lie, more of a wish, really.

Just as he goes to close the garage door, he sees a man standing in the driveway. His heart thumps in his ears as the man makes his way towards him. The street is completely empty and only their house has lights on, so who is he and what is he doing here?

He is big and tall, and he has a beard. It's the beard that relaxes Ben. He remembers Beth talking about the neighbour with the hairy face.

'Hey, how are ya doing?' says the man walking up the driveway towards Ben.

'Yeah, yeah, good,' says Ben.

The man holds his hand out. 'Bradley Williams, not sure if your wife mentioned me. I'm moving in next door. I was seeing if last night's rain affected the site much. Thought I might as well introduce myself.'

Ben shakes his hand. 'Hi. Yes, she mentioned you. You have family coming from Canada?'

'Yeah, Canada. Soon, real soon.' He puts his hands in his pockets and looks around. 'Weird that it's so quiet, right? I've never seen a street with so few people on it.'

'It won't be for long. When do you start building?'

'Another week or so.'

Ben nods and they both subside into silence. He feels a thumping in his head. He doesn't want to stand out here on the street making small talk with his neighbour. He just wants to get inside out of the cold and sit down. He is exhausted and heavy with despair. The silence stretches, grows awkward.

'Anyway, I'll see you around,' says Bradley and he smiles.

Ben nods and attempts a smile as well but he fails to make his mouth move correctly. He steps back inside his garage and pushes the button to close the door. He's been rude, he knows he has, but he doesn't have the energy to deal with that now.

The door leading from the garage into the house is slightly ajar. He knows Rachel is usually careful about locking it, but she must have forgotten today. He steps up on the single stair that leads into the kitchen and looks down to see another ugly little doll. He leans down and picks it up. These troll dolls are clearly Beth's next obsession. He takes it inside and places it on the kitchen table, right in front of Beth, whose tongue pokes out as she laboriously traces over letters in her workbook.

'Yay, another doll, thank you, Daddy!' she shouts.

Rachel walks into the kitchen. 'What are you shouting about?'

'Daddy got me another doll. Look, Mum, she's a bride and she's got bright yellow hair.'

'Where did you get that thing?' Rachel yells. Her raised voice is so unexpected that Beth bursts into tears.

'Rachel, why are you shouting? I found it in the garage. I thought you got it for her.'

'I didn't, I didn't... Where did it... Oh... I'm sorry. Please, Beth, stop crying. I'm sorry I scared you.' She goes over to her daughter and holds her tight. Beth buries her head in her mother's stomach and howls for only a minute, soon losing interest in crying. Ben supposes they are all a little on edge. There is an atmosphere in the house, something thick, lurking, as though the house has anticipated how their lives would fall apart. Ben suddenly hates the architect-designed, modern, three-bedroom, double-storey family home that had looked so perfect in the brochures.

His whole life seems to have disintegrated because of this house.

Rachel looks like she wants to throw up. How can a little doll have bothered her so much? But he realises that it isn't the doll. It is everything else. They are both dealing with too much right now. He thinks about the torn photo in his briefcase but he doesn't have the energy right now to ask her about it. She already seems angry with Beth and he doesn't want her to be even angrier if their daughter tore the picture. He will ask Beth about it later and explain to his daughter why it is wrong to damage something that doesn't belong to her.

'Maybe one of the builders in the next street dropped it or left it or…?' Ben tries but he has no idea how the doll could have gotten into their garage. 'Beth, did you take the doll from Charlotte?' he asks. 'You said Charlotte has troll dolls.'

Beth shakes her head violently. 'No, no, I didn't.' She sniffs dramatically. 'Can I still have it?'

'Sure,' Ben says with a shrug of his shoulders.

'Maybe someone brought one to school and dropped it into Beth's bag or something,' says Rachel.

She sounds like she's explaining it to herself. Ben doesn't answer her. Instead he heads for the liquor cabinet where there is a bottle of whisky that Veronica bought him for his last birthday.

Rachel follows him out of the kitchen, watching him pour himself a large slug. 'What's happened?' she asks. If he has a drink after work, it's always a beer. He rarely drinks whisky at all.

'I lost my job,' he replies quietly before downing most of the whisky in one gulp, and the silly little doll is forgotten.

Rachel's skin turns pale and she puts her hand over her mouth. She sinks down onto the sofa, wraps her arms around herself. 'What are we going to do?'

Ben sighs. He wishes he could have some time, just a night to work through this. He doesn't want to spend the evening reassuring Rachel that everything will be fine because right now he's not sure it will be. He looks at his wife, hugging herself, and he can imagine what she's thinking, can see the turmoil there. She has enough to deal with right now.

'It will be fine,' he says as he pours himself another slug of whisky, 'I promise we'll be fine.'

CHAPTER NINETEEN
Little Bird

It's the first day of the summer school holidays and the sun is shining, shining. Mummy has set up my paddling pool from when I was little in the backyard. I'm too big for a paddling pool but we don't have a real pool for me to swim in and I like to sit in the cool water. Mummy says she wishes we did have a pool and I wish we had one too. Mummy put a big umbrella over me and I am wearing an old pair of her sunglasses and her big hat and I am a lady at the beach, sitting in the sun, and my servants bring me cold drinks and ice cream. I don't really have any servants but Mummy stops cleaning the house sometimes and she comes out and gives me ice cream or some crackers and water because I am not allowed fizzy drinks because they are bad for my teeth. I look up at the umbrella, and the sunglasses make the red and white stripes look funny and I laugh. I have brought two dollies down with me and they are swimming in the pool. I have a boy dolly and he has reddy-pink hair and he is wearing a swimming costume with love hearts on it and his sister is a girl dolly and she has yellow sparkly hair and she is wearing a red swimming costume. They swim together and they don't fight and they always take care of each other like a brother and sister should.

I also have some plastic cups from when I was very small and I am filling them with water and pouring them over my shoulders when I get too hot.

'Are you okay there?' Mummy calls and I look up and see she is in my bedroom cleaning and she is staring out of the window.

'Hello, Mummy, I'm fine,' I say and I wave.

'I'll come down soon to get you your lunch, sweetheart,' she says.

'Okay.' I pick up a small cup, fill it with water and pour it over my arm. The water tickles and I laugh and then I look at my dollies and I can see they're laughing with me and they are happy to be in the pool on a hot day.

Kevin comes into the garden from the side gate. He has a key but I don't have a key. Mummy says that when I am thirteen like Kevin, I can also have a key.

'What are you doing, Tweet?' he says. Kevin likes to call me Tweet because that's the sound I make when I am being Daddy's Little Bird. He smiles at me and I smile back but a little butterfly flutters around my tummy because he looks happy but maybe he isn't happy and I never know.

'I'm a lady at the beach,' I say and he nods.

'You look cool.'

'Thanks,' I reply.

He sits down next to me on the grass because he is too, too big for the paddling pool. 'I wish we had a real pool.' He looks sad when he talks about a pool. We are not allowed to talk about a pool. Talking about a pool is a mistake. A big mistake.

'Me too,' I say, 'and then we could swim all the time.'

'Yeah, but you don't know how to swim.'

'I'm getting better.' I get a little bit cross because I can swim, I just don't swim very nicely, but I'm learning every week at lessons, and Jazz, my swimming teacher, says she'll have me in the Olympics in no time.

'I can help you learn if you like.'

'Jazz is teaching me.'

'Yeah, but you have to practise every day or you won't get any better. Want me to show you some stuff?'

'This pool is too small. It's only to sit in.'

'That's okay, the most important thing is to be able to blow bubbles underwater. See, watch me.' I know about blowing bubbles because I can do that already but I move to one side of the paddling pool and Kevin dunks his head under the water and blows lots of bubbles that tickle my legs. His blue T-shirt gets wet but he doesn't mind. I think he likes that the water is making him cool.

Kevin pulls his head out of the water and he laughs and wipes his face and smooths his hair back. He looks nice when he laughs, just like Daddy.

'Now it's your turn.'

'I know how to blow bubbles already.'

'I don't believe you, Tweet, show me.'

There are lots of butterflies in my tummy now and I don't know why.

'Are you scared of the water?'

'I'm not scared of the water!' I shout.

'Okay, okay,' he says and he puts his hands up. 'Don't shout, I was just trying to help.'

'I can blow bubbles, watch.' I push my head under the water and I blow lots of bubbles, just the way Jazz taught me to do. When I run out of breath to blow, I start to lift my head up but I feel Kevin's hand on the back of my neck, pushing me in. I try hard to get my head up, so hard, but he pushes me down and soon my whole body is under the water because Kevin's hands are big and he's strong, strong. I kick my legs and try to grab him by pushing my arms backwards but it's hard to move. I feel like the inside of me is going to burst and I need air to come into me but I can't get up. I can't open my mouth because I can't breathe in the water. I'm not a fish. My head hurts and then my body gets all funny and suddenly Kevin pulls me up out of the water and I cough and choke and he pats me hard on the back, hard as a slap so it hurts, but it makes all the water come out of my nose and my mouth.

Mummy comes running outside. 'What happened, what happened?' she yells.

'Kevin...' I start to say and then I look at him and I know if I tell on him, he will think I am someone who deserves a good smack, so I shake my head. I take lots of air into my body. Kevin smiles at me – a small smile – and I know that now Kevin and I also have a little secret together, but it is not a nice little secret like the ones I have with Mummy.

'What happened, Kevin?' asks Mummy quietly.

'I don't know, I came in and she was under the water so I grabbed her out. I only had to pat her on the back a few times but you really should watch her. She doesn't swim very well yet. Maybe those lessons aren't helping much.' He stands up and then he walks away into the house. Mummy helps me out and wraps me in a towel and then I cry and cry because I was so scared and I didn't want to drown under the water.

'It's okay,' says Mummy, 'it's okay, sweetheart, it's okay.' But it's not okay. Kevin is meany mean. I hate him, I hate him, I hate him.

At dinner Daddy says, 'And what did my Little Bird do today?'

'She went for a little swim,' Kevin says and he laughs and laughs.

'That's enough, Kevin,' says Daddy because he decides how much you can laugh in this house.

CHAPTER TWENTY

'So, you were seven, and why did he hit you?' asks Dr Sharma.

'Have you heard that quote from Aristotle that says, "Give me a child until he is seven and I will show you the man?"'

'I have,' she says. 'Sometimes it's attributed to someone else but I have heard it.'

'People have always talked about what that meant but basically it's come to mean that who a kid is at seven years old is who they'll be as an adult.'

'Yes, I believe that's how it's mostly been interpreted.'

'Well, my father saw it like that. In his mind, his kids were given leeway – not a lot of leeway but some – until they turned seven and then they had to be the kind of person that he was happy to have in his house.'

'And what kind of a person or child was he happy to have in his house?'

'Clean, neat, quiet, obedient. It wasn't that they didn't have to behave like that before. It was just that, until seven, you were not physically hurt. The mental shit that kept him entertained went on from the moment you could speak.'

'From the moment you could speak?'

'Yeah, when I was four, I woke up from a nap and found him in the living room. I asked for my mother and he told me she was dead.'

Dr Sharma shakes her head. 'Just like that? He told you she was dead?'

'Yes, and then he watched me while I tried to process the whole thing. I ran around the house calling for her and he followed me around and kept saying, "I told you she was dead, she's gone forever."'

'That's a terrible thing to do to a child.' She says this softly and slowly as though she is trying to process the idea of it herself.

'She was just at the store but he liked the way I cried. When I got tired of calling for her, I sat down on the carpet and just... I couldn't stop crying. I kept crying until she walked in and ran over to me to pick me up. I could barely breathe by then so I couldn't tell her what had happened and when she asked my father about it, he just shrugged his shoulders. "You really need to look into this child's behaviour," he said. I didn't even know what that meant but I've never forgotten the words.'

'That's... horrific,' she says.

I laugh. 'Yeah, but he thought it was funny.'

'Did you ever tell your mother what he said?'

'Nah, I don't know why but I think I knew it wouldn't be a good idea.'

She gives herself a little shake. I can see she's trying to rid herself of the image of me as a crying four-year-old. 'Emotional abuse can be worse,' she says.

'I know that.' What a stupid thing to say. Of course it can be worse. Here I sit in a hospital for madmen because it can be worse. It is worse.

'Your father liked to be in control.'

I think about resorting to silence because I loathe it when the psychiatrist states the obvious as though I'm an idiot who hasn't already figured this out for myself. But I keep going because I have an insanity defence to prepare for and my father is the number-one star in that defence. 'He did like control. He liked things in our house to be clean and neat and tidy. I don't mean just a general clean. I mean that if he came home and an ornament had been moved an inch to the left or right and not returned to its correct place, he went ballistic. He liked us to always be on our toes, waiting for his next instruction, making sure everything looked right.'

Dr Sharma nods, and for a moment I consider telling her about an incident from when I was six, but instead I just stare at the beige wall behind her head. I know that she would write the whole story down and she would be even more sorry for little old Kevin than she already is, but I don't need her pity. I don't want it. My father's seven-year-old rule didn't apply if you touched his stuff, you see. That rule was for everyone, no matter how young or old. I rub my leg where the scar is. He was just showing me what could happen because a pair of scissors is so sharp. It was a lesson. And the scissors belonged to him.

I let go of that little incident and remind myself of where I am. 'My mother didn't have a cleaner,' I continue. 'My father thought that she had little else to do with her day aside from take care of her children, and it was best spent making sure that his house looked the way he thought it should look. She spent every spare moment cleaning and tidying. When I was little, she confined me to one room for most of the day. We would sit there together, playing games and reading and doing whatever else you do with kids too little to go to school, and then about an hour before my father got home she would stick me in my cot or lock me in my room and she would tidy and clean and then she would come and get me and make sure I was tidy and clean. She did the same thing for my sister after she was born. One night he got home and he walked all around the house, opening every door, going into every room and checking her work, and she followed him around, her hands at her sides, her pale pink lipsticked mouth frozen in a smile. He nodded his head and smiled and then he came back to the kitchen where a bowl of fruit was on the table and an orange had fallen out. She must have balanced too many in the bowl.

"'And what is this?" he asked her and she grabbed the orange and put it back on top of the pile of fruit. I could see her hands shaking. He smiled at her and punched her in the mouth. Just pulled his fist back and punched her. Then he picked me up and said, "What a mess your mummy has made. Let's go and play a game while she cleans up."'

I let that little story sink in, watch how Dr Sharma struggles to maintain her composure. I am sure she's thinking about my mother and everything she went through, and I feel like I should mention to her that in the end my mother was more of a monster than my father was, but I don't. Of course I don't.

'That must have been hard for you to deal with,' she says. 'Did that happen when you were seven?'

'No. Before I was seven, if I dropped a glass and spilled some juice or if I didn't hold my knife and fork properly or I argued or whined, he would… I don't know how to explain it. I guess he would tell me what I was doing wrong and then instruct me on the correct way to behave and leave it there. "He'll learn," my mother always said, and he would nod and smile and say, "Give me a child of seven…" I had no idea what that meant but the day after I turned seven, I was sitting at the kitchen table colouring in a superhero colouring book when he came home. I was filling in a picture of the Joker – you know, from Batman?'

Dr Sharma nods and smiles a little. I remember she has kids.

'I was sitting there quietly when he came in. The kitchen was tidy and I was clean and dressed in my pyjamas and my mother had just gone upstairs to "spritz on some perfume". He came in and touched my head. "How's my big seven-year-old boy?" he asked. "Good," I said. "And what have we here?" I leaned back so he could see and he picked up the colouring book and looked at it. "You'll get better, I suppose,' he said and then he looked down at the kitchen table and saw that I had somehow gone off the page and onto the table with my red crayon. It was a wax crayon and all he had to do was wipe it off. My mother would have wiped it off if she had seen it. "And what is this?" he asked.

'I smiled and I started rubbing at the mark with my hand. He slapped me across the face so hard that I fell off my chair. That's when she came in and he didn't say anything, he just pointed. I was sitting on the floor, biting down on my lip and trying not to cry, but there were tears anyway. "Man up," he said, and she said…' Here I pause for a moment. I don't mean to be dramatic but I hate recounting this story, need to recount this story, am compelled to go over it in my head because she was showing me, she was letting me know exactly where her loyalty lay.

'She said…?' Dr Sharma prompts.

'She said, "I'm sorry, Leonard."'

'Oh,' says Dr Sharma and I can see her flicking through a mental list of appropriate things to say but she doesn't come up with anything.

'Yeah… oh,' I agree. I don't tell Dr Sharma that I should have known what that meant about my relationship with my mother. I should have known exactly who her priority was. I should have known, but I didn't. That only became clear much later.

CHAPTER TWENTY-ONE
Rachel

Rachel rubs at the back of her neck and then stands up, walking over to the window where condensation coats the glass. In the garden of the hospice, the liquidambar trees are bare, their grey branches stark against the blue sky. Dry, brown leaves scatter and flip in the whistling wind. In the garden she can see Luke, battling to hold down the pages of his book. She cannot help but smile at his stubbornness.

Outside the apartment where she and Ben used to live, she would watch the bare branches of the trees all winter and into spring, waiting for the green shoots that foretold the coming summer.

She swallows and wipes a stray tear away. Her mother won't be here next summer. She won't be here for spring either. Rachel cannot quite conceive of how her life will look without her mother in it. She has always relied on Veronica's quietly wise advice, her thoughtful way of expressing herself that never felt like too much.

She hears movement from her mother's bed and turns around to see that Veronica has opened her eyes. 'Mum!' she exclaims, and rushes back to her chair. She gently takes her mother's hand, hope flaring inside her. Could this be a sign? Miracles happen, anything is possible.

'Rachel, sweetheart,' says her mother, her voice whispery soft.

'Do you want some water?' Rachel asks, grabbing the plastic cup with the straw that she empties and refills every few hours, hoping that her mother will wake up and ask for some.

Veronica nods weakly and Rachel positions the cup so she can take a small sip, just enough to wet her lips.

'What time is it?' she asks.

'It's just after two o'clock.'

'And what day is it?'

'It's Wednesday. It's July and freezing outside. Do you want to sit up? Do you want something to eat?'

'No... no, sweetheart. I'm not hungry but maybe... could I sit up a little?'

Rachel presses the button on the control to raise the bed. A slight flush of colour blooms into her mother's face and Veronica smiles at her.

'How are you, sweetheart?'

'I'm... I'm okay, Mum, I'm okay.' Rachel begins to cry, even as she admonishes herself for spoiling the moment, but she is overwhelmed to see her mother sitting up with her eyes open. She cannot believe what she is seeing.

'Oh, don't cry... don't cry, my darling. It's okay.'

'I'm sorry, Mum... it's just... I've missed you. I've missed you so much.'

Her mother reaches over and grabs her hand, holds on tight. Rachel squeezes back, but not too tightly. The bones feel too light for her to hold on tightly.

'I need to tell you something, Rachel. I need to tell you something before it's too late.'

'I need to tell you things too... I don't know how to even begin. But we have time, Mum, don't wear yourself out.'

'Listen to me... Rachel, you have to listen to me... There isn't enough time,' she says and her chest heaves with the strain of having to speak.

'I'm listening,' says Rachel, rubbing the skin of her mother's hand. She decides instantly that she will not tell Veronica what has happened, will not tell her that he's found them both. Her mother doesn't need to know that or about Ben losing his job. Rachel takes a deep breath, wondering if her mother has heard anything she has been saying to her as she drifted along in her morphine-induced sleep.

'Are you in pain?' she asks, hoping that her mother will say no. She doesn't want to send her back to sleep again.

'A little,' says Veronica and her brow furrows, and Rachel knows that she's in more than a little pain.

'I can call Sam. He can raise the level of morphine,' she says, even though it would devastate her to send her mother back to sleep. She longs to hear her speak, to listen to her voice.

'No, darling, not yet. I need to tell you… I need to tell you the truth.'

'I'm listening, Mum.' Rachel nods.

'Your father… he…'

'Yes…?' she says and Veronica looks at her.

'You need to know… you need to know that he found us after we left, that he kept finding us,' says her mother.

'He… found us? I don't understand. How did he? How could he have found us? We kept running. We kept moving.'

'I don't know but he did. He always did. Every time we moved, it… it was because he had found us. He would just turn up at my work and just… just stand there. And then I would… we would run but he always found us… always.'

'You've seen him?' Rachel gasps. 'All this time I thought he didn't know where we were, but he knew? He always knew?' She cannot quite comprehend what she's hearing as she realises that it has not just been her and Veronica lying to the world but Veronica lying to her as well. 'So, when you told me we had to leave,' she says slowly as she thinks back on their years of running, 'because people were asking questions… it was because you saw him… you actually saw him?'

'I… didn't want you to be… frightened. It was easier… easier to tell you that I thought he had found us… than to tell you he had. You were so… so scared of him.'

Anger flares inside Rachel. She thought he had just found her after all these years but she and her mother have never been lost to him.

She should have been told. Maybe if her mother had told her, she would have made a plan to leave the country. But even as she thinks this, she knows it's not the truth. She would never have left her mother but she still wishes that she had been better prepared for his re-emergence in her life.

'He never… never came near you. I left as soon as I saw him. We… left… we always left.'

Rachel opens her mouth but she has no idea what to say as the images of her mother pulling her out of school more than once come to her. 'Pack up now, Rachel, we have to go!' her mother would yell, her voice filled with panic and fear. She remembers her picking her up from a friend's house one day in the middle of summer with the car already packed full of their stuff. Rachel was eight years old. 'Where are we going?' she asked. Not 'what's happening?' because by then she knew what her mother was doing. 'I don't know,' Veronica replied. It went on for years. When Rachel was ten and eleven and twelve, she would wake up some mornings and find that her mother had spent the whole night packing as she slept. And all she could do was sigh and drag her old suitcase out from under the bed she was sleeping on.

'But why did you agree to stay in Sydney then when I was sixteen? Why did you sign the lease on the flat for two years?'

'I hadn't seen him. I hadn't seen him for months and I thought he was done with us because you were so much older then. I thought… I hoped… that he had found someone else.'

'But if he kept finding us, why didn't he make contact with me? He would have known where I went to school. He would have known everything. Why didn't he try to talk to me?'

Rachel swallows the fear her child self would have felt at seeing him standing outside her school or outside the door of whatever flat they were living in. She feels her heart race at the thought.

He has not just found her. He has not been looking for years. He has only been watching. Watching and waiting. Rachel turns her head quickly, looking out of the window, expecting him to be standing right there. Her skin prickles.

Her mother's face scrunches up and then she tries to take a deep breath but can only manage a shallow gasp. 'I… I wrote him a letter after we left. Just after we… left when you were only seven. I wrote and told him…' Her mother closes her eyes, her breath coming in pants. Rachel strokes her hand as Veronica recovers her breath.

If she had been aware, she would have prepared herself for his return. She would have told Ben about him so that they could keep themselves safe, could keep Beth safe. The image of the baby troll doll assaults her. A baby, her baby. She shudders.

'We should have talked about it, should have planned what to do…' she says and then she stops talking. She knows she is not going to tell her mother about the dolls, about him making contact with her in his own sinister way. In her last moments, she doesn't want her mother to be frightened by the monster she has been frightened of her whole life.

Her mother's eyes flutter open again and Rachel wants to just talk about something else, anything else, but she needs to know everything now. She cannot stop herself asking. 'What did you tell him when you wrote to him? Why did you write to him right after we left?'

'I knew he would find us no matter what… I knew him… but I told him that if he left us alone… if he left us, I would never… never contact your brother. Never.'

'You wrote and told him that right after we left?' asks Rachel. She doesn't understand what she's hearing, how such a thing could be possible, how any of it is possible.

'Yes.'

'But if you promised not to contact him, why did you keep saying you wanted to? Why did you keep talking about him?'

Veronica shrugs her thin shoulders. 'He was… my son… I loved him.'

'He was like his father,' she whispers fiercely.

She wonders at her mother's ability to write a letter like that, to trade one child for the other. She cannot imagine it of her and yet there was no way she would have survived him being in their lives. He was like her father. He was her tormentor and she was sure that her fear of him was the reason Veronica never spoke to him again. But now she understands that there was another reason. She gave up her son to save her daughter. She is the one who was saved, so how can she be angry?

But despite that, she feels a moment of profound disappointment in her mother.

'It was to keep you safe, Rachel, so he didn't… didn't come near you. But he would turn up… just turn up and then I knew I had to run. I think he… he liked that I was always afraid and worried. I think he liked that. I'm so sorry, Rachel,' her mother pants and then her face contorts. 'Oh… oh,' she says. Her hand flies to her stomach, claws at her pink flowered nightdress, sweat covers her brow.

Rachel leaps up off her chair and goes to the door. She looks frantically up and down the hall. 'Sam!' she calls and is relieved to see him come out of a room a few doors away.

'Coming, love, coming. What's wrong?'

'She's… she's in pain. She opened her eyes and sat up and she's in pain.'

'That's all right, Rachel, I'm here now. Hello, Veronica, look at you, sitting up… well done, you… but maybe it's time for a little more rest. You've done very well.'

Veronica nods weakly.

Sam fiddles with the drip and then he strokes Veronica's arm, his voice low and soothing. 'It's wonderful to see you up. Rachel's here every day, sitting with you. You're lucky to have a daughter like her, Veronica. You are a wonderful mother.'

Veronica nods. 'I made… I made a lot of… of… mistakes,' she mumbles, almost asleep and lost to Rachel again. No matter what she has just said, what she has just revealed, Rachel cannot let her mother close her eyes thinking she was anything except a wonderful mother.

'You didn't make mistakes, Mum,' says Rachel. She sits back down in her chair and gently takes Veronica's other hand. Her disappointment has disappeared as quickly as it appeared. Her mother sacrificed everything for her. As a teenager, she can remember wondering why Veronica never dated or showed any interest in finding a relationship. Veronica was a beautiful woman until the cancer sucked everything away, and Rachel knows that there were men who had shown an interest. A sports teacher named Adam had called her once or twice a week for a few months but nothing ever came of it.

'Why don't you go out with him, Mum?' Rachel, who was fourteen at the time, had asked.

'I don't need anyone but you, sweetheart. I have no interest at all.'

Veronica dedicated her life to raising her daughter and keeping her safe and yet, when Rachel began to chafe a little at her boundaries, her mother quietly stepped back, allowing her the freedom she needed. Rachel has never given much thought to how lonely her mother must have been since retirement and her daughter's marriage. But she knows that there must have been some silent nights when Veronica questioned what had happened to her life. She cannot be angry at her mother for keeping this secret. She will not let anger mar this moment.

She watches as the medicine starts to work and Veronica's breathing slows and calms.

'There now, that's better,' says Sam.

'I wanted… to protect you, sweetheart. I didn't want you to be scared of him finding us. I didn't want you always looking over your… shoulder. I wanted to…' She doesn't finish the sentence. Her eyes close and her hand holding Rachel's slackens and then she is asleep.

They watch her for a moment, a deep sleep engulfing her. Rachel can see the question in Sam's eyes. He would like to know what Veronica was talking about but he will not ask. And she cannot begin to explain it all.

'It's good she woke up, right? I mean, it could be a sign of something… a sign she's getting better or something.'

Sam shakes his head. 'Rachel, I don't want you to get your hopes up. It's common for people to rally a little before… before the end. It's nearly time, love, you should prepare yourself.'

Rachel nods, too numb to cry, too confused to think straight. After squeezing her shoulder, Sam leaves her sitting next to her mother's bed, despair enveloping her.

An image comes back to her – black-red blood against a white tile floor. Her mother's horrified face, her own determined one. She hears the sounds of hurt and pain and relives the smell of fear, of sweat. He has hated her all these years, has watched her grow up and has been planning this – whatever this is – all along. His revenge. He has been planning his revenge.

The only reason he did not come to get her before is because her mother promised him her son. But soon her mother will be gone.

She rubs her forehead and then looks at her watch. It's time for her to fetch Beth, time for her to be a mother now. She is so tired, so incredibly exhausted, but it is time for her to be a mother.

She stands up and leans over, kissing her mother's forehead. 'I'll be back tomorrow, Mum,' she whispers.

In the car she opens the window, hoping the rush of cold air will help her think, will revive her a little.

She is going to have to tell her husband the truth, but she cannot think of where she should start, and Ben is struggling himself. She knows that he is desperately searching for work, following up leads and calling everyone he knows in the hopes that someone will be able to help. She wishes she could take some of the burden away from him but she can't.

Taking a deep breath, she finds a parking spot near Beth's school.

As she gets out of the car, she looks all around her in case another doll has somehow materialised. She has no idea what to do, no idea how to tell Ben the truth. She wonders what the police would say if she went to them and explained about the dolls. She fears they would laugh at her but then they have no idea about who her father is and what he's capable of.

Her mother opened her eyes today but Rachel cannot help her. Her husband has lost his job and Rachel cannot help him. Her father is threatening her and she cannot stop that happening. She cannot do anything.

As she walks towards the school gate, she tries to refocus her thoughts.

'Time to be a mother,' she mutters, because right now that's the only thing she can get right.

CHAPTER TWENTY-TWO

Ben

Ben uses a knife to slice open a box of books and begins placing them on the shelves in the living room. He would like to play some music or have the television on to make this whole exercise less boring but he is listening intently for his phone, for the ping of an email that could be the offer of an interview or an email from someone he's reached out to. He's only been home for a few days now, but he feels as desperate as if he's been here for months. And the pile of boxes seems to be growing rather than shrinking, and each time he finishes one and collapses it, he wonders what on earth he's doing it for since it's likely that he will have to repack them again very soon.

'You're doing everything you can, and you'll have a new job soon enough, I know it. Maybe just enjoy a little time to reflect,' Rachel said last night.

'What am I going to reflect on, Rachel? On how quickly we're going to lose this house?' he shouted. He regretted it immediately as he watched her green eyes darken with tears and her face flush.

'I'm sorry,' she whispered, 'I was just trying to… I don't know.'

He muttered 'stupid' at himself and left the room, feeling sorry for himself, angry at himself, ashamed of himself, for upsetting her when she was constantly on the verge of tears anyway. He opened his third beer for the night. He knew that was a bad idea but he didn't care. She was trying to help, searching for the right thing to say, but the only thing he wanted to hear was, 'You're hired.'

He hates that he's making Rachel even more edgy than she needs to be. He should be able to shoulder this burden alone, and to top it off, this morning he made things even worse by asking Beth about the picture. He thought Rachel was in the shower. He had sat down next to Beth at the kitchen table with the photo in his hand.

'What's that, Daddy?' she asked as she swallowed the last mouthful of cereal.

'This is a picture I found in my office. I think it must have fallen out of my briefcase and I know that sometimes you like to leave things for me to look at in my briefcase.'

'I left you a picture of me and Charlotte on the climbing frame at school,' she said smiling.

'You did and I put it up in my office.'

'Why aren't you at your office?'

'I'm taking a little break but, Beth, what I wanted to talk to you about is this picture,' he said, showing her the torn image, 'because I know you may have been doing craft or something but it's a photo of Mum and Nana and she will be sad to know that you've torn it.'

Beth looked at the image and then she shrugged her little shoulders. 'I didn't tear that. I didn't even see it until now.'

'But Beth…'

'Where did you get that?' Rachel whispered behind him. He turned, startled to see her standing in the doorway, her hair damp at the ends.

'I found it in my… I mean, I think it fell out of my briefcase. I thought Beth…' He stopped speaking. Rachel's face was pale, her body rigid and still.

'Rach, are you okay?' he asked.

'I'm fine.' She reached out and grabbed the picture away from him and then she turned and ran back upstairs.

He went after her to talk about it but she pushed past him as he entered the bedroom. 'I need to get to my mother,' she said and she virtually flew down the stairs and out the door.

It was stupid to bring the picture up with Beth but it feels like that was just another mistake to add to a long list of mistakes he's made in the last six months. He shouldn't have ignored the signs that the company was in trouble but he kept hoping that things would come right. He shouldn't have bought a house unless he was absolutely sure of his job, and he shouldn't be snapping at his grieving wife.

He picks up the knife he's using and slices open another box.

He's been surprised by the number of websites there are for jobseekers. He was optimistic about that at first until he realised that it must mean there are also a lot of people searching for jobs. He doesn't know how he's going to compete against younger people, all willing to earn less and all equipped with more up-to-date knowledge.

'At least I'm getting things sorted,' he says aloud to himself as he opens up another box of books. He wonders how long the bank will give them before they force them to sell the house or they simply take it away. He knows that if they sell, it's unlikely they will ever get back into the market again. He and Rachel will have to rent for the rest of their lives.

He takes the next book out. It's about sex, given to Rachel by one of her friends as a joke on her hen night. He looks at the cover with its lurid picture of a couple in bed. He and Rachel haven't been intimate for weeks. It feels like they're losing touch, like they're drifting away from each other, each of them wrapped in a bubble of their own problems.

They don't really talk to each other at all. Her mother's illness colours everything right now but he wonders if there is something else as well. Did the scare she had change the way she feels about their home and about him because he was the one who pushed for the house? Was she telling him the truth about there being no one in their home?

But why would she lie to him? It's possible that she resents being stuck out here without the security of neighbours and friends. The empty spaces where houses will one day stand can feel threatening in their openness. He finds himself checking the locks on the doors at night more than once before he goes to bed. He can imagine that she is finding the house a scary place to be. The missing money also hangs between them. He's seen no evidence of any shopping she might have done but he doesn't feel like he can confront her on that, not with everything else going on.

He places the book on the shelf and then pulls it off again. He decides to take it upstairs, to shove it in one of the drawers. Beth's reading skills are getting better every day and he can see a time when she will want to read the books they have collected over the years. He wouldn't want her to find such a thing. He picks up his phone from the floor and slips it into his pocket, not wanting to be away from it for a minute.

Climbing the stairs to their bedroom, he goes to the built-in wardrobe, opening the bottom drawer on Rachel's side and pushing aside the collection of gym clothes to shove the book underneath. As he is moving them aside, he feels some paper and, without thinking, pulls at it. It's an envelope, thickly stuffed with cash. He knows without having to count it that this is the $700 Rachel has taken from the account over the last two weeks.

He sits back on his haunches, staring at the plain-coloured envelope that contains his wife's betrayal.

Is she planning to run? Is that what she's doing? Will she keep pulling money out of the account until there is nothing left? Will she leave him when her mother is gone? He won't let her take Beth from him. There is no way he will let that happen.

He stands up, his hand gripping the envelope, and then he curses and shoves it back into the drawer. He won't tell her he's found it. Rage heats up his body, and he stamps downstairs and heads straight for the whisky, which after only a few days is nearly finished. Whisky and beer make it easier to get through everything. They just do. He pours the rest of the bottle into a glass, enjoying the anticipation as the amber liquid gurgles. He picks up the glass and tips it one way and then another, watching the colour lighten as it catches the sun, and then he glugs it down. How has this happened? Only a few weeks ago he had a good job and a happy marriage and now he feels like he has nothing. He goes to the fridge for a beer and then he slumps in front of the television, the sound up loud on a basketball game, placing his silent phone on his lap. He cannot be bothered to carry on unpacking.

What is he worrying for? Why does he care if he gets a new job at all? If his wife is going to leave him, then nothing is worth doing anymore. He thinks about not seeing his little girl every day, about not getting to lie next to her at night and read her a story as she drifts off to sleep. His rage fades with each sip as the whisky makes its way into his bloodstream followed by the beer; and then all he's left with is an unutterable sadness.

Something has happened to his life. Something has broken and he doesn't know what it is. Around him, in the silent house, in the eerily quiet neighbourhood, he can feel that things are hidden from him, that there are secrets being kept. But he cannot figure out how to make his wife reveal herself and tell him the truth. He cannot figure out how to get a job and get his life back on track. He sighs and stands up, clicking off the television.

'Unpack the boxes,' he mutters to himself, because that's the one thing he can do.

CHAPTER TWENTY-THREE
Little Bird

It's nearly the end of the summer holidays. I went to Maisie's house to play yesterday and she was so, so sad about having to go back to school but I don't mind. Maisie went on a holiday with her family to the beach and she and her mum went to see lots and lots of movies but me and Mummy had to stay home all the time because her head was sore a lot. She said it was her head but she keeps holding onto her side so I think it's maybe not her head.

Mummy and Mrs Jackson from next door are in the kitchen having coffee and I am sitting outside the door listening with my big ears. That's what Kevin says I have, 'big ears'. I looked in the mirror and I don't think they're big, just normal ears. 'He's just teasing you,' says Mummy. 'Just ignore him.'

I try to ignore Kevin but it's not always easy. Sometimes he comes to find me just to be mean to me. Yesterday he went into my room and pulled all the books off my bookshelf. I didn't know he'd done it until I went upstairs to put the book I was reading back in its special place on the shelf and found out. I had to pick up all the books quickly, quickly, quickly because I heard Daddy's car in the driveway and Daddy hates it when they aren't neatly on the shelf. My hands were shaking, shaking but I managed to get it done in time. I didn't tell Mummy what Kevin had done and I didn't say anything to him. I'm scared that he will do something else to get me into trouble with Daddy if I say anything. I think he wants to get me into trouble. I think he wants Daddy to give me a sore head like he does to Mummy.

I know Mummy doesn't like me to sit outside the kitchen door and listen but I'm bored, bored, bored. I have played with my dollies and read my book and watched some television and tidied up and I want to go out. Mummy said she would fill my paddling pool for me but I told her I was too big for the paddling pool but that's not the truth. I'm scared to go in there now in case Kevin comes home and tries to push me under the water again.

I made sure my room was sparkling clean after I played with my dollies, and now I don't want to mess it up again because it's the late afternoon and Daddy comes home in the evening when the sun is still in the sky because it's summer. Mummy says he comes home at six o'clock. She is teaching me to tell the time on the big clock in the kitchen. The clock in the kitchen is harder to read because it has hands and not just numbers like the one by my bed, but I'm learning. I know when it's six o'clock but I don't like six o'clock. Mummy also doesn't like six o'clock. When it's five o'clock she has to make sure that the whole house is sparkling clean and that she is wearing a pretty dress because Daddy says, 'I like to see my darling wife looking her best.' Mummy says she likes to look her best too but sometimes I don't believe her. Sometimes I think Mummy would like to be able to wear her comfy clothes all the time and have her hair in a ponytail like I do.

Mrs Jackson doesn't wear her hair in a ponytail; she wears her hair in a messy bun and bits of it are always falling out. She wears 'this old thing' all the time so she's always comfy. She comes over for coffee sometimes. Only when Mummy's head isn't sore. She is older than Mummy and she has three children but they've all grown up now and act 'like they raised themselves'. Mrs Jackson gets cross because her children, whose names are Ashley, Emma and Mitchel, don't call her on the phone. Mrs Jackson has a big

round tummy and today she is wearing black leggings and a pink
and purple top with shiny bits on it.

Mummy said, 'Don't you look sparkly, Peg,' and Mrs Jackson
laughed and said, 'Oh, this old thing!' Daddy says Mrs Jackson
is 'a disgusting woman who's lost control of herself'. Mummy
doesn't say anything when he says that but she looks sad because
she likes Mrs Jackson.

I put my big ear against the door of the kitchen and I can hear
Mummy laughing. I like to hear her laugh.

Mrs Jackson says, 'So I told her not to worry about some stupid
man. I keep telling her that but she's still obsessed with getting
married and I thought girls weren't worried about that anymore,
not in this generation.'

'She really shouldn't worry about it. She's only twenty-five and
someone will be along soon enough. She's so pretty and so smart.'

'Oh, I know, I know, and I do keep telling her that sometimes
marriage is the worst thing that can happen to someone. I mean,
Barry and I are happy but not everyone is, and it seems these days
that there are more and more unhappy marriages.'

Mummy doesn't say anything and I press my ear harder up
against the door in case she is whispering but all I can hear is the
sound of her teaspoon stirring her cup of coffee.

'You know, love,' Mrs Jackson says very softly, like she knows
I'm listening, 'if you ever need anything, any help or anything
like that, you know you only have to come to me. I promise we'll
help you any way we can, whatever you need, really. Money or a
place to stay – anything. You know that, don't you?'

Mummy still doesn't say anything and then I hear her sniff.
'Thanks, Peg. I know, you've told me often enough. I just… have
to figure this out for myself, I think.'

'Mmm,' says Mrs Jackson.

I wonder what it would be like to live in Mrs Jackson's house. I
went there once with Mummy to drop off a plate after Mrs Jackson

made us some Christmas cookies. They were nice – not as nice as the ones that Mummy makes but they had green and red icing and I licked off the icing before I ate the biscuit and my tongue turned a funny colour which made Mummy smile. I'm not sure I would like to live in Mrs Jackson's house because it is not very sparkling clean and it smells like dog because she has two dogs but they are old and they don't want to play with me because they just like to sleep. Mrs Jackson doesn't put all her dishes away in the cupboard and she doesn't clean everything so all the counters in her kitchen are covered in plates and other stuff. When me and Mummy were there to give back the plate, Mr Jackson came home and said, 'Hello, neighbours, how are you both doing on this fine day?' I smiled but I didn't say anything because Mr Jackson is kind of scary-looking and he has a long grey beard. I was sitting on a kitchen chair next to Mummy and I watched Mr Jackson to see what he was going to do about the big mess in the kitchen. I waited to see if he was going to tell Mrs Jackson she was 'an ungrateful pig' because that's what Daddy said to Mummy one night when he touched the top of the fridge and it was sticky. I thought Mr Jackson would say a lot of mean things to Mrs Jackson because there was sooo much mess.

But he didn't do anything, he just made himself a sandwich and went to eat it in front of the television. I don't think Mrs Jackson ever gets a sore head. Maybe if Mummy and me lived at Mrs Jackson's house she wouldn't have a sore head so much and we could go out to the beach and the zoo and the movies.

I hear Mrs Jackson push her chair back and I know that means she's stood up because it is time to go because it is nearly six o'clock and time for Daddy to come home and for everyone and everything to be sparkling clean. I stand up and go upstairs to have my shower so I am ready for when Daddy comes home.

When I am done, I sit on my bed and wait because Daddy says he needs time to have a drink and relax before I come and say hello to him. I hear him come home and go into the kitchen and he says, 'And what did you do with your little day today?' to Mummy.

'Oh, nothing much,' she says and I know she won't tell him about Mrs Jackson coming over for coffee because that is one of our little secrets because Daddy doesn't like Mrs Jackson because she is 'nosey'. But I like Mrs Jackson.

'Where's Kevin?' Daddy asks Mummy.

'He's at James's house, remember? I told him to be home by six but he—'

'He doesn't listen to you, I know… and why would he, my darling? Why would he listen to someone like you?' Daddy laughs but Mummy doesn't laugh with him so I don't think she finds it funny.

'I told him to be home at seven so he'll be here then.'

'But you asked me to tell him to be home at six, that's what you…'

Mummy stops speaking and she and Daddy are very, very quiet. I sit still on my bed and I can feel my heart beating in my chest. I wait and I wait and finally Daddy calls me. 'Where's my Little Bird?' he says and I jump off my bed and say, 'Tweet, tweet,' and I run downstairs to give him a hello hug. I sit in the kitchen with him while he has his drink and Mummy finishes getting dinner ready. I tell him all about how I played with my dollies and tidied up and he reads some of the newspaper and listens to me.

At seven o'clock exactly Kevin comes in and Daddy looks at his watch. 'Right on time,' he says.

'Yes, sir,' says Kevin and we all sit down to eat. We don't talk or laugh like the families on television do. We all look at our plates, and when Kevin and I are finished we wait for Daddy to say we can leave the table. Mummy doesn't eat much. Her eyes are red and she looks sad so maybe she isn't hungry. Sometimes I don't feel hungry at dinner either, especially if Mummy is sad. I wonder if she would be sad if we lived at Mrs Jackson's house? I think maybe, maybe she wouldn't be.

CHAPTER TWENTY-FOUR

'Today I would like to talk about your first incident, your first act of violence,' says Dr Sharma. It's Saturday so Dr Sharma is in jeans and a sweatshirt as though the casual clothes mean she's not wasting her Saturday here with the lunatics of the world.

'Don't you have somewhere else to be today?'

'No, I mean, I have…' She stops talking, aware that she almost, almost, told me something about her life. That's a big no-no in here. You never know who's going to turn up on your doorstep.

I know that outside the sun is shining but the air is crisp and cool. This morning at breakfast I looked out into the gardens and saw how bright it was but I only know what it feels like from listening to the nurses talk. Being allowed out into the gardens is a privilege. I have yet to earn any privileges.

In here it is always the same temperature, no matter the season or the time of day. I am wearing tracksuit pants and a T-shirt, which is how we all dress if we're not shuffling around in pyjamas. The passing of time is not obvious, especially since the lights stay on in the corridors all night. Between the drugs and the light and the temperature, I'm sure some people are confused as to whether they've been here three days or three months. I know how long I've been here because I am counting down from my twenty-one days. Twelve days to go. Dr Sharma is still unconvinced I'm insane.

'So, the first time you were violent,' she says again.

I think about it and I decide not to mention anything she wouldn't have on file. Instead I tell her something she already knows because it's right there on her computer. I tell her about the first officially recorded time.

'It was at school. I was fifteen.'

'Yes,' she agrees.

'If you know, why do I have to talk about it again?'

'I want to hear about it from your perspective.'

'I was talking to a friend in class and a teacher told me to stop.'

'Yes,' she agrees and she sits forward, legs slightly open, as though this is really exciting. She is wearing too much perfume today, something sweet and cloying. And she's wearing more make-up than she usually does.

'And,' she says and I hear an edge of frustration in her voice.

'She told me to stop talking, so I hit her.'

I can still remember the feel of my hand against her cheekbone, hear the sound of skin hitting skin, and most importantly, I can still feel the surge of power that ran through me when I realised what I'd done.

'Why? I understand you didn't want to be told what to do but why did you react the way you did?'

I shrug my shoulders. I have no intention of explaining that Miss Blakewell was a small pale woman who seemed scared of the bigger boys at school. I was the biggest there at fifteen. Big and filled with muscle from sport. I played everything. I wasn't brilliant at any one sport, but when I played rugby I just charged ahead, knocking everyone over. I enjoyed rugby the most. They like you to be aggressive. They celebrate your violence. The other stuff I played because it kept me out of the house and my father was happy for me to take part in as much sport as I wanted. If I was out of the house, I wasn't making a mess.

At fifteen I looked like I was twenty. The problem was that Miss Blakewell didn't just tell me to stop talking. She asked me politely to stop talking. 'Can you please concentrate on your work?' is what she said, and when she said it, I heard a slight tremor in her voice. She was unsure of my reaction. She was afraid of me and that made me angrier than her request to stop talking. I felt my body heating up and I knew that I was going to explode even though it had never happened to me before. I had, by then, perfected the art of moving into others' personal space. If I was standing, I would step close to them, and usually, no matter who they were, they'd back away. A few people didn't, of course. The principal and some of the sports teachers and my father. My father never backed away, but then my father is the one who taught me to step into someone's space, to threaten with my height and my size.

Miss Blakewell couldn't have known that I was talking to James because I couldn't really concentrate on my work. That morning my father had hit me from behind with a mug in his hand. He slammed the cup right into the back of my head. I had a headache. A low buzzing and pain that made me want to sleep. I probably had a slight concussion but I would never have mentioned that to anyone. I wouldn't dare.

That first time, the first time my rage boiled over into the world, the reason my father hit me was simple: I left the mug in the sink instead of putting it in the dishwasher. I knew what I was doing. I knew I was provoking a reaction, but at fifteen I seemed unable to prevent myself from doing that. I was as big as my father by then. As big but not quite as strong. But I'm as strong now, as strong, stronger, the strongest.

I know that when I stood up to confront Miss Blakewell, James tugged my arm to get me to sit down. I know that I watched my arm move like it wasn't my arm. I know that I hissed, 'You're pathetic,' after she fell backwards. I know that the girls in the class screamed and that someone ran frantically for help. James and another boy held me down while we waited but I wasn't really fighting them. I was shocked at what I'd done, completely shocked, but I was also, for the first time in a long time, at peace.

'Miss Blakewell was pathetic. She should have stood up to me, should have stood up for me,' I say.

Poor Miss Blakewell. I stood up and slapped her. She fell back against a desk and hurt her back. Cue expulsion and the first in a long line of psychiatrists that I wasn't actually allowed to say anything to. My father never did get me any professional help as the school psychologist suggested when I was fourteen. That only happened after I hit someone. It was a condition of Miss Blakewell – sweet, kind Miss Blakewell – not pressing charges.

'What do you mean she should have stood up for you?' I can hear the excitement in Dr Sharma's voice, see the curiosity in her eyes. She's having a lightbulb moment.

I look at her. I'm not feeling that sharp today. I accidentally swallowed the sleeping pill from last night instead of spitting it out. 'Slip of the tongue,' I say. 'She should have stood up *to* me.' Her face returns to neutral.

I never told anyone about my home life, and I only told James the truth about my father and what it was like to live with him after we left school. I'm surprised that James still has anything to do with me. He has a strange kind of loyalty to me, one that I can't really explain but one that I'm grateful for. He's so different to me, just a normal guy living his life. He has a wife and two kids, and even though I'm not allowed to be in his home, he calls me regularly to check up on me. He didn't even sugar-coat the not coming to his house thing – just said, 'You're my mate but I know how things can get and I can't have you near my family.' I thought I would be angry at him for that but I understand. I'm happy to meet him in a pub or for a walk. There's no pretence with James. I loathe the pretence that I lived with for years and years. Everything picture-perfect on the outside, writhing with shit on the inside.

Dr Sharma looks at me and I look back at Dr Sharma, and whatever hope she had for today's session dissipates into the air.

'Kevin,' she says, 'we are almost at the end of your stay and thus far I'm not sure that you have demonstrated any need to be here.'

'Fine, send me to prison.'

'I don't want to do that but you don't seem to want my help.'

I study Dr Sharma, considering explaining about my mother and what she did. I wonder if she could find a way to help me accept it and move on with my life because I'm forty-one now and I'm really tired of being this man, this really messed-up human being. I want to be different.

One day, when I was thirteen, I imagine myself saying, *I came home expecting everything to be normal – or as normal as my life at home could be – and everything, everything was entirely different and my life was never the same again. One day, when I was thirteen, I realised that not only did my mother not like me – which I understood, I was an arsehole teenager – I realised that she didn't actually love me either.* I know that if I told this to Dr Sharma, her face would light up like the sky on New Year's Eve and she would believe that she has finally found the one missing piece of the puzzle so she can put me back together again and make me whole. She would claw at me for details of that one terrible day, sucking the story from deep inside me where I need it to stay.

I'm not ready to open this particularly ugly wriggling can of worms. I'm not ready to discuss it and I will probably never be ready.

I know what I need. I need to feel different; I need to find some peace. In order to find some peace, I need to have justice. In order to have justice, I need a small window of time. Just a small window when I am back out in the world.

There will be a gap between my being released from this hospital and remanded in prison if I get a good enough lawyer. I know there will be a gap and that's all I need. A small gap and a little bit of time with him. And justice will be served.

'You're as useless as anyone else,' I say to her, knowing that it will mean I am sent to prison. 'You can't help me. None of you ever could.'

CHAPTER TWENTY-FIVE
Rachel

She is slumped on the couch in front of the television, a glass of yellow-gold wine in her hands. Ben is upstairs reading Beth a story. For the past three days there have been no more dolls. She has not heard from him at all. Perhaps he is done with her. Perhaps the dolls were a way to frighten her, to unbalance her just as he had done to her mother when he turned up at her work every time they found somewhere new to live. Is he done with her now? Is it over? She hopes so but she knows that it's wishful thinking. She knows, deep down, that she is fooling herself. The picture, the torn picture, could only have come from her mother's apartment. It was one of the few she had kept of the whole family. And Rachel knows that her mother kept it in her bedside table drawer, that she looked at it every night, stared at the faces until, perhaps, the truth of who that family was disappeared.

He's been in her mother's apartment, in her house, at Ben's work, at the hospice. He is everywhere. Everywhere. And it feels like each time he makes contact, he is closer to stepping out of the shadows and confronting her.

She would like to talk to Ben, to tell him everything, but he seems angry with her, almost as if he blames her for him losing his job. He's started asking her for all her receipts for grocery shopping. 'We have to economise,' he said. 'I can take over the weekly shop for now, while I'm not working. You just be with your mother.'

Her phone is right next to her all the time, and even though she checked five minutes ago she picks it up and checks it once more, making sure she hasn't missed a call from the hospice. Veronica has not woken up again. Sometimes her face contorts a little and Sam raises the level of morphine in her drip but nothing wakes her. Rachel hopes it is a peaceful sleep. Her mother's revelations have stunned her. Not only did she see her father over all the years they were running but she made a deal with the devil to keep Rachel safe. How could she have done that? But what other choice did she have?

Rachel keeps going over it, thinking about it from different angles, trying to imagine the choice she would make if she had been her mother in that situation. She knows what choice she made as a child. She remembers what she said and did and what she encouraged her mother to do. But she was a child. And then when she refused to discuss him, she encouraged Veronica to stay away from him. It was self-preservation but guilt scratches at her nonetheless. If Veronica had contacted him, her father would have known that the agreement was broken and come after them. There is no doubt about that.

She closes her eyes. Is that what happened? Did Veronica somehow reach out to her brother, breaking the agreement and sending her father after her?

Outside in the empty street she hears a car drive by and her hand grips the glass tightly. Who is there? Is it him? But the noise is soon gone and she realises it was probably someone just looking for another street. Today, as she left the suburb, she had to pull over to make way for three bulldozers, all heading to different plots of land. Something that should have frustrated her filled her with joy. It was starting. Soon there would be tradespeople up and down the street, noise and confusion, and help would be only a shout away. But not at night. At night the silence reigned. If it was summer, there would at least be the sound of insects to remind her that she and her little family were not the only living things in the street, but outside there is ice in the air, and in the morning she knows that a light frost will have settled over the grass they have only recently laid.

Maybe the cold will keep him wherever he is and away from her.

The merry-go-round of thoughts is making her dizzy and she wants it to stop. She should only be thinking about her mother now. That's all that matters.

She's only been home for an hour and she will go back soon. She knows she shouldn't have left but sometimes the walls of her mother's room begin to close in. She only meant to come home long enough to have dinner but then she saw the open bottle of wine on the counter and poured herself a glass. It's unlike Ben to be drinking midweek but there's no way she's going to mention it. He seems to be on the edge of another angry outburst all the time. She supposes her mother spent her whole married life not saying anything to her father. Her husband is not the same kind of man but she cannot think of what to say to him, of how to help him, especially after the last time she tried. She doesn't have the energy either. She can feel her mother's life trickling away.

Today she talked to Veronica until she felt her throat close over. She spoke about the few small holidays they took when her mother had managed to scrape together some money, about visits to the beach and movies they'd seen together. 'Do you remember when we went to see *Mary Poppins* when it was being shown at the cinema, Mum? It was so much better than watching it on television. Remember how you sang along to the songs and I got embarrassed and then I realised that everyone in the theatre was singing? Do you remember the chocolate cake you baked for my twelfth birthday? Remember how it flopped in the middle so you filled it with candy? Do you remember when we went bra shopping and the woman asked if you were my sister? Do you remember, Mum? I remember. I remember it all. I remember you coming over after Beth was born and you were so sick but you still told me I needed to go and lie down. You could barely hold your head up but you wheeled her up and down the street outside in her pram so I could sleep for an hour. I remember what you said on the night before I got married about Ben making me laugh and that being the best sign for a good marriage. I remember shopping for a wedding dress with you and we both got a little drunk on the champagne they gave us. I remember, Mum, and I won't forget, not any of it, I promise.'

'It will be soon,' Sam told her as she left today. 'You need to prepare yourself. Go home and get some rest and I will call you the moment I need to. We're only a few minutes away from you and I don't want you to make yourself sick.'

As Ben comes downstairs, Rachel looks up at him, feeling her thoughts of her mother drift away. 'She's out like a light. Apparently a very busy day at school. Are you going to drink that?'

'What… oh, yes,' she says, realising that her glass has tipped to the side, nearly spilling the wine. She takes a sip and then puts down the glass. 'I think I should go back and be with Mum. Can you handle getting Beth to school in the morning?'

'Of course. It's not as if I have to get to work. I've got an interview with a recruitment firm at eleven but that will be over by the time school is out. Just stay with her, babe, stay as long as you need to.' Rachel watches her husband as he says this. It sounds like he's rehearsed these words, as though he doesn't mean them at all. He doesn't look at her as he speaks.

'You're angry with me,' she says.

'I'm not.' He shakes his head. 'Why would I be angry with you?'

Ben slumps down on the couch and Rachel moves along until she is sitting next to him. 'You're a good guy,' she says. She rubs her hand over his cheek. He is letting his beard grow and she can see some patches of grey coming through. He doesn't react, but after a few seconds he moves his head away as though her touch is irritating him. She sits up, away from him, stung. He is worried all the time. When she stops for a moment to think about him, tearing herself away from thoughts of her mother, of her father, she understands that he's worried all the time. She wishes she could give him more, could be more encouraging, could even take on some of the financial burden, but she's trapped right now. Just like her mother warned her.

'I'm unemployed,' he says. 'Good guys usually have jobs.'

'You'll find something soon. I know you will, and if the worst happens…'

'Then what, Rachel? Then what?' He gets up to pour himself another glass of wine and takes a deep sip.

'We can sell the house,' she suggests. 'I know we've only just moved in but we can sell it and go back to renting.' It would be awful to lose their dream home but it no longer feels like a dream. In reality she would feel relieved to move somewhere else. She would like to leave this place and all the terrible things she associates with it behind. It is the house where she has lived as her mother is slowly dying and the house where her past has returned to torment her. She cannot look around at the clean lines and open spaces and enjoy them anymore. It is the house where she has lived as her whole world fell apart. She understands now why her mother didn't mind the shoddy rental apartments they lived in. The apartments meant she was away from her own beautiful, picture-perfect house where terrible things happened.

She may be safe from her father back in a rental apartment surrounded by people who watched everyone coming and going. Her father may not want to harass her if others can see what he's doing. She would welcome the noise that comes with having people all around her. The oppressive silence of the empty suburb forces her into the turmoil of her own mind. She would be happy to leave here but she cannot say this to Ben, who would be devastated that she does not appreciate this dream home he has worked so hard to provide for them.

'The way the market is now we'd probably land up still owing money on the mortgage and having to find rent as well.'

'I'm sorry, Ben, I wish I could help. I wish I could just get a job but right now…'

'Right now, you need to be with your mother so let's just get through right now. You said you were going. You should go.'

'Maybe you could ask your parents for some help?'

'I know I could but it means they will have to take money from their retirement fund to help us and I couldn't live with myself if I wasn't able to pay it back.'

'You'll get something soon, Ben, you will.'

'Yeah, soon.' He stares ahead at the television.

'Ben, listen,' she begins, reaching out for him.

The ringing of the bell startles her and she jumps, yanking back her hand.

'Who could that be?'

'I don't know, I'll go,' she tells Ben even as he's standing up.

'No, let me, you never know. After that scare you had, you don't need to be answering the door at,' he looks at this watch, 'eight o'clock on a Wednesday night.'

Rachel nods as he leaves the room. Heart racing, she picks up her wine glass and drains it. Is it him? It could be him. Have the dolls stopped because he means to show up here himself? She stands up quickly and goes to follow Ben.

Her husband is standing at the door, talking to two policemen, and for a moment she is relieved, sure they have simply come to check up on her since the supposed break-in.

'Um, Rachel,' says Ben, 'they're here to tell you, to ask you…' He shakes his head, seeming confused.

'Ma'am, are you Rachel Watson?'

'I am, I mean I was. I'm Rachel Flinders now.' She swallows. Have they come to tell her about her mother? Surely not, Sam would have phoned. He wouldn't have let her miss her last moments. Police don't come to tell you someone has died unless it's a violent murder or an accident. She looks down at her phone that she has clutched in her hand. Only the time is displayed. She hasn't missed any calls.

'We're very sorry but we're here to inform you that your father has passed away,' one of the officers says.

'My what?' Rachel gulps in air as her stomach twists into a knot. She bites down hard on her lip. 'My what?' she repeats. She has heard the words but they don't seem possible.

'Look, officer,' says Ben. 'I think you must have the wrong Rachel Watson. Rachel's father died when she was little, when she was seven or so. He died of cancer. I think this must be a mistake.'

The constable speaking is a large man with a belly hanging over his pants. He is young with his face freshly shaved and his pants neatly pressed as though he has just begun his shift. To Rachel he looks like a little boy with an overweight man's body.

'If you are Rachel Watson and your mother is Veronica Watson, then I am sorry to tell you that your father Leonard Watson is deceased. We wanted to ask you some questions about him. Would it be all right if we came in?'

'But I don't understand,' says Ben. 'When did he die?' He looks from Rachel to the constables and back again, and Rachel feels her stomach sink. The room begins to spin; she feels like she's going to faint.

'We think it happened sometime in the past week,' says the constable. 'Maybe as long as two weeks ago. We'll know more when the coroner has completed her examination. His body was found in his home in Blackheath. His neighbours hadn't seen him for a while and then they noticed…' The constable pauses and his colleague, an older man with a beard, jumps in for him. 'They noticed a smell coming from the house and alerted police.'

'Where… where was he living?' Rachel asks as she swallows repeatedly to stop herself from throwing up.

'In Blackheath as I said, the same place he'd been living for the last thirty-five years. Were you in contact with your father, Mrs Flinders?'

White. White walls, white door, white tiles in the kitchen. White towels in the bathroom. Red. Red blood on the floor.

The house appears before her.

I'll never tell, I promise.

The room begins to spin.

CHAPTER TWENTY-SIX

Ben

Ben stares at Rachel, at her pale face and her pink lips that have developed a bluish tinge. She looks up at him and says, 'Ben…' Her legs buckle and her eyes close and he catches her just before her head hits the floor.

'Oh, oh, jeez,' says the young constable. But the older man pushes him aside and helps Ben lift his wife. Together they move her to the couch.

'Perhaps get her some water,' the older man says.

Ben nods but for some reason he's reluctant to leave Rachel alone. He takes a blanket from the back of the couch, draping it over her.

In the kitchen he grabs some ice from the fridge and fills a glass with water, listening to the *crick crack* sound the ice makes as water hits it, and he tries to process what's going on. Rachel's father has been alive all this time. She didn't say that the police had made a mistake. It seems that she knew he was alive. Rachel has been lying about him for the last sixteen years he's known her and probably for her whole life. Why would she have lied about him? He thinks about the money she took. How much doesn't he know about his wife?

He died in his house and no one knew he was dead until he started to smell. Ben shudders. What a way to go. Lonely and unloved and unmissed by anyone. He cannot contemplate anything worse.

What kind of a person is Rachel to be able to ignore her father for most of her life? To simply pretend he was dead? He has so many questions and he vows that after the constables leave, he will ask her about everything. He will force her to tell him about her father and explain why she and her mother have perpetuated such an awful lie. And he will ask her about the money she has hidden in her drawer. He's been so reluctant to discuss anything that might upset her but he's had enough now. What is she hiding? He thinks about his little girl, safely asleep upstairs, surrounded by her flying butterflies. What if Rachel is a criminal with a terrible past? What will happen to Beth?

Putting the glass on the counter, he then gets another from the cabinet. He fills it with some water for himself and drinks deeply, savouring the way the cold slices down his throat. His mouth feels dry. His body feels weird and his whole life feels like it's completely out of control.

He would like to turn around, walk right out of the back door and keep going. Is that what Rachel was planning to do? Has she been taking money so that she can run away and leave him, leave their life behind? Would she have left Beth? A couple of weeks ago that would have been unthinkable but now he's not so sure. The woman lying on the couch in the living room is not the woman he thought she was. Her father never died of cancer. If she could tell a lie that huge, then it's possible there are a lot of other things she is concealing, including the ability to leave both him and their child.

Over the past few days, he has been questioning himself and his choices constantly. Now he realises that he should have been questioning everything else.

CHAPTER TWENTY-SEVEN
Little Bird

When school starts again, I am happy, happy. I don't mind walking there now because the best thing that has happened all summer is that the big growly dog moved away with his family. No one lives in the house with the red front door now and it has a big sign outside that says 'sold' on it. Daddy says that means that a new family is coming to live there and I hope that if they have a dog, it's just a small dog or a dog that likes to give licks through the fence. Maybe they could have a family with someone for me to play with. Maisie says her neighbour Estella is her best friend in the whole world and that makes me sad sometimes because I want to be Maisie's best friend in the whole world.

At school I'm not in Mr Stanley's class anymore. I'm in Mrs Berenson's class and she has grey hair and a cross face and everyone in my class is very quiet because we all know that Mrs Berenson likes to shout loud, loud.

I am very careful when I write down my new spelling words and Mrs Berenson says, 'Now that's nice and neat,' and makes me show the whole class. My cheeks get red and I feel happy inside and I can't wait to tell Mummy that Mrs Berenson didn't shout at me because I was careful when I wrote my words.

When I get home from school Mummy is lying on the couch having a nap because she has a 'summer cold'. A summer cold is different to a winter cold but it still makes her nose run and her eyes water and she feels really bad. Last night I heard her cough, cough, cough all night long. I wanted to go into her bedroom and tell her to take some of the medicine she gives me when I am sick but I knew that I wasn't allowed to get out of my bed except to go to the bathroom and I am never, never allowed in Mummy and Daddy's room when it's night time. Unless Daddy is not there but he is always there.

I tell Mummy about my day and she claps when I tell her about Mrs Berenson making me show the class my work. Then she blows her nose and blows her nose. I put my hand on her forehead just like she does when me and Kevin are sick and I feel that she is hot, hot.

'Do you want a drink, Mummy?'

'No, sweetheart. I'm fine for now. Can you get your own snack, love? I just need a bit more rest and then I'll get up and clean up and cook dinner.'

'I can, Mummy, but I can also bring you something to drink and I can be your nurse.'

'That would be lovely,' says Mummy, and she blows her nose and blows her nose and blows her nose.

I take a big spoon of peanut butter out of the jar and I use the knife to cut some apple but my cuts are not very good and the pieces are all different sizes, not like when Mummy does it and everything is the same size. Some of the peanut butter gets on the white counter and I quickly take Mummy's rag to clean it but I don't clean it very well and it just smears the peanut butter. I leave it for Mummy to clean because she is better at cleaning than anyone.

I eat my apple and then I pour Mummy some orange juice from the fridge because she always gives me juice when I have a cold and she says, 'Thank you, love, you're a very good nurse.'

I sit next to Mummy on the couch and I do my homework and she coughs and blows her nose and then she falls asleep for a bit and I watch television.

I don't notice the time going by and Mummy sleeps and sleeps and her breathing is loud because of the cold but I don't mind. I just watch television and then all of a sudden the door opens and Kevin comes in with Daddy because he has been at cricket practice and Daddy fetches him from practice because it ends late, late. If Kevin and Daddy are home it means it's after six o'clock.

'What's happening here, Little Bird?' asks Daddy in a kind voice and I stand up and go to say hello to him but I get lots and lots of butterflies in my tummy because the kitchen is not sparkling clean and I am not sparkling clean and there is no dinner. I think about the peanut butter on the counter and I am scared, scared because Daddy hates mess and this mess is not even hiding – it's right there. I want to run to the kitchen to wipe everything again but my feet feel stuck to the floor.

'Oh,' says Mummy, and she sits up. 'Oh, I'm so sorry, I must have dozed off. This terrible cold is making me feel awful. I'm so sorry, Len; hello, Kevin. I'll get dinner ready in just a few minutes.'

'Oh no, my darling,' says Daddy, 'don't feel you have to get up. Kevin and I can take care of things, can't we, son?'

'Sure,' says Kevin, but his voice sounds strange like he's not sure at all. I think that maybe Kevin doesn't know how to take care of things. I swallow because I hate it when Daddy cooks. His food is yucky.

'No, I'll be fine now, Len, I've had a rest, really.' Mummy stands up and smooths her hair. Her cheeks are red and I think that's because her face is hot and she has a temperature. I should have been a better nurse and given her some Panadol. That's what she gives me when my face is hot and I have a temperature.

'I said I'll take care of it,' says Daddy slowly. 'You go up to bed. Little Bird, go and have your shower and get clean, and by the time you're done I will have everything shipshape.'

'Tweet, tweet,' I say but Daddy doesn't smile at me. I don't think he's happy about everything not being shipshape.

Mummy comes upstairs with me. 'Why didn't you wake me?' she whispers.

'Sorry, Mummy,' I whisper back.

'Oh, it's not your fault, sweetheart, it's really not.'

Mummy helps me get all clean and sparkling and then I go downstairs and Daddy has made fish and broccoli but not the way Mummy makes it. Mummy puts crumbs on the fish and makes it all golden and crunchy and then she gives me tomato sauce to dip the fish into but Daddy has made the fish steamed and it looks yuck.

'Why don't you go up to bed, dear? You've had a long day and you need your rest,' Daddy says to Mummy and then he laughs but not a happy laugh. Mummy walks slowly up the stairs to bed because everyone has to do what Daddy tells them to do.

I eat all the food Daddy has made even though I have to chew and drink water to stop it from coming back up out of my mouth. Kevin eats it too. No one says anything and Daddy doesn't even ask me how my first day of school was.

Daddy hums as he cleans up after dinner. I try to help him but he doesn't want me to and he says, 'Just go to bed.' I want to tell him it's too early for bed and it's still light outside because it's summer but I don't. I go to my room and I lie on my bed with my new book from school and I read it over and over again. Mummy doesn't come to read me a story because of her summer cold.

I hear Kevin come upstairs and go into his room and close the door and then I hear Daddy come upstairs and go into his and Mummy's room. And then I hear a *crack* sound and I hear Mummy say, 'Please, Len, I'm so sorry. I'm so sorry.'

I hear another *crack* sound and Mummy says sorry again and again. The butterflies in my tummy flap their wings harder and harder. Mummy is sick and Daddy should be nice to her but I don't think he's being nice to her. I hear her crying and the *crack* sound comes again. I don't know what to do so I get off my bed and I go and knock on Kevin's door. I always have to knock on Kevin's door or he pulls my hair.

'What?' he says and I open the door quietly and go into his room. He is lying on his bed reading a comic book with Superman on the front.

'Daddy is not being nice to Mummy,' I say, 'and she's sick.'

'What do you want me to do about it?'

I look at Kevin, at his big feet and his big hands and his face that has some pimples on it. 'You're big,' I say. 'You can make him be nice to her. You're strong, Kevin. You can be strong, stronger than Daddy. You can be the strongest.'

'Go back to bed,' he says. And he turns the page of the comic.

'Make him stop,' I tell Kevin because Kevin and I both know that Daddy is the one who gives Mummy a sore head.

'Just go back to bed and mind your own business,' hisses Kevin like a mean, angry snake.

'Please, Kevin, you're big, please make him stop.'

Kevin throws his comic book on the floor and jumps off his bed. He smiles at me and the butterflies flap harder and harder because now I am scared of Kevin and I shouldn't have come to his room.

He grabs the top of my arm and squeezes hard. 'No way am I getting involved in that shit. She's pathetic and she deserves whatever she gets. You're pathetic too and I told you to go back to bed.' He pulls my arm and then he shoves me out of his room and closes the door behind me.

'Ow,' I say but not too loudly because I don't want Daddy to hear.

'Go to bed,' Kevin tells me through the door.

I rub my arm where his fingers have made it sore. I creep back to my bedroom and close the door and climb into bed. I hug my big soft dolly who sleeps on my bed and I cry and cry because I am not big enough to help Mummy.

In the morning when I try to go into her room to say good morning to her, she is curled up in a little ball and Daddy says I must leave her alone.

Daddy pours my cereal for me and I try to eat it but I can't because there are so many butterflies in my stomach.

'I suggest you finish your food, Little Bird,' says Daddy quietly. 'We don't waste in this house, do we, Kevin?'

'No, sir,' says Kevin and they both look at me and I have to crunch up my cereal faster and faster until it's all gone.

Then Daddy leaves for work and he takes Kevin to school because his school is far away and it's only for boys.

When he closes the door and I hear his car drive away I run upstairs to Mummy. She is still a little ball in her bed. 'I'm going to school now, Mummy,' I whisper and she uncurls a little bit and looks at me with two red eyes and a puffy lip. I want to run away because Mummy looks scary but then I tell myself that she is still Mummy. 'Is your cold better, Mummy?'

'I'll be fine, Little Bird,' she says and then she tries to smile but her lip starts to bleed and then she is crying and crying and I don't know what to do. I don't know what to do. I feel tears come into my eyes as well but I don't want to cry in front of Mummy because I know she is sad enough. I don't say anything to her. I go downstairs and I take my bag and walk to school.

I hate Daddy and I hate Kevin as well.

I wish me and Mummy could run away, just run away far. Far from here and far, far from them.

CHAPTER TWENTY-EIGHT

Twenty-one days after I am admitted to the Lyndon Public Hospital for observation and treatment, I am informed that I am being sent to prison. I have not been a particularly good or informative patient.

They found my meds hidden behind the toilet while I was in my last session with Dr Sharma, a session in which I said nothing at all. When I came back and discovered one of the nurses in my room, I felt the black sludge instantly bubble up. I clenched my fists and tried to see the bucket of cold water but it didn't help.

'I found these behind the toilet, Kevin,' said the nurse, a small woman with curly red hair. She opened both her hands to show me the sticky, damp collection of pills. Her name is Jacinta and she is perky and happy and I felt my arm move because I was going to smack her into next week. But just as I lifted my arm, nurse Bobby, great big nurse Bobby, walked in. He grabbed me hard, trapped my arms down by my side and squeezed until I thought I was going to pass out. I could tell he was enjoying himself. He's been waiting to get his hands on me to show me just how strong he is, just waiting. They sedated me and tied me down to the bed. And now they're sending me to prison.

It was a long shot to believe that I could get away with doing my time in a hospital. I am obviously not suicidal. I am seeking justice. I am not going to kill myself until I feel I have achieved it.

A woman named Annette Darcy informs me that I will be transferred to the local jail in the morning. She advises me to think about getting a lawyer. She says that legal aid will help me find a lawyer if I cannot afford one but that this may take a long time.

'I'll get a real lawyer, thanks,' I tell her. Behind her black-framed glasses, I watch her eyes widen and I speculate that Annette Darcy is probably married to or in a relationship with a lawyer who works for legal aid. People are so easy to read.

I call my father.

The first three times I dial his number from a phone in Annette Darcy's office, it rings out.

'He may be out,' I say. I have no idea where he would have gone since he gets his groceries delivered and has no friends at all.

'Maybe try again in a bit,' she says, her tone detached. She doesn't care what happens to me as long as I am no longer her hospital's problem. I have not met Annette Darcy before and she's lucky that they have Bobby in her office with me. His stance is wide and his chest is puffed out and he's just waiting for me to make even the smallest move. I can see he would love to get the chance to grab me again. I smile and Annette Darcy frowns. I am not supposed to be happy.

I try my father again and this time he answers so I know that all the other times he was just watching the phone ring. He must have known it was me, must have loved reading a little of my desperation into the endless ringing of the phone.

'Sir,' I say.

'Yes,' he answers, not 'How are you?' or 'What's going on?' or 'Are you okay?'

'I need you to get me a lawyer,' I say.

He sighs, a deep, heavy, disappointed sigh. 'Even the lunatics didn't want you.'

I chuckle because it's funny, he's funny. 'That's right and now they're sending me to prison so I need a lawyer so I can get bail.'

'How will you get bail?'

'I imagine,' I say slowly, 'that you will offer up the house as surety.'

'I'm not…' he begins.

'I may get bail anyway. They'll get me a lawyer from legal aid and I will get it anyway. I may get it anyway… Dad.' I hear him catch his breath. I'm not supposed to call him Dad like we're a normal father and son.

He's quiet. If he was younger, he would know that this is bullshit and that if I can't afford bail, I will simply be remanded in custody until I am tried. But he's getting on in age so he's not completely sure. He knows the world has changed, so he is aware that he no longer knows everything about everything. He is only sixty-five but he looks older than that. He is thin with disappointment and weighed down by those who have betrayed him.

I have enjoyed watching him become less and less sure of himself over the years, and I can imagine a time when he will be completely dependent on me, completely helpless. That will be justice of a sort, I suppose, but I'm not sure it will be enough and I'm also not sure how long I will get sent to prison for. I want to be there when he understands who is the strongest, who is the most powerful. I want to be there. I have to be.

I know, as I listen to him breathe on the other end of the phone, that he's worried that he will refuse me and I will somehow still make it out of prison and he will be the first person I come looking for.

When I was twenty-five, I spent a year in prison on a minor assault charge. Someone took my parking space at the shopping centre. I had gone to stock up on groceries and alcohol for myself and my father. He had handed me $200 and smacked me across the head. 'You should be ashamed of yourself. How can you have no money and still live with me at your age?'

'I'm sorry, sir,' I whispered. I was still his dancing monkey then.

But someone took my parking space. It was a woman, a large, overweight woman, who stuck her middle finger up at me when I pushed down on my car horn to let her know she'd taken something that wasn't hers. So I smashed my car into hers, once, twice, three times, and then, as she screamed and swore, I got out of my car and gave her a little slap across the face. She was a big woman and she barely even moved but I got charged anyway. Assault and destruction of property. My father got me a good lawyer who alluded to an absent mother and I was given one year. It was a tough year. I thought I was a real bad boy until I spent a year in prison and I learned what the real world can be like, what truly bad people can be like. I spent a lot of my year in prison covered in bruises until I beat the absolute shit out of someone and then learned to keep my head down. And when I got out, I hit my father back for the very first time.

I caught a taxi home from the prison, and when he opened the front door, he looked me up and down and shook his head. 'Loser,' he said. I didn't even have time to visualise the bucket of water. The black sludge overwhelmed me and I punched him in the nose. He stumbled backwards, blood going everywhere, creating a huge mess.

I was in shock. I should have turned around and run, just left and never come back. I often think that it was a sliding doors moment in my life. If I had turned and left, I might be an entirely different person now. I would be a man with a past, yes, but maybe I would also be a man with a job and a wife and a life.

Instead I just stood there, rooted to the spot, bewildered at myself. I had done what I was never allowed to do. I had fought back.

He grabbed me by the shirt, hauled me into the house and then he beat me until I could barely move. But I think he understood I was capable of hitting back, even though I was the one who landed up covered in bruises. I don't know why it took me until I was twenty-five to do it. I don't know why it took a year in prison. I don't know and I have a feeling that even though I understand, logically, why I feel powerless against him most of the time, I will never fully understand it enough to make any difference to my life. I will always, in some ways, be his dancing monkey. The only ones who don't have to dance are the ones who ran away. They should have taken me with them. They should not have left me here with him to spin and twirl as he played his harmonica. It doesn't matter how old I get; I have a feeling I will always be seven years old, trying not to cry.

But I grow more capable of hitting back each year.

I am strong, stronger, strongest now. That's just a fact. I may feel seven years old when he talks to me but I can see him for the round-shouldered, weak old man he is.

'Fine, I'll call a lawyer,' he says and he hangs up.

You have to love the legal system. They give you chance after chance after chance, certain that few people actually mean to really hurt anyone. The lawyer my father got for me was very good. I knew he would be. He was all shiny suit, slick hair and eloquent streams of words about how my mother left and my father is retired and can take care of me and how I'll be confined to the house and see a psychiatrist and blah, blah. According to my lawyer, I am no threat to anyone, not even myself. According to my lawyer, I will be in therapy every day while I await trial so I can figure out how to be a better person. According to my lawyer, my father will make sure I maintain all conditions of my bail and will dedicate himself to taking care of me.

So, they gave me bail. They gave me bail three weeks ago.

My father waited for me to be released and he drove me home.

'You have to stop this crap,' he said. 'You're forty-one and you should be ashamed of yourself. You need to stop blaming everyone else for your dysfunctional behaviour and get yourself a proper life.' And when we got home, he locked the front door and told me to go to my room.

He did try to keep me at home.

He really did.

CHAPTER TWENTY-NINE

Rachel

When she opens her eyes, she is on the sofa with Ben and the two constables peering worriedly down at her.

'You fainted,' says Ben.

'Oh, how embarrassing,' she says and she struggles to sit up.

'Now I think you just lie there for a bit, ma'am,' says one of the constables, the one that is older than his partner and has a shock of black hair to match his beard and kind, dark eyes. She nods and rests her head back on a cushion that Ben has wedged under her head.

'Um, look,' says Ben to the officers, 'it's obviously been a shock and you may not know this but her mother is currently in the Lady Grey Hospice, so I think it would be best if you spoke to her another time.'

Rachel wants to tell him to stop speaking for her but instead she closes her eyes. She needs him to speak for her. She needs time to get her thoughts together, to get the lies straight. She knows that her husband has no idea what to think.

He's dead. A week ago, or two weeks ago, they think. How is that possible? The dolls only stopped three days ago. When did they start?

She opens her eyes and looks at the constables, one of whom is writing in his notebook and the other sifting through his wallet. 'Let me give you a card,' he says to Ben.

'How did he die?' she asks.

'Um…' says the overweight one, 'maybe that's best discussed another time. If you could give the station a call tomorrow and maybe come in for an interview with one of our detectives, that would be most appreciated.'

'I will, call I mean, but how did he die? Why won't you tell me?' she asks again, determined.

'It was very violent,' says the constable with black hair.

'What happened?' asks Ben.

The constables look at one another and she can see that each of them is hoping the other will tell her what happened. How bad could it be?

'Just tell me,' she sighs, her heart hammering.

'He was beaten to death.'

'Oh.' She covers her mouth with her hand, nausea rising inside her. Lying back against the pillow, she closes her eyes again. She cannot deal with this right now, cannot think about what he would look like or who would have done that to him. She finds herself feeling surprisingly sad at how his life has ended, despite everything he did and how he treated his family. She has not seen him for more than twenty-eight years and she was terrified, absolutely terrified, that he had found her, but he was still a human being.

'Please call tomorrow,' she hears one of the constables say.

'I'll make sure she does,' replies Ben and then she hears them leave the room. She waits until the door closes and Ben turns the lock and then she sits up, trying to compose her thoughts.

Her husband comes back into the living room, his lips set to a thin line. He is not just angry but furious, she can see.

'You lied…' he begins as her mobile phone trills.

She looks at the screen; it's the hospice.

'Yes?' she answers without thinking.

'It's time to come now, Rachel,' says Sam gently. 'Bring your husband if you can but it's time.'

'Okay,' she whispers, 'okay.' She stands up. 'I have to go, Ben. Sam says it's time and I have to go.'

'Rachel, we need to—'

'I need to go, Ben!' she shouts. 'My mother is dying and I need to be with her. Everything else can wait.' She waves her phone at him and for a moment thinks she might actually throw it at him. It's time, it's nearly over, and while she had anticipated grief and despair, what she had not anticipated is this anger that has suddenly consumed her. She is so angry, angry. It's not fair, not fair.

Ben holds up his hands. 'Okay… I'm sorry… Do you want me to come with you, to come and be there? I can call my mother to come over and sit with Beth. She can be here in half an hour.'

'Yes, yes please,' she says, looking at him. 'Call your mother and meet me there.' The anger fizzles out, the grief and despair rearing up, ugly and confronting. It's time.

In her car she is too stunned to even cry. How can this be it? She has been waiting for it, has been expecting it, and yet it is completely surreal. How can this be it?

When she pulls into the parking lot, she is unsure of how she got there. She knows there are three traffic lights between her house and the hospice and yet she cannot remember stopping at any of them. She has not felt the pothole that has irritated her every day for the last two weeks as her car has bumped over it. She knows that she always turns left at the large white house with the balustrade balconies and yet she cannot remember seeing it. She has no idea how she got here.

The parking lot is half full of cars. She notices Elizabeth's BMW parked there and wonders, sadly, if she has been called in for Luke.

In the lobby she sees Elizabeth standing with her husband, whom she has only met once, and a young woman she knows is their daughter. Their faces are white, their eyes red. On Elizabeth's face she can read the heartbreak of loss and she feels tears on her cheek. She doesn't have time to stop and speak to them and yet she cannot simply walk by.

She takes a step towards them and Elizabeth looks up. 'Oh, Rachel, he's gone, my little boy is gone.'

Rachel nods her head as her tears dampen her shirt. 'I'm so… I'm so sorry, Elizabeth. I'm so sorry. He was the most beautiful soul… He was…' She steps forward and puts her arms around Elizabeth, feeling the weight of the older woman sag in her arms. 'It's too soon,' Elizabeth says, her voice muffled against Rachel's shirt. Rachel strokes her back. What can she say?

Sam comes into the lobby. 'Rachel, love, you need to come, you need to come now.'

'Oh, Rachel, I'm so sorry, I had no idea,' Elizabeth says, letting go of her.

Rachel gives her shoulder a squeeze and nods at her. She follows Sam. In the bedroom, Veronica is barely breathing. Rachel sits down by her bed, takes her hand, and quite suddenly her mother's breaths stop. 'Mum!' shouts Rachel, and Sam peers at Veronica, who abruptly starts breathing once more.

'Don't do that, Mum,' she whispers. 'Don't do that.'

Sam comes to stand next to her. 'Do you want me to stay or leave?' he asks.

'Can you stay, just until Ben gets here? Can you stay?' She cannot be alone here at the end. She has no idea what to do or say. She cannot bear for her mother to go. She cannot be alone.

Sam doesn't answer. He pulls a chair away from the wall and sits down next to her. 'I'm here, Rachel, but don't think about that, just let her know, let her know everything you want her to know.'

Rachel closes her eyes and rests her head on her mother's hand. Should she tell her that he's dead, that someone beat him to death, that someone used the same violence on him that he used on Veronica for her whole married life? She wonders if it would give her comfort to know this, but as quickly as she thinks about it,

Rachel dismisses the idea. Her mother looks peaceful, despite her laboured breathing, despite her life slipping away. Her mouth is relaxed and her pale skin is smooth and unlined.

'Tell her everything you want her to know,' Sam said, and Rachel thinks about what she would want her mother to know, about the words she wants her to take with her as she leaves the world. She doesn't want her to think about the times that she suffered, all those years that she lived in fear. She wants her mother to know that she was a gift of a human being, a gift to the world and to Rachel.

'I want you to know, Mum,' she begins, 'that you were the most wonderful mother and grandmother. You did everything for me, you lived your whole life for me, and I'm so grateful. I'm so grateful for everything you did for me. I'm going to miss you, Mum. You have no idea how much. And Beth's going to miss you. She's going to miss baking cookies with you and reading stories with you. I'm going to miss talking to you every day. I'm going to miss the way you describe the books you're reading and the sound of your laugh. I'm going to miss the times when we got the giggles over something only we remembered. Ben's going to miss you too. He always said you were the best kind of mother-in-law. We're all going to miss you, Mum, so, so much, but I understand if you need to leave now. I understand and I love you.'

Her mother moans quietly.

'Do you think she's in pain?' she asks Sam.

'She may be, love. I'm going to raise the level of morphine some more, but this will… You understand it may…'

'I understand,' she says, looking down at her beautiful mother. 'I understand.'

Sam stands up and adjusts the drip going into her mother's hand. The skin around the needle's entrance is bruised black and she wishes she could take it away and soothe the hurt there.

She and Sam sit silently while she holds her mother's hand. Rachel is unaware of the time passing but at some point, she realises that it is her husband who is sitting next to her and not Sam. It is after one in the morning when she hears a rattle from her mother and then, finally, complete silence. Ben, who has been resting his hand on her knee, leaps up and goes to call Sam, who is just outside.

'She's gone,' he says after checking Veronica over. 'I'm so sorry, sweetheart. She's gone.'

Rachel is too numb to cry anymore. She nods slowly, feels her husband's arms around her shoulders. 'Can you give me some time with her?' she asks and he nods and then it is just her and her mother.

She feels a slight chill, a small movement of air, and without thinking too much she accepts her mother's goodbye.

'I'll never forget you, Mum, not ever.'

It feels like hours later, years later, when they finally return home after she has done everything she needed to do to get her mother's body transferred to the funeral home Veronica herself chose, despite Rachel not wanting to discuss it at all.

She accepts a silent hug from Ben's mother, who quickly leaves, promising to return in the morning.

She stands in the hallway, listening to Audrey's footsteps in the silence of their suburb. She knows that if they were still in their flat, all the neighbours would know by now. Nothing was ever a secret – even things that happened in the middle of the night. And she can imagine that Mrs Andino would have already left a honey cake outside their front door, despite the late hour, so that they would have something sweet to help with their grief. But there is no one here now. No one except Ben and Rachel and a sleeping Beth. The profound loneliness of her mother's loss wraps itself around her in the cold stillness of the house.

She trudges up the stairs, needing to see her child, to see the little girl who carries her mother's genes and who will never forget her grandmother either.

She opens the door quietly, inhaling the strawberry smell that is Beth, and she tiptoes over to the bed.

Her empty bed.

Empty except for a doll.

A small troll doll.

As she stares down at the empty bed, her veins fill with ice, her heart misses a beat.

In the half light of Beth's room, the doll appears to be laughing at her.

She cannot bring herself to pick it up, cannot force herself to move. And inside her, a scream rises up. It fills her whole body. It is all the fear and worry and sadness of the past few weeks and months. The scream is all she is. She opens her mouth and she screams and screams. She cannot seem to stop.

CHAPTER THIRTY

Ben

Her screams travel down the stairs, where he is standing in the kitchen staring at the kettle, waiting for it to boil. The sound shocks him, and at first he assumes it's a scream of anguish, a howl at the world over the loss of her mother. But then, moments later, he realises that Rachel wouldn't make such a sound when Beth was near.

He bolts up the stairs, following the noise, to find Rachel in Beth's room.

She is staring down at their daughter's empty bed, screaming and screaming. The covers are thrown back, and lying in the centre, right in the centre, is another troll doll, with shiny purple hair and a leering smile. Rachel is standing still, frozen in place, staring at it.

It takes him a moment to process what he's seeing. Their daughter is not in her bed. He looks across the landing at the bathroom but the door is open, the light is off. He shouts because he needs Rachel to stop her terrible noise. 'Where's Beth?' he yells, expecting a response he can understand. Rachel doesn't move but she finally stops screaming. She is facing away from him. He walks around to look at his wife. Her face is pale and she is chewing on her lips, chewing hard enough to draw blood. Her green eyes are focused on Beth's wardrobe, staring at the wooden doors as though she can see through into the dark interior. He wonders if Beth is in the cupboard. 'What's going on?' he asks, and again she doesn't answer him. He opens the door of the cupboard and rifles through the hanging clothes. She is not there.

He walks back over to Rachel, who is still frozen but blessedly silent now, just staring down at the ridiculous doll. She hasn't even picked it up. He puts his hands on her shoulders and gives her a little shake. 'Rachel, where's Beth? Where's Beth?' Even as he does this he is not overly concerned, certain that there is just something he's missing and Beth will appear in a minute from hiding behind a door or that she will have be snuggled up in their bed. He is more concerned about Rachel and her disconcerting gaze. He doesn't know what she's thinking.

'Rachel,' he says again, holding her shoulders tightly, 'what's going on?'

'She's gone.'

'Gone? What do you mean gone? Beth, Beth, where are you?' he calls. He darts to their bedroom and switches on the light, checks in their bed, flinging back the covers. He looks in their en-suite bathroom, in the bathroom Beth uses, and does a quick circuit of the house, calling for his daughter. Only when he returns to her bedroom, finding his little girl nowhere, with Rachel still standing in the same position, still staring down at the ugly little doll, does he begin to panic.

'What?' he says to Rachel, trying to understand what's happening. 'What's going on? Talk to me, Rachel, talk to me now!' he yells.

She doesn't answer him. She doesn't say anything at all. And he is suddenly furious. Furious with her catatonic state, with the strange way she has been acting lately, and especially furious with how fragile she is and how much of his own pain he has kept from her because of that. And even though he knows that he would be this broken as well if it were his mother who had just drawn her last breath, he still cannot stop the anger.

He grabs her by the shoulders again, his fingers digging into her skin, and he shakes her back and forth. 'Where is Beth, Rachel?

What's going on? You have to talk to me.' Her head rocks back and forth, he hears her teeth click together, and then she finally, finally meets his gaze. He lets go and she slaps him violently across his face.

The shock sends him reeling backwards and he stares at her, horrified. Horrified at her and at himself. Shame washes over him.

'Don't,' she hisses at him, 'ever lay your hands on me like that.'

He holds up his hands. 'I'm sorry, I didn't… Where is Beth? You have to tell me where she is, please. Please, Rachel.'

She glances down at the doll again, leaning down and picking it up. She throws it on the floor and stamps on it again and again. 'Why aren't you dead? You're supposed to be dead!' she shouts. Ben is suddenly afraid for her. She is losing her mind. He is sure of it. Grief over her mother has broken her, but where is Beth? Where is their daughter?

He is surprised to hear himself whimper. He has never been more unsure of what to do in his life.

Rachel looks at him. 'He's taken her,' she states.

'Who, Rachel? Who's taken her?'

She takes a deep breath, straightens her shoulders, and for a second it looks like she's grown a little bit taller.

'I thought it was my father,' she says. 'I thought he was the one leaving the dolls. But he's dead. He wasn't dead before but the police told us he's definitely dead now.'

'What?'

'It's… I don't know… The police said he was definitely dead. They said he was…' His wife stops speaking.

'What are you talking about? What dolls? Rachel, you're not making sense.'

'The troll dolls,' she says, 'the dolls you've been finding, I've been finding. I thought it was my father leaving them for me because they used to be mine.'

'I don't understand,' he says. His worry for Beth becomes tinged with fear for Rachel, who isn't making sense at all.

Rachel walks over to him and holds him by the shoulders, gently. Her voice is quiet, her manner calm. 'You need to listen. I thought it was my father sending me the dolls. But now he's dead and Beth has been taken. No one else knew about the dolls except for my mother and…' She stops speaking and lays a hand on her chest.

'Of course,' she says. 'Kevin. It's Kevin. My brother.'

'You have a… a brother?' he asks weakly. He cannot imagine what else he is going to hear from this woman, from this woman he has been married to for nine years. How can she have kept an entire life from him?

'Look,' she says, her voice firm, 'I will explain. I promise I will explain everything, but right now you need to help me find Beth. All I can tell you is that two weeks ago someone broke into the house and left a doll for me to find. It used to be mine when I was a child. All the dolls used to be mine. I thought it was my father but he's dead so I think it's my brother. He's the only other person who would be angry enough at me to want to hurt me.'

'But you said no one broke in – you said… the police said…' Ben closes his mouth. He doesn't know what to think anymore. He feels like he's fallen through the looking glass. Nothing is as it should be. His whole world has tilted.

'I lied,' she says and she meets his gaze, lifts her chin, as if to challenge him. 'He broke in and left me the doll. Beth was right. There was a monster but it was a monster from my childhood. I thought it was my father but now I'm sure it was my brother, and I can tell you that he was as much a monster as my father was. And I have no idea how bad he would be now.'

'But… why didn't you tell me? Why didn't you tell me he was leaving the dolls?'

'I thought he was just… I thought it was my father and he was trying to torment me and that he would stop. He liked to play games and I thought he would stop, that it would all stop.

When it didn't, I was going to tell you. I was, but then Mum and your job and…'

'I don't understand…' He stops speaking. He doesn't have the energy left for all of this. He slumps onto Beth's bed. 'You should have… Why would he want Beth?'

'I don't know. But he has our daughter. And I don't know where he's taken her.'

'We have to call the police,' he says as her phone starts ringing. It's in her pocket and she drags it out and looks at it. She answers it, putting it on speaker.

'I'm in the park,' says a male voice. 'Come alone. Don't tell anyone. I won't hurt her.' And the call is ended.

Rachel sinks down onto Beth's bed. 'Okay,' she says, 'okay, okay, okay.'

'Was that him? Is it him?'

'I think so… I haven't heard his voice for nearly thirty years and he was only thirteen when we left… but I think so.' She chews her bottom lip and Ben wants to take charge, to make a decision, but he finds himself unable to come up with anything to say.

'What do we do now?' Ben asks finally.

'Now,' says Rachel, 'I go to the park and you call the police and tell them where we are.' She pushes her shoulders back.

'It's not safe, you can't go alone.' But even as the words leave his lips, she stands up and runs out of Beth's room and down the stairs, clutching her phone. She grabs her jacket off the hook near the front door and her beanie hat, and even as he is formulating his next words for his wife, she is out the door.

Ben stands on the landing for a moment and then he moves as quickly as she did, grabbing his coat and dialling the police as he runs, explaining to the woman who answers his 000 call that his whole life has suddenly imploded.

CHAPTER THIRTY-ONE

Little Bird

It is dark in the night and I am supposed to be asleep but I am awake because there is too much noise to sleep. There is a *thump, thump* sound coming from the kitchen. I slide out of my bed and creep along the passage towards the light. I hear Daddy grunt and say, 'Stupid, stupid bitch.' And then there is another *thump*.

I go past Kevin's room but it's dark in there and I know he's not home. He's never home. Mummy says he needs to be back by dark so he can do his homework but he just laughs when Mummy says that and Daddy says, 'Leave the boy alone. See if you can manage your own small life before you try to start managing his.' I remember that it is Saturday so Kevin is sleeping over at his friend James's house. I hate Saturday because Daddy is home all day. Today Mummy cleaned and cleaned and cleaned and Daddy followed her around all day saying, 'Are you sure you're happy with how that looks?' so she cleaned and cleaned again.

I am scared and shivering even though the night is sticky and hot. I try to move like a quiet cat down the passage. I should just go back to bed but I need to see what the *thump, thump* noise is. In bed I am safe. But I can't stay safe because I need to know what the noise is.

I stop on the landing and look down the dark stairs. Mummy is down the stairs. I know Mummy is down the stairs and not safe in her bed. I have to go to her. I have to.

When I get to the kitchen, I know I've made a big mistake. Daddy doesn't like it when I make big mistakes. I want to turn around and run away but I don't. My feet won't move. *Move, move*, I tell my feet but they won't listen.

It is bright and shiny in the kitchen, too bright for my eyes that have been sleeping, and I scrunch them up. I can't see and then I can see and what I see is Mummy lying on the floor. There is blood falling out of her nose and she is like a little round ball, holding onto her knees. Daddy is standing up, big and tall, and he is kicking her, *thump, thump, thump*. His hair is not neat and tidy but messy and his face is shiny and he looks hot.

Mummy's eyes are closed tightly like she doesn't want to see the kicks but I can see tears are falling and mixing on the floor with the blood from her nose.

I want to run away. I want to hide but I have to make him stop. How can I make him stop? I have to make him stop hurting Mummy. She's my mummy. I have to make him stop. I wish Kevin was here even though I hate him. I wish he would come home and make Daddy stop but I know that even if he did come home, he wouldn't make Daddy stop. He thinks Mummy is pathetic and he doesn't want to save her from Daddy.

'Daddy,' I say quietly and I hope he doesn't hear me but he does. He turns around and looks at me with dark, angry eyes.

'What are you doing out of bed?' he asks quietly. His voice sounds funny and his chest is moving in and out, up and down, like he's running. His face is shiny. It is hard work kicking Mummy.

'What are you doing?' I reply and then I start to cry because a little bit of wee has come out and I'm not a baby. Only babies wee in their pants.

'Go-back-to-bed,' he says in a robot voice.

Inside me I get angry at Daddy. He shouldn't be kicking Mummy. He shouldn't be hurting her. Hurting other people is bad. Mr Stanley said so last year. When Andy hit Maisie because she took his eraser, Mr Stanley said that was very wrong. 'We don't hit and we especially don't hit girls, Andy,' Mr Stanley told him. Mummy's a girl and Daddy shouldn't hit her and he shouldn't kick her.

'You shouldn't hurt Mummy,' I say and I want to sound big and brave and strong but my voice is only small and rattly. I'm so scared of Daddy, of how big he is, of how dark his eyes are. He looks like a monster, a scary monster. I don't want a monster in my house. I am scared but I am also angry. Daddies should be nice. They shouldn't be monsters.

'Go back to bed, Little Bird,' says Daddy and he smiles at me. It makes me even more angry because he shouldn't be smiling when he's hurting Mummy.

'No,' I say, making my voice loud.

Daddy turns away and kicks Mummy again, *thump*, like he doesn't care that I can see him being a monster. She makes a groaning sound, a crying sound.

'You leave Mummy alone!' I shout and a bit more wee comes out because Daddy is so big and his eyes are so black.

'Get back to bed!' he roars at me and he turns around and comes towards the door where I am standing. As he steps closer, he slips in the tears and blood puddle on the floor and he falls over and his head hits the kitchen floor – *crack*. He lies very still. He is very quiet. He is not roaring anymore. He is not kicking anymore.

Mummy says, 'Oh.' And she struggles to sit up. Her face is big and puffy and the blood keeps coming from her nose.

Daddy is lying still on the floor. He can't kick Mummy anymore. He looks like he's sleeping. I don't want him to wake up. I don't want him to ever hurt Mummy again.

'Go to bed, Little Bird, run, run to bed,' says Mummy but her mouth is filled with blood and she sounds strange. I don't like the way she sounds. He made her sound like that. I don't like that he hurts her and gives her a sore head. I don't like that he shouts at her and that he shouts at me and that he broke my favourite mermaid dolly. I don't go back to bed. I walk over to where he is and look down at him. 'I hate you,' I whisper.

'No, no, don't say that,' says Mummy, and she stands up, holding her stomach. She grabs a dishcloth and wipes her mouth and nose.

'He'll wake up soon. Just go back to bed,' she whispers.

'I don't want him to wake up,' I say. 'I don't want to see him again. Let's run away.'

'We can't, I can't, I… can't, Little Bird.'

Daddy makes a sound, a rumble, and he turns his head with his eyes closed and I know he's going to wake up and then he's going to go back to hurting Mummy. I look around the kitchen and see his hand weights on the floor. He likes to sit at the table and curl his arm up and down, up and down, making him stronger and stronger so he can hurt Mummy more and more and I know that he will start hurting me soon. He will hurt me like Kevin hurts me only it will be worse because Daddy is stronger than Kevin. I'm not going to let him hurt me and I'm not going to let him hurt Mummy anymore. I feel like there is a big angry fire inside me with the flames getting higher and higher. I am hot, hot, hot.

I go over to the weight and I try to lift it up but it is heavy, heavy. There is a number ten on the side of it and I know this means it is too big for me to lift up. I pull hard and my arms burn but I pick it up and then I take it over to Daddy, who is moving now. I can see he's going to open his eyes.

'What are you doing?' asks Mummy, but she asks quietly. She is sitting on the floor again, the blood coming from everywhere. She watches me but she doesn't move. I look at the kitchen door. The weight is pulling on my arms, making them ache and stretch. It's ten heavy and that's too heavy for me.

'Don't die, Mummy,' I say because she looks like the cat that got run over outside our house. It had blood coming from everywhere and Mrs Jackson took it to the vet but it died.

Mummy shakes her head.

Daddy groans and I stand above him with the weight making my arms and hands burn. His eyes are closed and he can't see me and can't see what I'm holding, but he will open his eyes soon and it will be too late. Too late for Mummy and too late for me. I can't let it be too late.

Now the fire is all over my body and I think that Mummy must be able to see the flames. I am burning inside and my arms are burning outside but I won't put down the weight. I won't be pathetic. Mummy doesn't deserve to be hurt.

I lift it high, high above my head. It makes everything hurt. It makes my whole body sore and Mummy still doesn't say anything. She just watches me as I drop the weight on Daddy.

Right on his head.

He stops rumbling. He stops moving. He stops everything.

'Oh… oh what… oh my God, what are we going to do, what are we going to do?'

Mummy's face is all blood and there is a gap in her mouth like she has lost her tooth but she is too old to lose teeth, only little girls like me lose their teeth. She looks at me and I stand up straight. Mummy has had too many kicks and she doesn't know what to do. But I know what to do – I know.

'We have to run away, Mummy,' I say and she is crying and bleeding but she nods at me and then she stands up.

'We'll run away,' she says.

'Kevin isn't here. What about him?'

'I don't know,' says Mummy. 'Should we wait for him? What if Daddy wakes up?'

I feel like I am Mummy and Mummy is the child but I don't mind because Mummy is bleeding and sore and I have to help her.

'He's just like Daddy,' I say and Mummy nods because she knows I'm right and we can't have someone who is just like Daddy run away with us. That would be like taking Daddy with us.

'I don't want Kevin to hurt us, Mummy,' I say, and she shakes her head.

'I don't want him to, I don't think… we should.' She doesn't know what to say. I think she is finding it hard to even make her brain work.

'We have to leave Kevin,' I say. 'He likes Daddy.'

Mummy starts to shake her head because she knows that Kevin is afraid of Daddy but then she nods. We can't wait for Kevin. Kevin is going to grow up to be Daddy and we can't take Daddy with us.

CHAPTER THIRTY-TWO

If she had recognised me, I believe I would have done things differently. If she had looked at me and said, 'I know who you are,' and maybe told me she had always thought about me, missed me even, I believe I would have done things differently.

As it was, she looked at me like I was a stranger, like I was just anyone.

She looks so similar to my mother, and her daughter looks just like she did as a child. Small, delicate, fragile, easily hurt, easily broken. The same curly brown hair and soft green eyes.

I've been watching her husband as well.

He left his car door wide open the first time I visited. I had to run when I heard the police siren but I wanted to see the chaos I had caused, so I hid and waited. I watched him come speeding into his street and screech to a stop outside their house and then just leave the car door open, as though he didn't understand that a threat was nearby. I couldn't resist gifting him one of the dolls. And then I left him the picture as a clue. I wanted him to show it to her, to ask the question, because I don't think he knows about me and my father. Or, at least, he doesn't know about me. I know that my mother made a deal, a deal to erase me from her life. I know Rachel just went along with it. I know she never expected to hear from me ever again.

I wondered if seeing the picture would make him angry. If catching her in a lie would make him furious. He's an average-sized man but even an average-sized man can inflict pain and suffering if he chooses to. I know that patterns of abuse are repeated. I know that women who grow up watching their mothers abused, or who grow up abused themselves, will sometimes unconsciously choose someone who repeats that pattern. I wondered if she did that. If the man with the brown curly hair and square jaw drove off to work every morning and then came home at night to beat the crap out of her. I know he doesn't look happy. He's lost his job and I know that because I watched him load the sad cardboard box filled with his things into the trunk of his car. It was easy enough to get into his office and walk around, easy enough to leave the photo for him to find.

I gave her every chance to recognise me.

It's unfair of me, perhaps, to have expected anything from her. I don't recognise myself sometimes.

Her little girl is sweet to look at with a big smile and dimples. When she smiled at me, I didn't get the sense that she was secretly worried, but you never know. I think my sister and I smiled plenty throughout our childhoods. I never had any obvious bruises and we both seemed to function just fine – up to a point. For me, I was fine – a little difficult, a bit of a loud mouth, but fine – up until my anger, the black sludge, gained control. By the time they started sending me to see the school psychologist in high school, I knew enough to just shrug when they asked me why I was so angry. I don't know if the school even knew my mother had left us. If they needed to speak to my parents, my father went, always lying that my mother was travelling or at work. I never contradicted him. You can live a whole life in secret if you choose to.

'Just go to your room. Go to your fucking room and stay there. You're absolutely pathetic,' he said to me when he brought me home from court, where I had been granted bail.

'I don't think I want to go to my room.'

'You know what,' he spat, coming right up to me, right into my space, 'I shouldn't have agreed to stay away from them. I shouldn't have accepted you as the fucking consolation prize. I should have told her to come and get you and then at least I could have had my daughter with me.'

'What are you talking about?' I asked and I stepped back, away from him, even though I was looking down at him and I knew he couldn't really hurt me. I stepped back.

He laughed, a wheezy old man laugh. 'Didn't know that about your precious mother, did you, Kevin? She gave you up in exchange for our little girl. As easy as clicking her fingers,' he said and he snapped his finger and thumb together. 'She didn't want you at all – she probably never did.' His eyes were dark with the thrill of the pain he knew he was causing. Even though I hated her, even though I understood she had betrayed me in the worst possible way, there was still always some part of me that hoped she missed me and thought about me. That they both did. I was family, after all. But I knew he was telling me the truth and the black sludge moved so fast I didn't have time to even think about stopping it.

I don't think he was expecting me to hit him. There was a look on his face after I landed the first blow. It was a punch to the stomach. He bent over double and coughed. And then he looked at me and I could see the shock on his face but I also saw something else. Fear. He was afraid of me. I am strong, stronger, strongest. He wasn't expecting me to hit him but I wasn't expecting to not be able to stop. Nothing could have stopped me. Forty-one years of mental and physical abuse rushed out of me through my hands and I went until I was sweating, until my chest was heaving, until I had justice.

In the end, I was exhausted. I don't think anyone would believe how tiring it is to beat another human being to death. I slumped down next to him and dropped my head in my hands.

'Kevin,' his voice rattled and I jumped and moved away from him. He was still alive.

He reached out a blood-covered hand to try and grab me, and I moved further away from him.

'Read the letter, Kevin,' he wheezed. 'Desk drawer, read it. She never… never wanted you. I was the best… best you had. I was…' And then he stopped speaking. And he stopped moving. And he was still. Even at the end, right at his end, he couldn't resist hurting me. He couldn't resist it.

I showered and cleaned up and then I went to look for the letter. If I hadn't found it, I would simply have run. I would just have left and kept running.

That was the plan. I had my justice. He was lying in the living room, covered in blood, with his face puffing up and the hands that had hit and punched and smacked finally stilled.

I know his banking details. I have a passport and I was just going to run and keep running for the rest of my life.

But then I read the letter.

His desk drawer was locked and I couldn't find a key so I beat it open with a hammer. It took four blows, and on the final one the wood cracked and splintered and I pulled it open, spilling its secrets onto the slate-grey carpet of his pristine office floor.

It was mostly filled with the buff-coloured envelopes that Inspector Gadget brought over the years, and I tore a few open to read where they had gone, where they had run to.

16/22 Greenview Terrace, Kilburn, Adelaide. Rachel attends Kilburn Public School. Veronica is a cleaner for an office complex.

24/23–27 Hurstville Place, Essendon, Melbourne. Rachel attends Essendon Girls School. Veronica is working at Essendon Books.

43/124 Valley Road, Erskineville, Sydney. Rachel attends
Erskineville Public School. Veronica teaches at the primary
school.

There were endless addresses, endless schools, and then they
were in Sydney and that's where they still are.

I found the last envelope that detailed Rachel's wedding to a
man named Ben, and Veronica's job in a primary school in Sydney.
I learned my sister is a teacher as well.

They did fine. They just went on and lived their lives as though
I had never existed.

I folded the last sheet from the last buff-coloured envelope my
father had received, just two months ago, and shoved it into the
pocket of my jeans. It told me my sister and her husband were
planning to move into a new house on a new housing estate. She
created her own picture-perfect Christmas card life – a life that
doesn't include me.

My eyes were gritty with exhaustion, and everywhere was
beginning to hurt as blood pulsed into bruises and cuts. He had
fought back as hard as he could.

But I needed the letter he was talking about. I knew there
would be a letter. I knew it would be a letter that would break
me. I knew that because otherwise he wouldn't have told me. I am
strong, stronger, strongest, and he couldn't defeat me physically
but he could still maintain his psychological hold, his control,
his power over me.

I scrabbled through the envelopes on the floor and finally found
it. A small, pale blue envelope with our address, written in my
mother's neat, square handwriting. I held it up to my nose, my
bloody nose, and inhaled its scent, as though it might possibly
still smell like gardenias, like the perfume she used to wear, but
there was no trace of her. I liked that she had chosen blue for
the envelope, that she had not chosen the white he would have

approved of. And I knew, as I held it, that I didn't want to know what she had written, that it would break the heart of thirteen-year-old Kevin, break it completely.

I ripped open the envelope, noticing how my hands were shaking, and then I sat down on the floor of my father's office to read it.

The letter was dated one week after they'd left. One week after I'd come home and found them gone, just gone. I read the letter that is twenty-eight years old and I could see her writing it, how she would bend her head to the paper, how she would hold the pen to her lips as she thought. I could see her writing it and I felt her next to me as the horror of the deal she made became clear. My mother, my mum.

Dear Leonard,

I have thought about how to begin this letter for days, hoping to somehow find the perfect words to reach you. But I realised last night, as I watched Rachel settle into another strange bed in another motel, that I can never reach you with just words. I would have done that already if I could have.

I imagine you are looking for us already. I'm sure you will hire a private investigator and find us quickly enough. And I know what will happen if you find us, Len. I know.

Peg Jackson told me to file for divorce over and over again. She told me she would help me, that Rachel and I could live with her and Barry, and that she would help me find a lawyer and go to the police about your abuse. She used to paint a picture for me of a life lived without you whenever she came over for coffee, but I knew it wouldn't be that easy. I remembered your words, you see, the words you used after the first time you hit me: 'Run from me, try to leave me, and I will kill you.' I knew you meant those words and I knew you would kill me.

I couldn't let that happen to Rachel. The thought of her being raised only by you was beyond devastating. You broke my spirit but you had yet to break hers, although I know you were looking forward to doing that.

There is something wrong with you, something terribly wrong, and even though I have encouraged you over the years to try and find a way to fix what is broken inside you, and I have accepted the beatings that came with those suggestions, you don't want to be healed or get better.

You left me no choice, Len. I knew what you would do to her after what happened that night. I knew what you would do to me and so we ran.

I know you will find me but I am writing to ask you to leave us alone.

I remember the day that Kevin was born. I remember how your eyes filled with tears I had never seen you shed before. I remember you held him in your arms, that tiny, perfect bundle, and then you leaned down and kissed me and said, 'Thank you for giving me my legacy.'

So, this is my offer to you. If you leave me and Rachel alone, I will never try and contact Kevin. I will not go to the police and I won't try and get him back. I will leave you your legacy.

I will accept the deep and despairing heartbreak that comes with this choice. I will accept the guilt that I know will simply become part of my soul because I will always feel it. I will accept the terrible suffering of losing my boy, my son, if you leave me and Rachel alone. I hope that the suffering and the guilt I will endure as I think of my child every day for the rest of my life will be enough for you, Len. I pray it will be.

Just leave us alone.

I know you will find us and you may decide that killing me and taking Rachel is easy enough, but you may also get caught,

*Len. You will get caught. And that would ruin your tidy life
in your tidy house.*

Just leave us alone.

*And if you can bear to do it, let my son know that I love
him, that I have always loved him and that my heart is broken
in two to have to make this choice. He is still my little man,
my baby boy, no matter how big he gets, and I will miss him
with every part of me.*

Let him know and leave us alone.
Veronica

She traded me for Rachel. She gave me up to save my sister. I
tore the letter into two and then I kept tearing it into smaller and
smaller bits as I cried like a fucking baby and then I roared my
pain so loudly, I knew the neighbours would come.

Then I understood that I didn't just want justice, because I am
and have always been just like my father. I wanted revenge. Good
old-fashioned revenge.

I needed to find the women who had left me behind, who
had just upped and left me, and make them pay for that choice.

The bedroom where he slept alone no longer smells of my
mother. He threw out everything that belonged to her soon after
she left. But my sister's room was still exactly the same – until I was
done with it. I ripped, tore and broke everything in there, even as
my bruises grew and my nose dripped blood everywhere. And by
the time I was done, by the time I was sitting on the floor, holding
her pink blanket to my nose, I had a proper plan for revenge.

The moment I left the house I knew the clock was ticking. No
one would miss him for a while but eventually someone would
wonder where he was, why the mail was piling up, what the smell
was. And part of my bail conditions is that I check into the local
police station every day. They would be out looking for me. I was

glad I had let my beard grow in the hospital, glad that I wouldn't look exactly like the mugshot they took before I went in.

I took his car, his precious 'don't you ever touch it' car. And as I drove, I thought about what I would say to my mother and to my sister, and I practised an accent, settling on Canadian because I wanted to make it as hard as possible for them to recognise me. I wanted them to be able to see through the beard and the accent to the son and brother they abandoned because maybe then I would know that they had thought about me, had imagined me growing up and living my life without them.

But it was too late for my mother, she wouldn't even wake up to look at me. Maybe it was the cancer but it felt like it was denial as well.

I don't know why I took the dolls. I think some small part of me wanted to give them to my sister as a gift, a kind of way to say, *See, these are from your childhood just like I'm from your childhood. Remember me?* I imagined saying. When I saw her, saw how she was just a carbon copy of my mother, I realised that any hope I had of some emotional reunion was ridiculous. She looked like her so she probably thought like her. Would she leave her child the way my mother left me? Probably. Would she care if her child was taken from her?

I wanted to force them to see me, to see what I had become because they made the choice to leave me alone with him.

When my mother left with Rachel, any hope I had for a life not governed by violence ended. Any hope I had disappeared because until then I had possessed just a little bit of hope. Just a sliver.

Every time he hit her or hit me, I would see something in her eyes, something that told me she wouldn't accept this forever, that at some point she would make a change.

I had heard Mrs Jackson speaking to her and I kept hoping that the woman would get through to her, would convince her that it was time to leave him.

And the longer it went on, the older I got and the longer she stayed, the more I hated her. But it was a weirdly complicated hate, bound up with all the love, the intense love I had for her. I wanted her to stand up for me. I wanted her to love me more than she feared him. But instead, she took the child she actually loved; she took her and ran.

She left with the child she loved. She left me behind, at his mercy. I was hard work and I knew that but I thought she loved me. I was her son, wasn't I? Her flesh and blood? Only after she left, only after I came home and found him holding a dishcloth over his bleeding face, did I realise. She didn't love me enough to save me as well. She didn't love me enough to take me with her when she ran away. She only took her precious Little Bird, her darling Rachel.

I was destroyed, broken, shattered. My father spent my whole life telling me I wasn't worthy of being loved, and when she left, she confirmed that was the truth. I wasn't the kind of person anyone could love. I was the kind of person you hurt, you abandoned, you forgot about. I was barely worthy of being a person at all.

I want Rachel to feel that terrifying pain. Destroying Rachel will allow me my revenge.

Will losing her child destroy her? I hope so.

I wanted to do that to my mother first, to destroy her, but when I went to her flat a stupid neighbour told me about the cancer, told me she was in a hospice with only days left to live. She even gave me the name of the place. I told her I was Veronica's nephew. She never questioned me and I went to the hospice and sneaked into her room. That took some doing. The nurses are everywhere all the time. But I managed. I didn't recognise her when I saw her. There is nothing left of her now, just skin and bones. She is a shrunken old woman in a bed.

I sat down next to the bed and took her papery dry hand. 'Mum,' I whispered. 'It's Kevin.'

But she didn't move.

I wanted to scream at her to wake up, to speak to me, to tell me she was sorry for leaving me, but I knew it would be of no use. She is dying. My mother is dying and I will never get an apology or a goodbye.

I sat in the car park of the hospice and I waited for Rachel. And then I followed her home. It was so easy, so simple.

And then I introduced myself one morning and she looked right through me.

I left those dolls everywhere, the dolls that were hers, that she loved and named. I know she wanted me to love her, to be kind to her when she was little, but I just couldn't sustain it. Every time she got away with something that I wouldn't be able to get away with, I hated her a little more. I knew it was an age thing. I knew it would stop when she was seven and then we would be in the same boat, but that never happened because they ran. They ran and left me.

I gave her chance after chance to recognise me, but she still didn't even register who I was.

I have been put so thoroughly out of her mind, it's like I never even existed.

I need her to understand this pain, to experience this pain of loss and despair.

That will be justice and revenge, and then maybe, maybe it will be enough and the black sludge will stop rising and I will be able to move away and start over.

Maybe.

CHAPTER THIRTY-THREE
Rachel and Ben

By the time he catches up to her she is nearly at the park. She is puffing in the cold wind as is he.

'Did you call them?' she asks him, knowing that he will have done it, wondering how on earth she will ever explain this all to him, hoping that she is not too late, that they are not too late. She has some idea of what he's capable of, but she is not sure how far he would go. Her father was beaten to death. Is Kevin the one who killed him? Is that possible? But of course it's possible. She had known all those years ago that he would grow up just like her father. He was already just like her father. The guilt over telling her mother to leave him behind has pricked at her flesh all these years but it has never been sharp enough for her to reach out to him. She hated him. She knows she hated him but he was still a child himself. And he must be so filled with fury and anger at her. Even as her fear for her daughter churns her stomach, there is a small spark of understanding about that anger. She would have felt it herself.

I had to tell. I couldn't keep it a secret anymore, Mum, I had to tell. I should have told sooner.

'I called them,' he pants. 'They're coming, but, Rachel, we should wait, we can't confront him on our own. We don't know anything about him.'

He is surprised that she stops running and looks at him. 'I know what he's like, Ben, and I've known all my life. And if he is anything like the father my mother and I spent our whole lives running from, then Beth isn't safe.'

He nods, understanding he can't stop her, and together they jog the last few hundred metres to the entrance of the park.

The park is a beautiful space during the day, surrounded by a metal fence with a safety gate to keep children securely inside. In the middle there is a brand-new play area for children with sprung matting and a complicated rope climbing frame that Rachel has seen older children enjoying. There are three slides for different-aged children and enough swings so that a kid never has to wait too long for a chance. The park, with its man-made lake in the middle that will be filled with ducks in summer, charmed Rachel when she first saw it. She could see herself bringing her daughter down on a spring day and one day maybe pushing a pram with a baby while Beth was at school.

It is a different place at night. The cold wind whistles through tiny trees, and the only other sound is the creak of the chains on the swings. Lights illuminate small patches of the park, creating shadows that disappear into dark unlit areas where anything and anyone could be hiding.

Rachel releases the catch to the safety gate, the metal freezing against her hands, and Ben follows her into the space, walking into the play area.

'When did you last see him?' Ben whispers.

'Not since I was seven,' she replies. 'He was violent then.'

'I won't let him hurt her,' says Ben. 'I won't let him hurt you.' He glances at Rachel as they walk, making sure they step quietly, wanting to maintain some small element of surprise. He sees her swipe at her cheek, vanishing her tears. 'I won't let anything happen to you,' he says again and she nods. Everything he has been thinking, every question he has formulated about his wife and her secrets, disappears from his mind. The only thing that matters is keeping her safe and keeping their daughter safe. It occurs to him that he has been so worried about not having a job and paying the mortgage that he has forgotten that this is his most important job. This is what makes him a man and a father: the ability to keep his family safe.

Together they come around the back of the public toilets and then stop, hidden from view but able to see the play area.

Large lights around the play area cast everything in an eerie glow.

Ben starts to move forward but Rachel grabs him. 'Wait, just wait,' she whispers.

Beth is on a swing that moves back and forth in the wind.

As Rachel and Ben watch, her head lolls backwards.

CHAPTER THIRTY-FOUR
Little Bird

Even though Mummy is bleeding and hurting, she is very quick when she packs up some things.

'Take a backpack, just a backpack with your clothes and a toothbrush. Don't take anything else,' Mummy whispers.

'But what about my dollies?'

'No, Little Bird, we can't take them all. Take one or two but you need clothes. I don't have much money. You have to carry your backpack yourself.'

'Where are we going to run to?' I ask her and she looks at me. There is dried blood on her face and she can't stand up straight. 'Don't you worry about that. We'll be fine. I'll make sure we're fine.' Mummy sounds like her brain is working now but I don't know if it really is. Her eyes look worried and sad.

I go into my room, pack up my clothes and get my toothbrush, and I take my coat even though it's hot now because one day it will be cold and I like my coat. I look at all my dollies lined up neatly on the windowsill and then I touch each one. 'I'm sorry I can't take you,' I say. 'I'm sorry I can't take you. I'm sorry I can't take you,' and then I am crying and there is stuff running from my nose because I love all my dollies and I have to leave most of them behind. But I love Mummy more and we have to run away. I take the dolly who is a mermaid – even though her head is only glued back on and she looks strange – and I also take the one who is a princess, and I shove them deep into my backpack.

We creep quietly, quietly through the house. When we go past the kitchen I look inside and Daddy is still lying on the floor. He is still, still.

'Is Daddy dead?' I ask Mummy but she doesn't answer me.

We creep on tippy-toes out to Mummy's car. It is warm, warm even though it's late in the night. I look up at the big black sky and I can see a million billion stars all around. The moon is a banana and I lift my hand to touch it but I'm too small. I wish I could take the stars with me so I can always see them twinkling, and I want to ask Mummy if there will be stars where we are going but I don't. I don't think Mummy knows where we are going.

Mummy helps me get into the car and puts on my seatbelt.

Her whole face is ugly, ugly and I wish I could wipe it for her and make her better.

'Maybe I should tell Peg?' she says. 'I should go and tell her and then they can call an ambulance and the police.'

I get scared when she says that. I dropped the weight on his head. I think that will make the police very angry. The police put bad people in jail and I think that dropping a weight on someone's head must be very bad. They will put me in jail. I don't want to go to jail and leave Mummy.

'Don't tell anyone, Mummy,' I say. 'Let's just go. This can be our little secret.'

'Our little secret,' she says and she nods but then she starts crying.

'I'm so sorry,' she says but I don't think she is saying it to me. 'I'm so sorry,' she says over and over again as she reverses out of the driveway and into the street.

She sounds sad and she sounds scared and I know that I have to keep her safe. I kept her safe from Daddy but I have to keep her safe from everything. It is time for me to grow up now. I sit up straight in my car seat and I feel I am getting taller and taller. Maybe I will get as big as Kevin and then I can really keep Mummy safe forever and ever.

It is very dark and very quiet. I don't see any other cars while we drive. Mummy doesn't say anything. She doesn't even turn on the radio and I listen to her breath going in and out and I listen to the hum sound the car makes.

The more we drive the less I am burning inside and outside even though my arms are still sore. When all the burning stops, I start to feel tired and I get very scared because I hurt Daddy, and Mr Stanley says you're not supposed to hurt other people. I feel bad for hurting Daddy and I feel sad as I was his Little Bird and he used to let me sit on his lap and ride high on his shoulders. And then I feel bad for Kevin and I want to tell Mummy that we have to go back and get him but then I don't want her to get him either because he tried to drown me in the water.

I start to think about Daddy and my heart goes *boom*, *boom*, *boom* in my chest and it feels like I can't get enough air inside me. I am scared of what will happen if I hurt Daddy so much that he is dead. I am scared of what will happen if he isn't dead. If he isn't dead, he will be angry, angry and he will find me and Mummy and give us both a good smack.

'Is Daddy dead? If he's not dead, he's going to be angry, Mummy.'

'Don't worry, I won't let anything happen to you – I won't,' she says.

I lean forward in my seat and I can see she is leaning over her steering wheel like it's hard to see because one of her eyes is almost closed.

'But Daddy will hurt me,' I say. 'He'll hurt me like he hurt my dolly.' I start to cry because I am so scared that Daddy will wake up and come to find me and break my head off.

'Don't,' she says. 'Stop crying, he can't hurt you, he won't hurt you. I won't let him hurt you, but you have to promise me that you won't tell anyone about what happened, that you won't ever tell.' She turns around in her seat and looks at me with her hurting face. 'Promise me, you have to promise me that you will never tell anyone.'

Inside me the butterflies are flying around and around and I feel like they want to come out of my mouth because I am so scared about Daddy waking up and coming to break my head off.

'I'll never tell, I promise,' I say. 'I'll never tell anyone about Daddy and about what happened. It will be our little secret forever and ever.'

'Forever and ever,' she says and her voice is sad, sad.

The butterflies stop flapping their wings and then I am sad too. I loved Daddy. I think I loved Daddy and now I will never see him again.

I am only seven years old but I feel like I am an old lady. I want to close my eyes and sleep but I need to watch Mummy. I need to keep Mummy safe.

We drive and drive and drive and we don't talk about leaving Kevin or about me dropping the weight on Daddy. We don't talk about anything. Even though I am trying to stay awake my eyes close because they are burning and I listen to the hum sound the car makes.

When I wake up the sun is high in the bright blue sky and Mummy is still driving. The moon and the stars are all gone and everything is different. The sun is big and burning and my eyes are scratchy. My mouth is very dry.

'I'm thirsty, Mummy,' I say.

We stop at a petrol station and Mummy fills up the car and then she gives me some money to pay the man standing inside because she can't let anyone see her. Her face is scary-looking. One eye is closed and her cheeks are puffed up and the skin is blue with hurting flowers. When Mummy is filling up the car, she holds her side because that's where Daddy was kicking her.

'In there,' she says as she hands me the money. 'Pay him and tell him tank number four. And get me a cold drink, Little Bird,' she says.

I take the money and I look at her.

'Don't call me, Little Bird,' I say, 'not again, not ever. I am not Little Bird anymore.'

Mummy nods her head. 'Not again, not ever, I promise, Rachel.'

CHAPTER THIRTY-FIVE
Veronica

Veronica watches her daughter's tentative steps towards the store at the petrol station. The little girl clutches the fifty dollar note tightly in her little hand, looking left and right. A small child in pink patterned pyjamas who looks too young to be going into the store alone.

Every muscle in Veronica's body is screaming. Her skin is on fire. Her body holds the result of all his anger, all his pain, all his fear. It cannot hold any more.

She could not, cannot, save him or change him. Her love was not enough. She is not enough.

In the car she keeps her head down, not wanting to meet the eyes of anyone else, not wanting to invite questions. She has enough of those for herself.

How has she let it get to this? How has she let this happen to her life? And how on earth will she take care of this child, this damaged little girl who has seen too much?

She dabs a tissue to her split lip where the blood has dried and congealed. She is afraid to look in the mirror. She cannot allow herself to see what he's done.

A sob escapes her but not because of the physical pain. She is used to that. This is for a deeper pain. She knows, as the salt of her tears slips into the cuts on her face, that the sting they create is for the pain of real loss.

This is the pain of the loss of a child, the loss of her little boy who is nearly a man, the loss of who he could have been and the fear for who he will become now.

How can she leave him behind? How can she just walk away? She can't. She can't leave him.

She sits up straighter in her seat, her hands determinedly on the steering wheel.

She will go back, she decides; she will go back and wait for him. She will accept the consequences, however terrible they may be, and then they will leave together – all three of them.

Rachel walks out of the store, her tongue pointed out of her mouth as she concentrates on carefully carrying the drinks she is holding and not dropping the change crumpled in her hand.

Her daughter who, at seven, is too young to have suffered what she has suffered. She will not allow her to suffer anymore. She cannot allow it and if she goes back, he may stop them. He has stopped her before.

Rachel will become a target for him. He has been waiting until she was seven and now she is seven.

She imagines a bruise on her child's pretty face, blooming on her cheek and half closing one green eye.

And in her seat, she slumps over, rests her head on the steering wheel.

They cannot go back. She cannot go back. She has to protect her daughter the way she never managed to protect her son.

And the only way she can do that is to run, to run from the man who hurts and the boy who is learning to hurt.

She has no choice.

They have to run.

CHAPTER THIRTY-SIX

The feel of her hand in mine was unexpected. I have never held a child's hand before.

I almost called her Little Bird. Almost.

She looks just like her mother did as a child but she doesn't have Rachel's hesitancy. She didn't scream when I put my hand over her mouth. She just opened her eyes and looked at me.

'Want to go somewhere exciting?' I asked and she nodded quickly.

She should be more afraid of strangers but I'm not really a stranger. I'm the nice next-door neighbour with a little boy named Jerome.

'Can my mummy and daddy come?' she asked.

'No, because they're not here. They went to see your grand-mother in hospital.'

'Nana is very sick,' she told me. 'She has bad stuff inside her.'

I nodded, agreeing with her. It was strange to hear her call my mother 'Nana', strange to think that my mother is a grandmother, and this thought brought with it a heavy sadness. I will never be a father. She will never be a grandmother to my child. I shook it off quickly. I was in the house, in her bedroom, because of everything that had been taken from me. I was there to take something.

'Did they ask you to babysit me?'

'No, your other grandmother is here.' I wasn't sure who the older woman, sleeping on the couch under a thick blanket, was. I guessed.

'Granny Audrey always gives me treats when she babysits me.'

'Yes, but she's sleeping now. Get dressed quickly. We don't want to wake her. If we wake her, it will ruin the surprise.'

She immediately jumped out of her bed and shed her pyjamas. I found myself turning away from her, giving her a little privacy.

'What's the surprise?'

'I'll tell you when we're outside. Get your coat, and do you have a hat? It's cold outside.'

She just listened, doing everything I told her to do. Perhaps because I woke her up and she thought she was dreaming.

'Where are we going?' she asked. 'Is it to see the fairies?' Her green eyes were round with the thrill of an adventure.

'Definitely to see the fairies.'

I left the doll in the bed, the doll my sister named Polly Purple for her purple hair. I made sure it was lying exactly in the middle. Beth didn't see me do it. She was jumping up and down, desperate to get to the fairies.

It was as easy to get into the house this time as it was that first time. I didn't just learn to keep my head down in prison. I learned a few other things as well, like how to move a sliding glass door so the catch gives way. It would have taken more than just one lock to keep me out. I was worried about the alarm being on, but as I held my breath and waited, there was only silence. Alarms only work if you turn them on.

'We have to be very quiet,' I whispered to her. 'If you wake your granny, you won't be able to see the fairies.'

'I'll be quiet like a mouse,' she whispered back.

We crept out of the house together.

For three nights now, I have parked my car a street away and used a pile of building materials on the plot of the house next door for cover. I have waited in the cold. I have been patient. Tonight, I was waiting for them all to be asleep, and then I was going to make my move. I saw the police arrive and I knew what they would be telling her. I realised that I left the buff-coloured folders strewn around the office. It wouldn't have taken the police long to put two and two together. It took them a couple of weeks but there they were, looking serious as they delivered their news.

And then she got into her car to leave and I could see on her face where she was going. I felt like what I wanted and needed was being given to me right then. When the older woman turned up and her husband left as well, I couldn't believe my luck. An old woman would not be able to stop me. She remained asleep, undisturbed by my entry into the house, but she wouldn't have been able to stop me even if she had woken up.

I didn't know when they would be back. I didn't know if they would be back.

I knew I would call her phone when we got to the park. If she answered, I would tell her to come to me. If she didn't, I would leave her child for her to find.

That was the plan and it was very clear in my head.

She answered.

And now I will wait. Beth is walking slowly, practising patience, her eyes darting around the hidden dark patches in the park as she searches for the longed-for fairies.

I know Rachel's coming. I can feel her getting closer. I had a plan. I know that. I had a plan. A plan for justice and revenge, but now, now I'm not so sure. She is so little.

It's really cold now and I keep looking at her to make sure she's warm enough. It's a strange feeling, something I've never felt before, this worry and concern for someone else. Perhaps it's because of her absolute trust in me. She assumes I'm going to keep her safe because every other adult in her life has always kept her safe. In her world adults can be trusted. I know without thinking about it too much that Rachel is a good mother. My mother was a good mother for the thirteen years that I had her. I never gave her credit for that. I understand that now, after all these years, after all these therapy sessions. I never gave her credit for the things she did do because of the one thing she wouldn't do: leave him. But then she left both of us and I could only see her as worse than him. I could not forgive her.

She was the mother who baked cakes and did your homework with you and read you stories and whose kiss could make a scratch heal itself.

She was the mother who left her son. A truly good mother would not have left her child, regardless of what he was like. A truly good mother would have waited and would have taken me with her. Instead I was left at the mercy of the monster. And then she gave me up – she sacrificed me to save Rachel. The black sludge begins to rise and I caution myself to wait. I have to practise patience just like Beth does. She is waiting for something magical and I am waiting for my justice, for my revenge. I breathe the cold air into my lungs and imagine it going down to my feet, cooling the sludge so I can wait.

I watch Beth as we walk towards the play area and I remember the day that changed everything.

I came home the morning after they left to find him with a black eye and a giant bruise on his forehead. He wouldn't tell me what happened, wouldn't explain anything. 'They've gone,' he said. 'We're better off without them.'

I believe that for a few days I thought this might be the case. He was quiet. He didn't do room inspections or cook crappy food. He ordered takeaway and we watched television together. He took time off work and he took me to school and picked me up in the afternoon so I didn't have to get the bus. It was a little like living with a zombie version of him, to be honest. After a bit I got used to it and I even thought, *Maybe she was the problem all along?* He was so calm once she was gone.

But I was an idiot, of course. Around ten days after she left, and when his bruises had faded, he walked into my room, tossed everything out of the drawers and cupboards and said, 'Clean this shit up in twenty minutes.'

Everything had been neatly folded. My room was tidy. I was just lying on my bed reading a book. I had barely wrinkled the duvet. But it was a message, a warning. He was letting me know that he was ready to resume normal activities. And it just got worse from there.

There would be whole weeks that went by without him touching me. Even if I messed up – like if I spilled something or my bed wasn't perfectly made or if I left some washing in the machine – nothing would happen. He would just say, 'Oh and don't forget to empty the machine,' or, 'I straightened your bed for you.' And I would feel my guts churn and I would start to sweat because I was sure that he was going to lay into me. But nothing would happen. He would sit on the couch and watch television or he would go and work in his study and nothing would happen.

And every time we had a week like that, I thought – despite everything I knew – it was over. I thought we had reached a point where we were just going to live together, just get on with our lives. And every time I was wrong. The very next week, a rumpled duvet meant a punch in the stomach, unfolded washing meant a belt across my back. A spilled glass of water was a slap across the face.

Eventually I worked out that it was my fear he was getting off on. I could never relax and that was what entertained him.

Beth runs towards the swings. 'Yay… will you push me, Bradley?' she asks.

'Shall I tell you a secret?' I ask as I help her up onto the swing.

'I love secrets!' she says.

'My name is not Bradley. It's Kevin, and do you know what else?'

'Uh-huh,' she says, her legs beginning to pump to get the swing moving.

'I'm actually your uncle. I'm your mother's brother.'

'I don't have an uncle, only an aunt… my aunty Lou. She's the principal of a primary school and she has the best craft stuff in the world.'

'Well, now you have an uncle as well. Isn't that great?'

She drops her head back, looks up at the stars and she giggles.

'Push me, Uncle Kevin, push me.'

And so, I do.

CHAPTER THIRTY-SEVEN
Rachel and Ben

She giggles. 'Push me, Uncle Kevin, push me,' she says in the same commanding voice she uses for her parents. 'Push me so I can go really high.'

Ben starts to move again but something in Rachel tells her they need to wait. They can see their daughter, can see she's safe. But if they charge out at him, if he is holding a weapon, he may hurt her. 'Not yet,' she whispers to Ben.

They watch as he moves his hand from resting lightly on her neck to her back. He gives a mighty push and then steps back as Beth pumps her legs back and forth. Rachel stares at him, at her brother, trying to make out his features in the low light. He has their father's broad shoulders, and his dark hair is cut short. He is huge in size, even bigger than her father was. He turns a little and she gets a better look at his face.

'Bradley,' she breathes.

'What?' whispers Ben, and she looks at him.

'That's Bradley Williams, our neighbour, the man I told you… told you about, but that's not his name.'

'I met him, he introduced himself, but I didn't… How did you not know?'

'I don't know why I didn't recognise him. I don't know why I didn't see it.' It is obvious to her now. He stands with his legs apart, his shoulders back, just the way their father did.

'You saw his face and didn't know? How is that possible?'

'I don't… I was seven when we left and he was only thirteen. He has a beard and an accent. I didn't think, I just didn't think.' It occurs to Rachel as she says this that Kevin would have probably felt mystified by this. Mystified and possibly angry. He gave her every opportunity to recognise him. He even handed her one of her dolls, he had the audacity to do that, but she didn't really look at him, not really. She has been caught up in her own world, mired in grief over her mother, in disbelief over the dolls, shrouded in fear. But if he wanted to be recognised, why not just tell her who he was? Even as she thinks this, she knows the answer. She would have been terrified, would have slammed the door in his face. She would not have welcomed her brother back into her life with open arms.

And then she remembers a conversation with her mother when she was eighteen. They were having dinner together at their favourite Italian restaurant to celebrate Rachel's birthday. 'It's Kevin's birthday next month,' her mother said. 'He'll be twenty-four.'

Rachel didn't know what to say, felt fear rise inside her at the thought of her brother older and bigger, stronger.

'I wonder if now… now might be a good time to contact him,' Veronica said tentatively.

'Do you know where he is? What happened to him?'

'I would have to—' began Veronica.

'Don't… I don't want to know, I don't want to talk about him, he's probably just like Dad.' She dropped the fork she was holding back onto her plate and took a big gulp of wine, the butterflies returning in her stomach. 'He'll want to hurt us, to hurt me… he…'

'Okay, okay fine… don't worry, Rachel, don't worry.'

She had stopped her mother from contacting Kevin. First, she had told Veronica to leave him, had encouraged her mother to drive away that night. And then, when she was an adult and the spectre of her father had faded, she told her not to contact him. She didn't want him in her life.

But Veronica had given him up long before that. She had made a deal with their father. She had sacrificed one child to save another. Rachel is the one who was saved, so she cannot turn her heart against her mother, but what might the child who was sacrificed feel?

Ben looks hard at the man because there is something familiar about him. And then he realises he has seen him at work, not just when he introduced himself as his neighbour. The man got into a lift with him, actually got into a lift with him, and Ben shivers at the thought that this man, Rachel's violent brother, has been watching them both, stalking them both. Did he leave the picture? He must have been the one to leave the picture. And now he has his child.

Rachel thinks about her mother as she watches her brother. Her mother is gone. Does Kevin know this? Will he care? He seemed to hate her at thirteen but what if he didn't? What if, somehow, she got him all wrong?

He is dressed in jeans and a jacket, and Rachel notes that her daughter is wearing a jacket as well as her beanie. He has made sure she will be warm. It's not something she would have expected of him but then she doesn't know him. She only knows who he was when he was thirteen – an angry young man who seemed set on the path to become the same violent and abusive person his father was.

'Can you push me higher?' asks Beth, and Rachel hears the creak of the chains on the swing, watches Kevin place his hand on Beth's back and send her high into the air. Beth giggles again and Rachel lets out the breath she has been holding. They have only been standing in the park for a few minutes but it feels like they have been still for a lifetime.

'Maybe I should go out alone to him,' she whispers to Ben.

'Good idea. I'll try and go around. If you keep him distracted, he might not see me.'

Rachel clenches her fists, takes a deep breath.

'I like to go high,' says Beth. 'Do you like to swing?'

Kevin doesn't reply. Rachel waits.

'My mum takes me to this park in the day,' says Beth. 'I've never been here at night. It's kind of scary.'

'You don't have to be scared,' says Kevin. 'I'll keep you safe.'

'When are the fairies going to come?'

'Soon, very soon. You'll see fairies very soon.'

Rachel wonders how he explained who he was and what he said to Beth to make her trust him.

Then she realises that he isn't a stranger at all. He is their new neighbour with a son named Jerome. Of course, Beth would have trusted him.

'My dad keeps me safe,' says Beth. 'When did he say he and Mummy would be home from visiting my nana?'

'I don't know,' says Kevin.

'You can take care of me until they come home because you're my uncle. I didn't know my mum had a brother.'

'Yeah, well, I've been away.'

'I wish I had a brother. He would play with me. Did you play with Mummy when you were little?'

Their daughter is completely comfortable, unaware that she might be in danger.

'I… sometimes I wasn't very nice to her.'

'Why? She's nice to everyone.'

'Is he nice? Your dad?'

'Yup.'

'Does he get angry at you?'

Rachel looks out behind Kevin and sees movement. She knows that this is Ben moving around to the other side. She prays that Kevin doesn't see or hear anything. She will give Ben another minute and then she will step out into the light so Kevin can see her, that way they can rush him from both sides if he becomes violent. At the thought of anything happening to Beth, Rachel feels her stomach churn. She can't let anything happen to her child. She won't. She feels herself stand up straighter and taller. She won't let anything happen to her.

'Sometimes he gets angry,' says Beth finally.

'And what does he do when he gets angry?'

Rachel can feel Kevin waiting for Beth's answer, waiting for her to tell him some terrible truth about her father because all he has known about fatherhood is anger and violence and cruelty. What might their father have done to Kevin without Veronica around to bear the brunt of his terrible anger? From what she can remember, he was always easy on Kevin as long as he did what he was told and kept his room neat. He got hit, but not as often as her mother did, and she knows that at seven she had somehow understood that one day she would be hit, just like her mother was.

How bad would things have gotten as her father processed her mother leaving, as he realised that he had lost control of his wife and daughter? That's what her father thrived on, control; even at seven she understood that.

The guilt that is always there, that she has been carrying for years and years, brings tears to her eyes. They left him. She told her mother to leave him, and while she knows that she was a child, she also knows that Veronica was incapable of thinking anything on that terrible night they packed their bags and disappeared. She wonders at the guilt that Veronica has carried all these years, at not just leaving her son behind but at making a deal with the devil in order to save her daughter. It would have been an enormous, unfathomable burden.

'One time when I touched his computer and made all the words go away, he made me have a time out. I had to sit on a chair in the kitchen for ten whole minutes and then I had to write a note to say sorry.'

'And then what happened?'

'I gave him the note and he gave me a cuddle and said not to do it again.'

'He sounds like a good dad.'

'Is your dad a good dad?' Beth asks.

'My dad is dead, but no – he wasn't good.'

'We can share my dad. You're big but we can still share.'

'Thanks,' Kevin says and Rachel thinks she hears something in his voice, something breaking, the holding back of tears. She nods, knowing that Ben will be watching her, so he understands it's time for him to move and she steps forward, away from the protection of the wall of the bathroom block.

'Kevin,' she says.

Her brother is standing behind Beth, and when he hears her voice he starts and then steps towards the swings, lifting his hands to grab Beth. He hauls her backwards off the swing.

Rachel darts towards him. 'Please, Kevin,' she says.

'Ow, you're holding too tight, put me down,' says Beth, her legs kicking.

'Get back or I swear I'll hurt her,' he says.

'Please,' says Rachel. 'Please, Kevin, just put her down. Please, I'll do anything, I'll give you anything, just tell me what you want. Put her down and let her go to her father.'

Ben steps forward out of a shadow on the other side so Kevin and Beth are now between the two of them.

'Put her down, mate,' he says quietly. There is, in his voice, a sense of quiet menace, of threat, and Rachel almost doesn't recognise him for a second. He is standing up straight with his shoulders back and his arms away from his sides. He looks threatening, even to Kevin, who takes a step backwards, his head turning from her to Ben and back again.

Rachel is glad she has never seen this side of Ben, and at the same time glad that he has this side and that he is here to help her. She knows he has always felt like he has to protect her, and perhaps she shouldn't have let him, but after a life of fear she needed protecting. Ben has no idea how dangerous she can really be, no idea at all, and as she watches her brother, she thinks that he probably has no idea either. Beth will not be hurt, even if others, including herself, have to die.

'You're hurting me, Uncle Kevin,' says Beth softly as though she knows that she needs to speak gently, that she needs to stay calm.

Kevin sets Beth on the ground, and for a moment Rachel thinks that he's going to let her go, but then he holds her little arms behind her back with one hand and places his other hand around her neck. His big fingers encircle her small, fragile throat and Rachel's heart feels like it might explode.

'Do you see, Little Bird? Do you see what I can do?' he sneers.

'No, Kevin, no please,' she whispers because she cannot make the words come out with any more force. She is only a few feet away from him but she knows that he could snap Beth's neck in an instant. His hand is huge against her frailty, and Beth's eyes bulge with fear.

'Please, Kevin,' she says again. 'I'm begging you, please just let her go.'

Kevin's hand tightens, enough to force an intake of shocked breath from Beth. Rachel takes a step forward.

'Move back or I'll do it. Move back, both of you,' he growls.

Rachel holds up her hands. He's going to hurt her. He's going to hurt their little girl and she's not going to be able to stop him. Adrenalin surges through her body. Her heart races and her palms sweat as she struggles to take a proper breath. He's going to hurt her.

'Just wait,' she says. 'Just wait, Kevin, don't do anything you'll regret. Please, she's just a little girl. Let her go and you can do anything you want to me. I promise, I promise.'

I'll never tell, Mummy. I promise.

'You were just a little girl too, Tweet, and look what you did. Did you tell her to leave me? Did you tell her to just get in the car with you and leave me like I meant nothing? Did you tell her to make a deal with him, to give me up forever?'

'I…' Rachel lifts her hands again. 'I didn't…' she begins but she cannot make the lie come out. She did tell her mother to leave him. She wanted to leave him. 'I was… I was a child,' she stutters.

'Give me a child of seven,' Kevin spits, and his hand tightens a little more around Beth's neck.

Rachel watches her daughter's eyes bulge, sees the incomprehension of fear and pain etched on her face. She glances at Ben. He is slowly moving closer to Kevin, his fists clenched, his eyes narrowed.

If Ben can get there and hit Kevin, maybe the shock of the blow will force him to let go. She doubts Ben could hurt her brother but they just need a second, just a second, and they can get Beth away from him.

She falls onto her knees. 'Please, Kevin!' she cries. 'Don't hurt her… You're hurting her. Please just let her go. I'll do anything.'

'There's nothing you can do now, Tweet. Just like there was nothing I could do when I got home and found you both gone.'

'Please,' begs Rachel.

'Say, "Tweet, tweet," Little Bird. Tell your chick goodbye now.'

'No, no,' Rachel moans. 'No, please no.'

Kevin's hand tightens around Beth's neck. Rachel watches her beloved daughter and then she sees her eyes begin to close as her slender throat is squeezed.

'Tweet, tweet!' she cries, a child with no power again, her stomach filled with butterflies, her baby being broken. 'Tweet, tweet.'

CHAPTER THIRTY-EIGHT

Ben

Ben leaps forward, a howl emerging from him, a howl like nothing he has ever heard come out of his own mouth. He feels like he could tear apart the world as he lands a blow on the side of Kevin's face with such force he feels the bones in his hand crack.

Shocked, Kevin falls sideways and lets go of Beth, who sinks to her knees, coughing and choking, gasping for breath.

In his peripheral vision he sees Rachel dart forward and pick her up.

Ben doesn't check on his child, is incapable of thinking straight. He feels fury roar through him as he jumps onto Kevin, punching his face over and over despite the hideous pain that ricochets through his hand.

He uses every bit of strength he has, aware that the man he is punching is much bigger than he is. He uses both fists, again and again. He needs to hurt him. He cannot seem to stop.

He is dimly aware of sirens and then the sound of running feet, but he keeps going.

'Step back now,' he hears, the voice loud and strong, and he stops to take a breath.

'Hands in the air!' Another voice, even louder.

He turns to look around. There are four uniformed police around him. All of them have their guns out, trained on him and Kevin.

He is on top of Kevin, who has his hands up to protect his face. He has no idea how he got to be sitting on top of him.

He catches sight of Rachel, who is holding Beth tightly. Beth is hiccupping and crying. 'It's okay,' he hears Rachel say. Beth is okay. His daughter is alive and Rachel is alive and help is here. He doesn't have to keep doing this now. They are safe. He can stop. He feels like he has a hangover, his head pounding, his mouth dry, as he struggles to his feet and lifts his hands.

'Down on the ground,' one of the constables shouts, and Ben complies, lying down on his front as he has seen criminals do on television. Beth is safe and Rachel is safe. He drops his head onto the black matting of the playground. He is suddenly incredibly tired.

He is dimly aware of Kevin standing up, and he turns his face to look at him.

'Down on the ground,' a constable shouts.

But Kevin does not comply. 'Get back!' he yells.

Ben lifts his head so he can see him better but he does not move his body.

Kevin pushes a hand into his jacket pocket and it seems as though he may have a weapon.

'Drop the weapon,' Ben hears, and he feels his heart rate speed up again. Does Kevin have a gun? What if he tries to use it on Rachel and Beth? He starts to stand up.

'Stay down,' a voice barks, and he remains where he is. The police have guns. They definitely have guns.

'I have a gun,' says Kevin.

'I'm going to need you to put that on the ground and raise your hands,' says one of the constables. His voice is firm and his words come out slowly as though he is controlling himself.

Kevin steps back. *Please let him not have a gun*, Ben prays. Kevin is outnumbered, trapped, a bear surrounded by hunters. Ben has no idea what he will do now.

'I'll kill you all,' he says. He doesn't sound panicked or afraid. He sounds resigned as though this is a decision he has made, as though it is something he has planned. And Ben understands that Kevin would do it, that he would kill them all and that he would start with his wife and daughter. He starts to stand up again. He can't let that happen.

'Get down.' But Ben can't listen to the authoritative voice. He can't take the chance. If Kevin is going to shoot someone, let it be him.

He stands up, holding his arms high in the air as the police raise their guns.

'Shoot me first, Kevin!' he yells.

Kevin focuses on him, his hand beginning to move out of his jacket pocket.

'Shoot me first!' he yells again.

CHAPTER THIRTY-NINE
Rachel

Rachel opens her mouth to scream, 'No,' to tell Ben, 'Stop,' to tell her husband, 'Don't.' But no words come out as she cradles her sobbing daughter.

Kevin moves his hand and she knows her husband is about to die. The constables lift their weapons. Kevin moves forward, his hand emerging from his jacket pocket.

She closes her eyes and covers her little girl's eyes with her hand. They cannot see this happen, cannot watch it. She bows her head.

Kevin has no choice now. He is a trapped animal. Rachel feels her throat close. She has never had any sympathy for him, never had any empathy for him, but he was as trapped as she and her mother were. She had not thought so because he was big and because he was violent and strong, but he was still a child, and her mother should have gone back for him or sent for him. They should have done something. Rachel wonders now, through her guilt, at her mother's ability to simply abandon her son, to leave him at the mercy of the man who was their father. She has always seen Veronica as a victim, as a perfect mother who did what she had to do to save her child – but Veronica had two children, and to save herself and her daughter, she sacrificed one of them. Rachel has no idea what she would have done but she does know, as she holds her daughter tightly, that Veronica made the wrong choice. And she knows, without a doubt, that she was the reason her mother made that choice. It's her fault. This is all her fault.

'I needed a mother, Rachel!' shouts Kevin, and she looks up, sees that he is crying, watches his hand move into the open air. 'I needed a mother just like you did. I needed a mother,' he moans.

'No!' shouts Ben.

'Stop!' screams a constable.

And then there is just noise.

CHAPTER FORTY

It doesn't hurt. It's a jolt, a smell, a sound, but it doesn't hurt.

I stumble back, feel my knees sag and then I am on the ground, staring up into the heavens. The moon is a glowing orb and I breathe in the air, feeling the beauty of the sky fill me up. I have never noticed the splendour of a star-filled sky before. I think about Beth, about her little hand. I wouldn't have hurt her. She was going to share her father. I wouldn't have hurt her. I want to believe that. I need to believe that.

My eyes feel too heavy to keep open.

But I feel at peace.

The sludge is gone. I… I can't seem to concentrate. The stars are winking at me and I can hear the whistling wind.

The sludge is gone. I don't know why I can feel this, but I can.

My mother's face comes to me, a rare smile on it, her eyes lighting up at the sight of me. I can't remember when that stopped, when her eyes stopped lighting up at the sight of me. She was beautiful and kind and I loved her. I know that. I still love her and I know that as well.

My eyes fall closed and I blink, struggling to keep them open so that I can hold onto this moment of peace, so that I can be here and just feel the peace.

But they will not stay open. I take a breath and let go. Nothing hurts now. I'm so grateful that it doesn't hurt.

Finally, finally, it doesn't hurt.

CHAPTER FORTY-ONE
Rachel

Standing in the sun, Rachel unbuttons her coat, allowing the warm rays to touch her skin. It's cooler in the shade but she can feel the spring weather that will be here soon enough.

'You can take your coat off if you're too hot, Beth,' she says, knowing that she has dressed her daughter in many layers in anticipation of a normal winter's day, knowing that they would be outside for a while.

'I'm fine,' says Beth. She keeps her hands in her pockets and Rachel knows that it's not because she's cold but rather because she is holding onto at least five troll dolls she brought with her. 'Can I take Pinky and the baby and the bride and the boy dolly to visit Nana?' she asked this morning.

Rachel had begun to shake her head but then she shrugged her shoulders. 'Sure, just keep them in your pocket so you don't lose them.'

She had imagined that seeing the dolls, all the dolls she used to own, in her daughter's hands would trouble her, but she can look at them now as just toys. They come from her past but their meaning has changed. They are the special dolls that her daughter loves, and she is happy to see them loved and played with again. They are no longer a threat or a message, just the dolls she used to adore.

They bring with them a memory of her mother and herself at a different time. It was a terrible time but there were moments of joy. She can look at them now and remember the moments of joy.

Rachel leans down and places the bunch of vividly purple chrysanthemums against the grey granite headstone.

'What does it say, Mum?'

'It says, "Veronica Watson. Adored mother of Rachel and Kevin and beloved grandmother to Beth. Your spirit will live on forever."'

'That's a lot of words.'

'I know, but I wanted to have them there.'

'I miss Nana,' says Beth, her voice barely above a whisper.

Rachel crouches down next to her daughter and puts her arms around her. 'I do too. And it's okay to miss her because it means you loved her very much.'

'And it's okay to cry,' says Beth solemnly.

'Yes, it's okay to cry,' she says as the tears she is so used to begin to fall again.

'I'm here, Mum,' says Beth, hugging her back, hard.

'I know you are, baby, thank you.'

I miss you more than I ever thought possible, Mum, thinks Rachel.

'Can we go now?' asks Beth.

Rachel nods her head and takes her daughter's hand. She comes by herself at least once a week but Beth wanted to come today to visit her nana. If Beth is not with her, she kneels by her mother's grave and talks to her, tells her what she's doing and the changes that are happening in her life. It helps with the grief, she thinks.

Ben has gently suggested a therapist or a group where she could talk to other people who would understand the depth of her sorrow, but she prefers to simply be here at her mother's graveside, speaking as though Veronica were listening. She knows her grief will change with time, will become more manageable.

As she and Beth make their way to the car, she looks around the cemetery with its wide expanse of green lawn and rows and rows of graves, some of which have people standing by, speaking to a lost loved one as she does. She is not unique in her pain, and this thought helps her on days that are more difficult than others.

She has not been to visit her father's grave in Blackheath, where he was buried with no ceremony and only a priest for company.

He died a terrible, sad death but he chose to live a life where he hurt and tormented those around him.

Kevin committed a heinous crime in causing his death. There is no excuse for what he did but perhaps there is some way to explain it, to understand it.

At seven she had wished her father dead. And the only emotion she experienced when she thought it was him leaving the dolls for her was terror. She had loved him as well – she is sure of that – but she knows that love would have withered as he began to hurt her as he did his wife and son. He was the monster in the house. He was always the monster in the house.

She is glad that the monster is finally gone.

'Open the car, Mum,' says Beth, and Rachel obediently clicks her remote control and then watches as Beth climbs into the car and secures her seat belt.

'So,' she says, as they pull out of the cemetery parking lot, 'what do you want to do with the rest of the day? It's your last day of school holidays so we can do anything you like.'

'Yay, can we get a milkshake and then go to the park?'

'Sure,' agrees Rachel. She and Ben are watching Beth closely for signs of trauma. She has spoken with a therapist a few times but seems to be coping with everything that happened. Rachel imagined the park would become a scary place for Beth but instead she seems to need to go there often, almost as though she is reminding herself each time that she is safe, that they are all safe.

'And then when we get home, I'm going to draw a picture to send to him.'

'To who?'

'To Uncle Kevin, Mum, of course,' she says and she laughs.

'Of course,' says Rachel, marvelling at how her daughter sometimes seems to know what she's thinking about. 'Of course.'

EPILOGUE

Dear Kevin,

Hello from what feels like the noisiest place on earth.

The houses on either side of us are about halfway through now, and I keep hoping that things will get a little quieter, but so far, no luck. I know I complain in each letter but I don't mind, not really. We've met both families now and they both have children Beth's age. There is an eight-year-old boy on one side and an eight-year-old girl on the other. Beth can't wait for both children to move in and is already campaigning to be allowed to walk to the park with them without adult supervision. I'm not sure about that but we'll see. I've enclosed a picture that Beth drew of her birthday party last week. I had twenty little girls over to do crafts and I'm still finding beads and sequins everywhere. They all had a lovely time.

Ben is already in line for a promotion at work so he's putting in some long hours, but he doesn't seem to mind because he's so happy there. Everyone is younger than him so he's the old man of the marketing department, but they seem to value his experience and opinion. I am working part-time at Beth's school, just substituting for teachers who are away sick when they need me, and I'm happy to keep doing that until the baby comes. He's really moving around now, keeping me up at night sometimes and just generally making it known that he's on the way.

I hope all is well with you and you're enjoying getting your engineering degree. I promise you won't regret it. I'm sending along a money order for you to top up your trust account. I'll send more next month.

Mum's flat sold last month. I am putting half the money into an account for you to have when you are released. I will do the same with the house you and Dad were living in.

When I was cleaning out the last of her things, I found a box of some stuff she must have had when we were babies. Our hospital bracelets are in there as well as some pictures and the first Babygros we must have worn. Blue for you and pink for me.

There was also a letter. A letter from her to you. I haven't opened it. I don't know what it says, but I hope it goes some way to explaining why she did what she did. I hope it tells you that she loved you because I know she did.

I know I say it in each letter, but I'm saying it again – I'm sorry. We should have waited for you or come back for you. I should have encouraged her to contact you because I know she wanted to. I know she did.

I'm sorry. I don't deserve your forgiveness, but I am truly so sorry.

Thinking of you.

Love,
Rachel

Dear Kevin,

Happy birthday. Today you are thirty-four years old. Today is also the day I started chemotherapy.

It's not like I thought it would be. I am in a room with about ten other people and we are all hooked up to whatever cocktail they believe will kill our particular cancer.

The other patients have all been here before, I can see. They are familiar with the nurses, and the women are wearing scarves on their heads or wigs. There is only one man and he's completely bald but he's wearing a cap. Everyone nodded and smiled as I sat down and I'm sure I will get to know them well over the coming weeks.

There is a smell in here, a chemical smell from the drugs, a slight smell of sweat from those who are struggling with the medication, and it all mixes with the flower-fresh smell of the nurses. I'll get used to it, I'm sure.

Rachel would be here if she could but she has just given birth to a little girl, a beautiful little girl. Her name is Bethany but I'm sure she will only ever be called Beth. She has silky brown hair and green eyes like her mother does, like I do.

I brought a book to read but quite suddenly I knew I needed to write to you, to leave something for you, because while I am hopeful that I'll find myself in remission, I am also aware that doctors don't have all the answers. Sometimes the cure doesn't work.

I have not seen you for twenty-one years now. It seems to me to be an unbelievable span of time. In the beginning I counted the days and the weeks and the months since I'd seen you.

I have thought about you every day. Every single day.

When we left, when Rachel and I ran away, I made a terrible, awful choice. I left you. I shouldn't have left you but I also knew that if I stayed, if I waited for you to come back, he would wake up. And then, I was certain, he would kill me and then kill Rachel. I knew that for sure and it was about the only thing I was certain of as blood poured from my face and I ached all over. I had three broken ribs and a fractured wrist. I knew he would kill me if I stayed.

Rachel was just trying to help, to save me. She was too little to understand the consequences of her actions and I couldn't let him hurt her. I just couldn't.

But I thought that there was a good chance that he would not hurt you. I know he was hard on you and I know those words don't do justice to how he treated you, but believe me when I tell you that he loved you above all else.

You were his legacy, his son. You looked like him, and as you grew older you acted like him as well. I don't mean that to be a bad thing. I know that some of your behaviour was because of how he treated all of us. I mean that you had most of his good traits as well. You were so clever, like him, and so good at sport and really funny. You liked the same things he liked. I thought, I hoped, that he would understand that he had to embrace you and care for you because Rachel and I were gone. I believed, in some part of me, that I was the problem, and that if I was gone, he would be better. I pray every day that's been the case.

I am not justifying what I did. I don't know if he will ever tell you about the letter I sent him, begging him to leave us alone and telling him I would never see you again if he agreed. I cannot explain and I will never be able to explain how impossibly hard those words were to write. They caused my fingers to cramp and my heart to break because I loved you. You were my first child, my baby boy, my little man. When I was pregnant with Rachel, I was sure that I would not be able to love her as much as I loved you. But I did, of course. I loved her as I loved you but I believed, in the end, that she was more in need of my protection than you were.

I made a choice and it is a choice that I have wished I hadn't had to make – or that I hadn't made – every day. But fear kept me sticking to what I told him in the letter. Fear for my life and Rachel's life.

I know your father loved you deeply in his own, sometimes terrible, way.

I am saying that I thought that out of all of us you had the best chance of surviving a life with him. And I thought, much to my horror at myself, that if he had you, he wouldn't try that hard to find me and Rachel.

I made a choice. A terrible, awful choice to save my life and the life of your sister. And I have worried every day since that I left you with a man who is capable of great harm and great pain.

At least once a week for the first couple of years we were running and hiding, I would find a call box and dial Peg Jackson's number. It was always my intention as I punched the numbers into the keypad to tell her where we were and hopefully get her to find a way to get you to come out to us. Despite the letter, despite what I wrote to him, I wanted to try and get you to come and be with us. But each time I only got as far as listening to the ringing of her phone on the other end of the line before my heart began to race and my stomach flipped over and I felt sweat bead on my forehead. And then I hung up. Your father is a clever man. If Peg spoke to you, if she managed to get you to us, he would have killed us all. I knew I had to stick to what I said in my letter, and although he never let me know that he had read it or that he had agreed, he only ever turned up to let me know he knew where we were. He never went near Rachel and he allowed us to run again. It became a game to him, I'm sure, and then one day it just stopped and I thought it was finally over. But it will never be over because I left you.

I admit that there was another reason I did it. I was worried that you were just like him in the bad ways as well, that you would hurt us. You were already bigger than me, and I was scared of you. I wish I hadn't been but I was. I am ashamed to say that, but it is true.

When you got to eighteen, I called and waited for Peg to answer because I knew that you would be an adult and I hoped to be able to reason with you. But the woman who answered the phone was not Peg. She told me they had bought the house *from Barry after Peg died and I felt like my only lifeline to you had been severed.*

I could have found a way to speak to you, I know that. I could have written you a letter or contacted your school, but my fear of your father made everything seem impossible.

It's not an excuse, not a justification, just the truth.

I have hated him for twenty-one years for making me leave you behind. But I have also, strangely enough, never stopped loving him. I loved you, and when I looked at you, I saw him.

If this doesn't work, if the cancer takes over my whole body and I die, I will leave this letter for Rachel to find. I hope that she will find a way to get it to you.

I hope that you and your father found a way to live together without hurting each other. I hope that you have love in your life and happiness. I hope that you are not too angry at me and at your sister even though what I did should only engender anger. I hope that you have found a way to be a better man than your father.

I love you, Kevin. I miss you and think about you every day. I dream of a time when we will find each other so that we can be a family again – you, me and Rachel. I am holding onto that hope and I will keep holding on until there is no reason to do so.

With all my love,
Mum

Dear Rachel,

Thanks for sending the money. You don't have to, you know. I can get by without most of the stuff, although I have to admit that chocolate is my weakness in here.

And thank you for the letter from Mum. It threw me for a bit. I have read it over many times now.

I wish I could say I forgive her but I'm not there yet. I'm just not there. I understand her is the best I can do. I understand her because after she left, I got the full force of who he was, and if I'd had the choice, I would have run too. As it was, I was afraid and trapped, and by the time I was old enough to leave, I was hopelessly enmeshed in this dysfunctional relationship we had going. I understand her choice but I cannot accept it.

I have started seeing a therapist once a week. I like to think that this time it will be different. This time I will tell him everything there is to tell. This time I really want to find a way through the memories into a more peaceful place. This time I finally want to change. I can see, from the way he listens when I speak, that I'm not the first person he's heard this kind of stuff from. I showed him the letter from Mum. I don't think he knows quite what to say about it.

I want to thank you again for testifying at my trial. I know that hearing about our childhood and about what he did to Mum helped with the sentencing. It was self-defence. He wasn't strong enough to hurt me when they let me out on bail before my trial but he had been hurting me for years. Every time I came home, he would hurt me again. And it didn't matter how big I got or how strong or how old. I was always powerless against him. Until I wasn't.

I'm trying to untangle it all but it's going to take time. I have no excuse for what I did to you and Ben and Beth. All I can come up with right now is that I was trying, in some really messed-up way, to reach you, to make you understand. I wanted to talk to Mum, but it was too late. You were the next best thing.

It was so incredibly wrong and I can only comfort myself with the fact that nothing happened to any of you and that the constable who fired the gun only gave me a flesh wound because he suspected I had nothing in my pocket.

It feels strange to say this because I'm in prison, but I feel like I've been given another chance at life.

I'm also really grateful to have your support. I feel like you and I have to learn how to be a family. We were never really taught that by our parents. Mum tried, I think, but she was too busy trying to survive, really.

I'm really enjoying the course. Engineering was always a passion of mine and I regret that I got myself kicked out of university in first year. It was inevitable, I suppose. Once my anger met alcohol, there was really only one way things were going to go.

I'll be here a long time and I know that you may get tired of writing letters and sending money, so I want to let you know that I will understand if you do.

I wish I had been a better big brother to you when you were little, but I guess I was also just trying to survive. It's strange to think that one man could have tried to so thoroughly destroy the three people in his life who only wanted to love him. I know that he came from his own messed-up childhood, but at some point that can't be an excuse anymore, can it? It's no longer an excuse for me. I accept what I've done but I can't change it, so all I can do is try to do better, a lot better now. I am trying, Rachel. Believe me, I am trying.

I should get on with some of my work now.

Thanks for the drawing from Beth.

Please write to me again. I really like the letters, and tell Beth I love the drawing and it's going up on my wall with the others she's sent me.

Thinking of you.

Love,
Kevin

A LETTER FROM NICOLE

Hello,

I would like to thank you for taking the time to read *The Life She Left Behind*. If you did enjoy it, and want to keep up to date with all my latest releases, just sign up at the following link. Your email address will never be shared and you can unsubscribe at any time.

www.bookouture.com/nicole-trope

For a long time, I was told to 'write what you know', but that never really worked for me. Instead I write what I fear.

I write about families in crisis, about lives changing in the blink of an eye and about people who somehow manage to survive very difficult situations.

As human beings, we make choices every day, and as parents and guardians of the next generation, we make them knowing that we are impacting the lives of those we have brought into the world or care for, in a profound and permanent way. When writing this novel, I thought about having to make a choice as difficult as the one Veronica had to make, and I had to ask myself, 'What would you do?' I admit I have no idea, and I also admit that I found myself in a quandary over Veronica's choice. I hated that she made it, but I also accepted that she felt she had no other option. She should have felt she had an option because all women should feel they have options, but that's not quite the case yet. I look forward to a time when it might be.

I have loved writing about the bond between a mother and daughter and about the bonds of family that stretch through the years. I hope you've enjoyed the story of this particular family, however sad it may be.

I usually end my novels on a note of hope because that's what I want for the world and for those women and children who suffer.

If you have enjoyed this novel, it would be lovely if you could take the time to leave a review. I read them all, and on days when I question whether or not I have another book in me, they lift me up and help me get back to work.

I would also love to hear from you. You can find me on Facebook and Twitter, and I'm always happy to connect with readers.

Thanks again for reading.
Nicole x

NicoleTrope

@nicoletrope

ACKNOWLEDGEMENTS

I would like to, once again, thank Christina Demosthenous for her wonderful editing and for always getting back to me quickly when I send her desperate emails with the header 'Does this work?' As always, she has pushed me to write the best possible novel, and I have loved working with her.

I would also like to thank Kim Nash, Noelle Holten and Sarah Hardy, publicity and social media gurus, for helping my novels into the world. Thanks to the whole team at Bookouture, including Alexandra Holmes, Ellen Gleeson, Lauren Finger and Liz Hatherell. Thanks to DeAndra Lupu for another excellent copy edit.

I would also like to thank, as always, my mother Hilary, who knows how quickly she needs to read any novel I send her.

Thanks also to David, Mikhayla, Isabella, Jacob and Jax (Where are you going? What are you eating? What have you got there? Stop that!).

And once again thank you to those who read, review and blog about my work. Every review is appreciated.

Printed in Australia
AUHW011634161020
335628AU00004B/513

9 781838 882280